Midwinter Tales

REVIEWS FOR DAVID WELLING

FOR CINEMA HOUSTON

By allowing us to remember what we lost, Welling refines our perspective on what is worth preserving.

— Aaron Carpenter, *Cite Magazine*

If (the theatre is) clean and comfortable and the interiors don't clash, great, but, hey, who cares. David Welling cares.

— Louis B. Parks, *Houston Chronicle*

Welling has done a great service in preserving memories.

— Russell Herron, reader

FOR MIDWINTER TALES

Midwinter Tales is a literary holiday cookie tray. It's a happy-making jumble of updated seasonal favorites and nuggets that are anything but sweet, all lovingly infused with modern mythology.

— Kathy Biehl, author of *Confessions of a Third-Rate Goddess* and *Eat, Drink & Be Wary*

Get cozy with these *Midwinter Tales...* Welling's stories are rich with relatable characters, vivid settings, and surprising twists along the way.

— Melissa Algood, author of the *Enhanced Being* series

Midwinter Tales

A Seasonal Anthology

by

David Welling

CALIGARI'S BOOKSHELF PRESS

MIDWINTER TALES
Copyright © 2024 David Welling
Cover illustration by Jamie Farrant, www.enjoy.co.nz
Interior design by David Welling
Header ornamentals by Balora

ISBN: 979-8-9909308-0-3
Library of Congress Control Number: 2024912113
First Edition

Printed in the United States of America

Caligari's Bookshelf Press
caligarisbookshelf.com

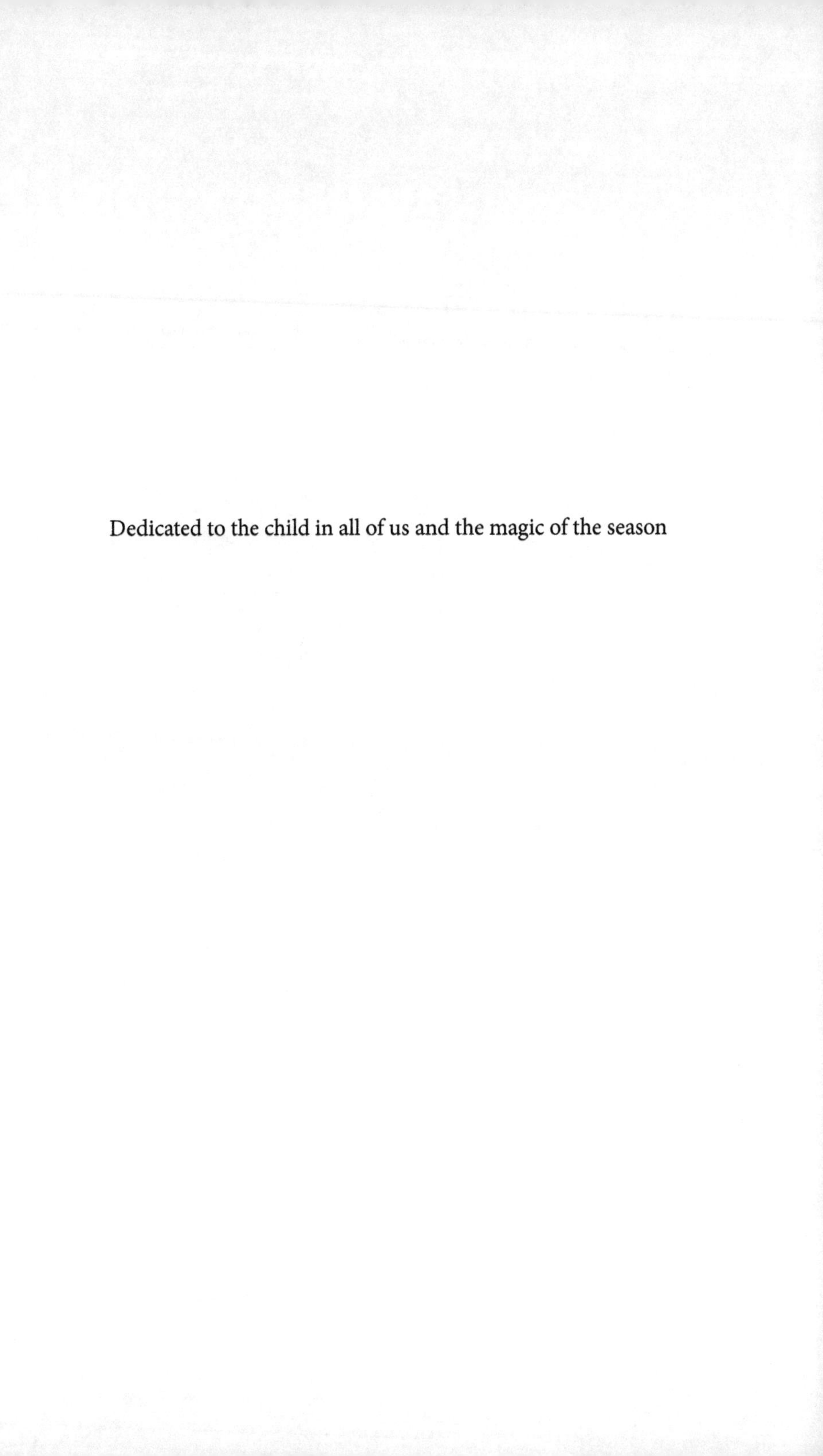

Dedicated to the child in all of us and the magic of the season

ACKNOWLEDGEMENTS:

AS THE SAYING GOES, books are not written in a vacuum. Neither are even the shortest of stories. Thanks begin with the participants of my critique group who have heard many of these stories and offered their sage advice. Their opinions have always guided me in improving the stories and I would be lost without them.

Also, to my editor, Tina Winograd, who adds invaluable polish to these works. To my wife, Denise, who lends an ear as I read aloud, usually at the end of the day when it's chill time. Lauryn and Dylan have been additional influences, especially during their early years. They served as a degree of inspiration for some of the Neuwirth stories.

Our dogs, Disney and Cooper, camped out by my side as I wrote, offering comfort, a snuggle, and occasionally a snore as they slept. To all the family, friends, and acquaintances who gave their time to read, especially in the early days, thank you.

Finally, to my mom, dad, and two brothers, and all the Christmases we spent together, there's more than enough love and memories there to fill volumes. And that is what the season is all about.

CONTENTS

"But I am sure I have always thought of Christmas time,
when it has come round—apart from the veneration due to
its sacred name and origin, if anything belonging to it can be
apart from that—as a good time; a kind, forgiving, charitable,
pleasant time; the only time I know of, in the long calendar of
the year, when men and women seem by one consent to open
their shut-up hearts freely, and to think of people below them
as if they really were fellow-passengers to the grave, and not
another race of creatures bound on other journeys."
— Charles Dickens, *A Christmas Carol*

INTRODUCTION

THANK'EE, CHARLES. It started with you.

In 2002, I began the first draft of a period holiday story inspired by Dickens' *A Christmas Carol*. By all rights, I should have been terrified. Never before had I tackled a fictional project of this length or scope.

That I had the sheer audacity, the hubris, to wade into the words and thoughts of the great Dickens might have caused others to run from their keyboards. Yet I felt surprisingly (and foolishly) confident. Already, I knew the opening scene as well as the closing words. I only had to travel from A to Z. To paraphrase Robert Frost, I chose the road less traveled and it made all the difference.

I'm hardly alone in bowing in reverence to Dickens' literary presence. Since he penned *The Carol* in 1843, the story has been adapted countless times to radio, film, and television. It is re-enacted on the stage every year across the land in towns big and small.

The story of redemption and compassion hits a core deep within, touching the humanity in all of us. As a result, it, along with *It's a Wonderful Life*, has become a permanent fixture in my holiday season viewing. Not a year goes by when I don't pull one of the many movie adaptations from the shelf, most often either the 1951 version with Alastair Sim or the 1984 television production with George C. Scott (although I also have great love for Michael Caine and the Muppets (C'mon, Kermit embodies the very essence of Bob Cratchit, albeit a bit green).

Under the influence of mistletoe and holly, I followed my "Carol" project with a smaller story as a way to wind down. The great thing about short stories is that they are just that—short. They are a different animal. Rather than deal with tens of thousands of words, a story can be told in as few as a hundred-plus, a simple sketch as opposed to a detailed oil painting.

The year following, I wrote another tale to share with family and friends, the way one might send a Christmas card. At the time, the rationale was one of discipline. Even if I had written nothing else over the previous twelve months, this would force me to stretch my creative muscles.

Then came the next year, and the next. With each, new yarns arrived, sometimes more than one at a time. Christmas is all about traditions and this became one of mine. The collection grew.

In time, I realized the season is the gift that keeps giving, offering so many stories that plead to be told. Perhaps, I'm simply the medium for channeling these stories. After all, there is a belief that artistic creations live and breathe to the same degree as those who create them. They are simply waiting to be born. I like that thought. It has a bit of magic to it, and if the holiday season is anything, it is one of magic.

With over two decades gone, this book represents the fruit (or fruitcake) of those endeavors. The themes range. Some are humorous, some not so much, some happy, and some sad, and all points in between. A few are reflective of the times in which they were penned due to social, political, or world events. War. Intolerance. MeToo. Cancel culture.

Likewise, lengths range with the longest in this volume being yet another variation on *A Christmas Carol* ("Can I Take Them All At Once?"). I'm especially fond of that particular piece, with absurdist humor tempered by affairs of the heart. It may be the first time in literature to assemble in a single story the ghosts of past, present, and future, along with Hamlet, Edgar Allan Poe, and a rubber chicken. Some of these stories have appeared in other collections while others are in book form for the first time.

I'm a sucker for Christmas, relishing the multi-color lights, the trees and garland, the decorations, and the crass commercialism as well as the spirit of the season. For me, it can be wrapped with a bow and summed up in the message of "peace on Earth, good will toward men."

For all the classic films, from *Christmas in Connecticut* and *Remember the Night* (both with Barbara Stanwyck) to the Christmas movie mammoth that is Hallmark, I watch them all. I love *Miracle on 34th Street*. I also enjoy *Violent Christmas* and *Bad Santa*. Likewise, holiday music hits the speakers well before December 1, usually starting with Bing, whom my wife and I consider to epitomize the true musical spirit of the season. Diana Krall and Aimee Mann soon follow.

As an entertainment junkie, you will find numerous references to music, movies, and art in these stories. *Gilmore Girls*, a show as fresh to me now as it was when it first debuted, earns a rightful reference within these pages. That story is easy to spot as it kicks off the anthology. Other nods may be more obscure, but that's the fun thing about Easter eggs. They are hidden in plain sight.

A final note about the title: traditionalists may wag their fingers at me for the liberal use of the word *Midwinter*. Why not *Christmas*, *Yule*, *Winter Solstice*, and so on? Understandably, some adhere to the literal meaning referring to a period well past the Christmas holidays.

Yet, there are differing views on its exact beginning or end, or how it currently applies to the larger season. Unlike the solstice and Christmas, which fall on a particular date, I prefer the broader spectrum to the midwinter, thus covering the December holidays and into the New Year with the days growing in length. If it still bothers you, feel free to take a marker, scratch out the word, and write in your favorite name. Books should be personal.

Having shared these stories with a small group up to now, I am thrilled to see them find new life with a larger group of readers. I hope they kindle all the proper emotions that belong to this time of year. And if you like what you've read, feel free to regift it to those you think might enjoy it. After all, it's the Christmas season. That's what we do.

Happy holidays!

David Welling
February 2024

AN INTRODUCTION

OF GILMORES, PIGS, AND GREETING CARDS

I love *Gilmore Girls*, always have, and followed the series from the day it first aired. My daughter soon discovered it and likewise became a fan. I still have the theme song as her personal ringtone.

This short story has always been a favorite of mine with the aftermath of a "meet cute" and how romance is so much more magical at this time of year. Plus, it has an adorable dog in it, the kind that makes you say, "Aww."

This one is in memory of Jean.

OF GILMORES, PIGS, AND GREETING CARDS

DIVERSIONS abound.

Life is full of them. They come in all forms–large and small, animate or inanimate, time or space-based, an addition of or absence thereof, and might be identified by color, sound, or smell. Yet whatever the form, they have the ability to serve as a catalyst for change. In a twinkling, happenstance can be altered by the simplest ones.

In this case, diversion took the form of a greeting card.

Patrick noticed her for two reasons as she exited the store. The first was the girl-watching instinct so profoundly engrained in the male genetic code. He eyed her from top to bottom, finding her attractive in that indefinable way as neither a model nor a moose. It was more a natural kind of loveliness. At least, that was how he saw her from across the parking lot.

It might have been her walk, the way she shifted her weight from side to side, her poise weighed down by the two full bags of groceries she carried. Or it could have been the blondish-brown hair that fell past her shoulders and kicked up by the cool December wind; or her clothes, which accented all that hid underneath in a modest, flattering manner.

Most likely, it was a combination of the entire package. All this analysis took place in a matter of seconds as he looked her over.

The second reason was the greeting card.

The girl tripped just enough to cause her to take a couple of quick steps in rapid succession before regaining her balance. In that moment, a small card jostled loose from the bag and fell to the ground. She didn't notice and continued to her car.

Patrick saw it fall, and as she walked away, he felt a distinct shift in his role. No longer a passive observer, he now felt a connection to her. He was privy to something she did not yet know, and by a simple action, could do what any decent person would do in such a situation. There was a brief interval of consideration before allowing circumstance to draw in and intertwine their two separate paths.

"Miss?" he called across the lot. "Hello?"

When this brought no response, he trotted toward where the card had fallen, stopping halfway to let an impatient car pass by. The card was still partially sandwiched in its envelope, itself a pale pink color, and otherwise, much like any other envelope in size and appearance. He picked it up and looked for the woman once more. Across the lot, she had just stepped into her car and closed the door.

"Miss?" he called again, feeling foolish since she would not hear him as he ran across the lot, card in hand.

Then came the stumble, not a minor wrong step like the one she had taken a minute earlier, but a full-fledged nose-dive, sending him forward with his hand outstretched to break the impact.

Skin met asphalt, and he let out an "Ouch!" as the pain registered. He looked first at the already reddening bruise on his palm where the skin had been torn, then back to the spot where the lady had disappeared.

Not good timing. Her car eased forward, and even as he rose, he knew she might be gone before he could catch up. Now jogging toward her car, he waved the card in the air, calling out to her, but still gaining no response.

Within a second, an impulsive and irrational idea formed, and he changed course from her car to his parked a few rows away. Holding the card in one hand as he ran, he pulled the keys from his pocket. His arm outstretched as if aiming a revolver, he pressed one button after another, with the car chirping when he first hit the lock button. Narrowly bypassing the panic button, he pushed the correct one.

By the time he reached his car, it had unlocked. He tossed the card onto the passenger seat, started the engine, and after checking briefly for oncoming vehicles, pulled away from his spot and drove out, looking ahead for the other car. Her car.

"This is really, really a dumb idea," he said to himself.

She pulled onto the street. So did he. For the next fifteen minutes, he kept her in sight. All the while, a running commentary played in his head.

"Patrick, you're an idiot."

"She's going to think you're even more of an idiot."

"What are you going to do when she stops? Get out of the car and say, 'Oh, lay-dee, duhhhh, here's your purdee card.' Real bright."

"Why am I doing this?"

"How long will this trip last? For all I know, she could drive for hours."

And the obvious question running through his head like a mantra: "Does this mean I'm a stalker?"

It could certainly come off that way. A total stranger follows a woman he doesn't know across town—sure appears like a classic case of stalking.

"What if I lose her in traffic?"

That never quite happened. She remained in position a few cars ahead for most of the journey. Keeping the vehicle in view was difficult at times, her blue Ford Focus disappearing in front of the larger SUVs that populated the streets. At one point, a traffic light turned red, bringing him to a halt as she went through. The fates were kind; it was a short pause, and he quickly regained his spot.

He reached behind him with his free hand, feeling around on the rear floorboard, and finally found a spare napkin left from the previous day's drive-thru lunch. At the next stoplight, he dabbed it against his bruised hand, creating an inkblot pattern of dirt and blood. After completing his delivery, he'd treat it properly with antiseptic and a bandage.

He kept casting sideways glances at the envelope on the passenger seat, wondering what kind of card it was. Holiday? Birthday? Funny or sweet and sentimental? The act of selecting a card could be a highly individualistic and personal task, and thus be rather revealing of the giver of such a gift. So what breed of card was this?

He picked it up for closer examination. The front was a typical holiday design with the words "Season's Greetings" in a large gold script and adored with a combination of floral wreaths, ribbon, pinecones, and holly berries. In all, it was of the style one might send to their grandmother. He opened the card, read its contents—and nearly drove into the oncoming lane.

After giving fresh attention to the road before him, he held up the card and reread its message, making sure he read it correctly the first time. The words had not changed:

> *'Tis the season of holiday cheer,*
> *And I'm so happy that you're not here.*
> *Merry Christmas, Dickhead*

Patrick looked at the car ahead, suddenly aware that perhaps this might not be as good an idea as he first thought. After all, he had no idea who this woman was. For all he knew, she could be crazier than a Christmas fruitcake. If the card was any indication, she was not someone to piss off. Anyway, what kind of store would sell such a card?

Whomever the card was intended for, her feelings were pretty clear. No words minced. "Whoa," he said to himself, considering the implications of the greeting and how it might be received. Obviously, someone had done the lady wrong, possibly an ex-boyfriend.

The thought led to the logical follow-up questions: Domestic spat? Incompatibility? Not the proper amount of respect for her... or was it the old standard of him cheating? She could have been treated horribly, and thus, justified in picking out a card that summed up her feelings. Somehow, this rationale made her more appealing, if only as a mystery.

With that, any thoughts of turning back were squashed, and Patrick continued the pursuit, more interested now than before. The journey continued, first on the main street, then onto a freeway for a short distance, then off again, and finally into a suburban neighborhood.

It was a quaint, older street with small ranch-style houses probably built in the fifties or early sixties. At one time, the area might have catered to the upper-middle-class family, but the ensuing decades had brought a downturn to the block. On the real-estate market, these homes would now be considered quite affordable. Still, it had a very neighborly feel to it.

Ahead, the Ford slowed, and without as much as a signal, turned onto a driveway. Immediately, Patrick slowed and pulled to the side a few houses away, now unsure of how to proceed. Her car edged forward as the garage door opened, then pulled in, and the door closed once more.

He considered his options. If he were to knock on the front door, would she open it for someone she did not know, and how would he explain his actions? It had all the hallmarks of creepiness. Then again, what could be the worst thing to happen?

Quite a lot, actually. She could slam the door in his face, that is, if she even opened it. She could scream bloody murder, spray Mace in his face, and *then* slam the door. She could call the police. He could be hauled away in handcuffs and thrown into jail, thereby, spending the holidays in a non-festive atmosphere. Each successive scenario seemed worse than the previous.

"Right," mumbled Patrick to himself. "Think of something positive. I hand the card over. I leave. End of story."

He tried to put himself in her place. If he opened the door of his home to find himself standing outside, would he look threatening? First appearances were everything.

Fortunately, Patrick was reasonably good-looking, or so he had been told on occasion. Clean shaven and well dressed, he would come across as an unknown, but at least his appearance did not scream "psycho killer." His smile was warm, his personality likewise, other traits that might work in his favor.

Of course, he could just drive away. It was not too late to abandon this folly, and she'd never be the wiser, albeit cardless. No foul on his part. No one else would have come this far to return a $3.99 piece of paper.

Another option: He could remain anonymous. Simply leave the card on the doorstep, ring the doorbell, and leave before she opened the door. Of course, that might come off as far more disturbing, finding the card she had just purchased missing from her bag and lying at the front door. No, if he was to return the card, it should be done in person, regardless of what she might think of him.

"All right, let's do this," he said to himself as he pulled up to her house and stepped out. Almost without thinking, he went through the motions of checking his hair, making sure it was in place and that his shirt was tucked in. Yes, appearances carried weight, even in matters of doing a good deed.

Yet even as he approached the door, he questioned whether he would have done the same if the person on the other end had been a grumpy old man instead of this beautiful woman. Probably not, he quickly answered, knowing how base it sounded. It was all about the woman. Moth to a flame, he was motivated purely by attraction. He could at least admit that much.

The moment at hand, he rang the doorbell and waited while noticing a medium-size box placed at the right side of the door. He could just make out the Macy's logo in the sender address, as well as the name of the addressee: Shelley Helpern. Quickly, he felt guilty as if he were prying through her mail.

Half a minute ticked by before a figure appeared. Shadows shifted beyond the small, beveled glass pane on the door, growing darker as someone drew closer on the other side before peering through the window. More seconds passed as he was examined. Then came a voice from the other side.

"What do you want?" Even muffled behind the door, he could detect a texture to the mid-register voice, a combination of softness with a slight rasp, rather like Stevie Nicks back in the day. Laced on top of this was the tone of due vigilance when addressing an unknown.

"Miss, you dropped your card at the store." Patrick held the card up into view, giving it a little shake for emphasis and immediately feeling ridiculous for the gesture.

So he waited.

Then came a *click* as the door unlocked. It opened just wide enough for a face to appear, looking at him with an expression of caution. The chain lock stretched across the narrow opening.

"What?" she said, not yet grasping the meaning.

"I'm sorry to disturb you, miss, but you dropped this card on your way out of the store. I tried to catch up to you in the lot, but you had already driven away."

She continued to look at him, an unreadable expression on her face. He noticed her eyes, intense olive-green interspersed with specks of brown, and as cliché as it sounded, intoxicating.

"I just wanted to return it," he added in an attempt to fill in a very uneasy silence.

Her eyes narrowed, looking at the card and then back at him. "Do I know you?" she asked at length.

"No. I don't think so."

Without shifting her gaze, she carefully extended her arm, hand open. He passed the card. She snatched it, and her hand shot back through the opening of the door, which then slammed shut. Its abruptness was startling, and he immediately thought of the toy banks from when he was a child where the little plastic hand comes out of the box, grabs the penny, and snaps back out of view. This was a reenactment in real time, a card instead of a coin, but just as fast.

He turned to leave, a job well done. As Good Samaritan deeds go, this should fill his quota for a while. And it had been worth the effort; funny how a pretty face could be a motivating factor. No, he would not have driven across town for a grumpy old man.

He was halfway back to the car when he heard the door reopen and a voice call out.

"Excuse me."

He turned to see her at the door, this time more visible.

"I just dropped this card at the store?" she asked, holding up the envelope for him to see.

"Yes."

"And you drove over here to return it."

"Yes."

"Oh." She thought about this, looked at him a moment, then retrieved the Macy's box at her feet before disappearing behind the door once more. The door shut again with a sound less emphatic than the first, but still with the lock clicking into place afterward.

Patrick smiled, realizing that he thoroughly confounded the woman and walked back to his car. He was nearly in when the voice called out once more.

"Excuse me."

Patrick looked up to see Shelley, again standing at the door, with that same perplexed look on her face.

"Do you work at the store?" she asked.

"No," he replied, stepping back to the front lawn. "You stumbled on your way out of the store, and the card fell out of your bag."

She considered this. "Why?" she asked at last. The open-ended question might have had many meanings, so he chose the most appropriate response.

"It seemed the right thing to do," he replied and smiled. "Sorry to inconvenience you."

"No. No. It's okay. I'm just..." The end of the sentence drifted off into the vast wasteland of unfinished trains of thought where men and women alike let go of their verbal skills.

"And I probably startled you, as well," he added. "My apologies."

"No, you did fine. This is just—unexpected. I was rude just now." Then she offered just the barest hint of a smile. "Thank you."

"You are very welcome."

Again, a pause. He felt himself under the microscope, knowing his motivations were being justly scrutinized.

"How did you find me?" she asked.

"My car was right there. I hoped to flag you down, get your attention, so I just, uh, followed you, um..." The last word came out as a lame admission. "...home." His feet began to do an involuntary shuffle as if their motion would make him any more comfortable. The dance did not help.

When no response came forth from her, he continued. "Right, that sounds kind of weird. I couldn't think of another way to return the card, and so I just drove, and I didn't mean to throw you off. I mean, this could appear like I'm sort of..." His sentence died midstream as he changed track in order not to use the S-word.

"It's just, uh, it belonged to you, and I had it, and if it didn't get returned to you, then it wouldn't belong to anyone, and so you had every right to close the door in my face, and, uh, okay, I'm babbling now. Please stop me before I sound any more ridiculous than I already do."

All the while, that glimmer of a smile on her face kept increasing by the barest fraction.

"You can stop then."

Another lapse into silence followed—less awkward for her as she watched but more so for him. He smiled, one of the sheepish sort.

"Well," he said at last, "I should go."

Before she responded, another shape came into view, this one a quick blur of brown and white, passing out the door at her feet and straight toward Patrick. With it came the jingling of metal and the sound of paws against the ground.

"Rory!" she cried as the furry shape, accented with large eyes and a tongue in front, made a final leap at Patrick's leg.

"Well, what do we have here?" Patrick asked as he bent down, his arm outstretched to the furball—a small dog of the Spaniel breed that had become so popular in recent years. Immediately, his hand was covered with a series of slobbering licks.

"Rory! Down!"

"No, it's quite all right," Patrick said while using his other hand to scratch the back of the dog's head. The wag of its tail sped up. "She's an affectionate one."

"I'm sorry," the woman said as she approached. "We've taken the training classes for all the good it did."

"Interesting choice for a name."

"It's from an old TV show. *Gilmore Girls*."

"Oh. I'm surprised you didn't go for Lorelei."

She smiled. "I'm impressed. Most men don't know the series. It's a girl thing."

"I was seeing someone that loved the show. It was a while back."

"The name seemed appropriate. There are some parallels between my life and the show, and since I think of Rory as my daughter, the name fits."

Patrick picked up the dog, and before he could turn his head, was rewarded with a doggie lick on his lips.

"Oh yeah, I should have warned you about that," she said.

"S'okay. She's just excitable."

"Here, let me take her."

She reached out for the dog, and as if by instinct, Patrick looked at her left hand. No ring. He handed the dog back.

"So, were you coming or going?" she asked.

"Pardon?"

"From the store," she clarified.

"Ohhhh. Neither. I was going to the Starbucks next door." He gave his shoulders a shrug. "Coffee junkie."

"So I deprived you of your caffeine fix?"

"Just a delay."

She went silent, looked at him in careful consideration, and the pause again put him ill at ease. Some people were excellent conversationalists. Patrick could hold his own only if the other party was equal to the task but had never been adept at jump-starting the dialogue. Instead, his eyes wandered away to an innocent blade of grass nearby.

"There's a coffeehouse around the corner," she said at last.

The shop was no Starbucks. One of the small, last sanctuaries of independence in a growing world of corporate takeovers and retail chain domination, the GrindHouse was an intimate venue for the art-house set.

At one time, the building housed one of those 24-hour convenience stores, but it had been remodeled extensively inside, now bearing walls of dark wood littered with paintings by local artisans and flyers for upcoming folkie performances. With its well-worn furniture and low lighting, the atmosphere was true bohemian, befitting the tone of a coffeehouse.

"The selection here may not be as extravagant as what you are used to," Shelley noted as they looked over the large wall chalkboard menu with its coffees, salads, sandwiches, and beers (for the late-night musical crowd) listed in multiple chalk colors.

"No, this is good," Patrick replied, surveying the surroundings. "I like it."

They placed their orders, his a basic black, no sugar, and hers a latte along with a couple of carrot muffins, and then they took a table near the back. Except for another couple sitting near the front window and the shop employees, they had the place to themselves.

At first, there was only the slurping of coffee, each holding on to their cup as if it were a safety net. She broke the silence first.

"A name would be nice."

"I'm sorry. I should have introduced myself earlier. I'm Patrick."

She nodded. "Good name. Not too common, just enough so."

"And you are..." he prompted, already knowing her name but following proper etiquette.

"Shelley." Another pause, another sip of coffee. "So is chasing after people with their dropped goods an occupation for you?"

"Afraid not. I have to work for a living."

"Which is?"

"Communications—well, retail actually. Cell phones."

"So you just chase after people on the side. Rather like a hobby."

"No. This was pure chance. Like I said earlier, I tried to catch up to you before you drove off, but I, well, I tripped and fell."

"Seems to be a lot of that going around today," she answered.

"Really, I did." Without thinking, he held up his injured left hand for inspection. "See?"

"Ugh," she responded, turning her head away.

"Sorry. I didn't mean to gross you out."

"No, it's okay," she answered after he lowered his hand. "I don't do well with blood."

"So I take it you're not a nurse."

"No," Shelley answered but offered no more.

"So what's the Gilmore connection?" he asked.

"Oh, that. There are some personality traits—quirks—in the lead character that I can identify with."

"Such as?"

"Just things," she answered vaguely.

"Well, from what I remember, there was not a single *normal* person in the entire show. Everyone was slightly off-kilter."

"You see? What does that say about me?" she quipped.

Patrick laughed, but more to himself than what she had just said.

"What?" she asked.

"Just a line that popped into my head. The time has come to talk of many things. Of shoes, and ships, and sealing wax."

"Of cabbages and kings, and why the sea is boiling hot, and whether pigs have wings. Well, I don't like cabbage. Sealing wax is hardly worth discussing, so that leaves the pigs with wings."

"Good memory. You remember the line better than I."

Shelley smiled and took another sip of coffee. "I studied Lewis Carroll in college. Actually, it was one of my favorite classes, interpreting the Looking-Glass and Wonderland stories as allegory rather than a simple children's story. The adventure is seen as a journey from childhood to adulthood, a rite of passage, and the Alice that comes out the other end is not the one who began the adventure. There are also the social and political interpretations to the story. So, yes, I remember the line."

"I can't say that my university courses were quite so memorable," Patrick said, visibly impressed she was so well read. Smart as well as cute... probably smarter than he. "It seems like a long time ago."

"It does at that, but they were good times for me." She took a nibble of her muffin. "Well... what do you think? Do pigs really have wings?"

He laughed. "Heavy question. So the conversation's gone from decaf to espresso, huh? There was a time when I thought so. I believed in a great many things, but..." Patrick took a deep breath while letting his gaze take in the room around him. "One by one, I discovered the pigs for what they were, not what they appeared to be, and as much as I wanted the wings to be real, I could see the attached strings and the papier-mâché."

"Optimistic much?"

He considered this before answering but instead changed direction. "How is it that two strangers jump into deep thoughts within a few minutes of meeting? What happened to light discussion, like weather, music, or favorite foods?"

"You were the one who brought up Alice," Shelley responded and smiled. "Now you know better."

"Then how about you? Any winged pigs?"

"Of course," she responded without hesitation. "I see flying pigs every day."

"Optimistic much?"

"Absolutely."

"Yeah, right," Patrick observed. "You always find the bright side of things and see the best in people?"

"I... try," she answered, and for the briefest of moments, something dark passed behind her eyes, then it was gone. "I have my down periods, but I prefer to accentuate the positive."

"Interesting. I wouldn't have guessed it from the greeting card you dropped."

Shelley's composure toppled. "You read the card," she said slowly, not as much as a question as a new fact to consider. He nodded in response. "This is... embarrassing. You see, I..." She paused, looking at her cup, and then back at Patrick. Then her demeanor changed. "That was personal. You shouldn't have looked at that."

"It was just a greeting card. I expected a simple happy birthday, thank you very much."

"At least you could have had the decency not to have mentioned it." She reached for her purse and started to get up. "I should go now."

"No, wait!" said Patrick. "I'm sorry. I didn't think anything of it when I looked. It was as much an impulse as trying to return the card to you, and... I've enjoyed talking with you. Please don't go."

Shelley eyed him with an unreadable expression before settling back into her chair.

"Can we pretend I never read the card?" he asked, hoping humor might charm himself back into her graces.

"Had roles been reversed, I might have looked myself," she finally said. "But it is personal, so you caught me at a disadvantage. I tend to keep private. That card—it was a bookend of sorts to wrap up something in my life. And..." she considered her words before speaking, "I think the optimist in me was speaking out in that card."

"You're kidding? I'd hate to see what you think on your gloomy days."

She laughed at the remark, yet it sounded hollow. Patrick failed to notice. "This is the place where you're supposed to say 'Would you like to talk about it?'" she said.

"You said yourself, you like to keep things private. I would not presume."

"You're right, but I guess I owe some sort of explanation. Otherwise, you'll probably be thinking the wrong thing of me."

"You don't have to."

"No, it's all right. After all, you did return the card."

Behind her, a bell rang—Christmas bells hanging on the door as it opened—and a couple entered. Shelley glanced at them briefly as they walked to the counter, then turned back to Patrick.

"I was in a relationship. It just ended. He was all the things that could have possibly been wrong for me. I just didn't know it at the time. It took me a while to walk away."

Patrick nodded. "He must have really done you wrong for you to want to send him a card like that."

"He did, and I didn't... well, I haven't. I wasn't going to actually *send* the card."

"Then why did you buy it? Souvenir?"

Shelley contemplated this for a moment, again letting her eyes wander across the coffee shop interior before answering. "This has more to do with ritual than payback. Let me see if I can explain this properly. When I mentioned Alice's adventures, I spoke of a rite of passage. She goes through a series of experiences which lead her into adulthood. The events occur around her, but her choices are a part of it. She plays out a ritual to mark her own growing up. Do you see this?"

"Errr, no, not really."

Shelley began looking around the room, letting her mind search for a better explanation. She lingered on the anorexic Christmas tree in the corner, colorfully lit and decorated with a random collection of ornaments. Then the proper analogy struck her.

"Okay. Were you a Boy Scout?"

"Yes."

"Good. I did the Girl Scout thing. You remember the award ceremonies we were all paraded through to get the little patches and pins?" He nodded, and she continued. "Those were the rituals which marked each step in our progression as a scout. They were supposed to represent our growth in learning, and the step up in ranks were like steps toward adulthood. That's the rite of passage. Got that?"

"Sure. So how does the card fit in?"

Shelley opened her mouth and then shut it abruptly. "Christ, I don't know why I am telling you this. I don't even know you."

"But isn't that how all acquaintances begin? As strangers?"

"True," she replied, "but not everyone is followed home without their knowledge. I mean, what motivates a person to drive all across town just to return a dropped card. The 'good deed' line only holds so much weight. If I had been a little old lady, would you have done the same?"

He laughed. "Funny thing, a similar thought had occurred to me on the way."

"And?"

"I don't know," he answered with a shrug of his shoulder.

"I think you do." She looked at him intently, rather like a visual interrogation, looking for some physical twitch that might give him away.

"Are you married?" she asked.

He held up his left hand, sans ring, for her to see.

"That doesn't mean a damned thing."

"No, I'm not," he answered.

"Engaged, involved?"

After a moment to choose his words, he replied, "The polite response would be that I am between relationships. For what it's worth, I was recently burned as well."

"Messy?"

"Pretty much so. It would be easy to point fingers, but there was more than enough blame to share."

"A noble and honest answer." Shelley's eyes grew cold. "My finger-pointing is purely one way. You read the card, so you know my feelings."

"And you consider this a rite of passage? I don't understand."

"Simple. I choose to do many things in response to this person that I... knew. I can do nothing. Forget everything that happened, pick up where I left off, move on. Tomorrow's another day, right? Except I'm still damned angry."

"Can I ask what he—"

"Another woman," she answered before he finished the question. "He decided that two girls were better than one but neglected to fill me in. I found out the hard way. I could have taken the offensive, thrown eggs at his windows, slashed his tires, all sorts of mean, nasty things. Except that they are mean, nasty things, and I am not, generally speaking, a mean, nasty person.

"I could get all sad and melancholy and wallow in sorrow for a good long time, but he's not effing worth it. So I had this idea and went searching for a card to sum up my feelings. That was the one you found."

"And you thought to mail him a Christmas card just to tell him he is a jerk?"

She laughed. "You are being way too polite, and as I said before, I did not plan to mail it. I had something else in mind—my personal rite of passage. I plan to spend Christmas Eve at home with Rory and take stock of the bad baggage that I have accumulated.

"Then I will cut away all the unpleasantness that has filled my life, of which he—the jerk, as you called him—is a part. You see, it's not enough to simply chalk him up as a bad relationship without repercussions. A purging is in order. So you might say the card you found is something of a farewell card."

"But why Christmas Eve? Wouldn't you be spending time with family?"

"Parents are dead. No brothers or sisters. Other relatives live up north. That's okay. I'm giving myself a good present: a clean slate, no bad baggage."

She smiled at him, but there ran an undercurrent that belied her grin. Behind her, the other couple began to chuckle over some joke shared between themselves.

"More coffee?" Patrick asked, attempting to fill the void left by her lapse into silence.

"No," she replied, automatically putting her hand over the cup. "So, how about you? Spending the holidays with family?"

"Yeah. Warm-up Christmas exercises tomorrow night, parents, brother, sister-in-law, eggnog, a few presents. I'm sure my niece and nephew will force us to watch the Grinch movie yet again."

"That's nice, though. At least you have people to share it with."

Patrick considered this, along with the obvious question to follow. "Look, I know that we just met, but if you would like—"

"No," she answered before he had a chance to finish. "I know what you were going to ask, and it is awfully sweet of you to think of it, but no. I will be best off spending my evening as planned. I have a fire waiting. But thank you, just the same."

"Then would it be too forward of me to ask for your phone number?"

"No, it's not too forward, but I'm not ready."

"Fair enough," he replied, doing well to mask his disappointment. He reached into his pocket for a pen, then wrote his number on a napkin. "Then take this. If you change your mind, I'd like to hear from you again." She took the napkin from him without looking at it and put it in her purse.

"Why?"

"I could use a positive role model. You seem to have all the answers."

"You might be surprised," she replied without as much as a smile. "Every silver lining has its cloud."

They stayed a short while longer. He downed the remainder of his coffee. She left hers half full but finished her muffin. They said their goodbyes and parted. The meeting ended with the jingling of the Christmas bells from the door of the coffee shop as it closed.

Christmas Eve.

Bing sang "White Christmas." Nothing spoke of the holiday better than Crosby, Shelley thought, especially this song. White *anythings* were few and far between in this region, much less a white Christmas, so the song conjured the magic of faraway landscapes full of snow, glistening treetops, and sleigh bells. The music fit well into the background, with just the right touch to finish off the mood.

The room was illuminated from various points: the smallish Christmas tree inset with white lights which stood in one corner, several red candles scented with holiday spices positioned around the room, a table lamp, and the fireplace ablaze with gas-fed flames that licked up around the fake log.

Shelley settled herself into the chair opposite the lit fireplace, with the unopened parcel resting on her lap. There was no surprise to what it might contain. This was her Christmas present to herself, an impulse buy from earlier in the week, and she had grown worried that it might not arrive before the twenty-fifth.

She picked up the razor blade box cutter from the side table and pushed up on the safety handle. The blade slid into place with an audible click. It was short work to slice open the box and push back the tissue paper. Then she pulled out the object of her desire, a wool shawl that was soft, thick, and as white as the hard-driven snow of a thousand holidays past.

After setting the box cutter on the table, she pulled the scarf around her shoulders, enjoying the same comfort as a down blanket might offer at bedtime. Sometimes the simplest of things could make all the difference.

Shelley watched the unscripted choreography of the flames for a while, occasionally taking a sip of merlot from the glass she had set next to the box cutter.

Another year come, another year nearly gone, and she considered how she fit into its scheme. In the grand picture, there was little to suggest that it was any different from the year before. Oh, the day-to-day activities might have varied, but what about the significant accomplishments that marked the year as a success?

The highest highs were also marked with the lowest lows, and all were tied to an individual to whom she had opened herself up emotionally. Could she have known better? Could she have read the signs in advance? Perhaps so, not that it mattered now. He was gone, good riddance, and she had found him a card. Oh, what a card.

She looked at the side table, examining the objects that rested there: a lit votive, a pen, a half-read book she had been working on for the last several weeks, a small brown paper bag, a stack of unopened cards all addressed to her, several blank cards—and his card. Next to it was the box cutter, its razor blade still exposed and gleaming from the reflection of the lit votive.

Shelley picked up the cutter and worked the razor blade loose from its protective sheath. It slid free without resistance. She held the blade up, attempting to see her reflection while angling it from one position to another.

What she saw was cold metal but little else. No, the blade would give up nothing more than what it was designed to do. This, it could do quite well.

She ran her fingers across her left wrist. With her thumb, she found the gentle pulse of the vein and focused on the rhythm.

Thump-thump.

Thump-thump.

Shelley closed her eyes, feeling the internal tempo while letting her mind wander on matters concerning the fragility of life.

Thump-thump.

She had been neither entirely forthright nor honest the previous day. Oh yes, it was easy to speak of feeling upbeat to a stranger when he was unaware of the ticks and tocks that make a person. Some of it was true. As to the rest—well, everyone had their shadow side.

Thump-thump.

She thought of her friend, Angie, from long ago. They had known each other for years, close if not best of friends, and had shared all their ups and downs, wondrous romances, failed outcomes, and other details of their lives. Then, as often happens, they took separate paths. They spoke less frequently, allowing more distance to come between them, much to Shelley's regret.

For Angie, the world had grown to be too much to occupy, and she had chosen the quick way out. She took to the blade, let her life ebb, and departed for whatever lay beyond. In her wake were a number of friends who mourned her absence and their loss. Angie had so much to offer, so much to give—if only she had reached out a little. She was deeply loved and deeply missed, and Shelley was among those who cried for her.

Thump-thump.

At the heart of the matter, Shelley questioned her own involvement. They had, at one time, been really tight. If she had remained in close contact, might the outcome have been different—or was this Angie's final and unchangeable rite of passage, and nothing done or said could have altered that course?

What a waste. How could anyone possibly do that to themselves? It was reprehensible.

As tears welled in her eyes, Shelley reached for the stack of cards, all addressed to her, and began to slice each open with the blade.

Really, one of these days, she was going to get herself a real letter opener.

The cards came from all over. Distant relatives from up north who wished her the best of the season, associates from work who thought enough of her to drop her a card, friends from far away who missed her, and other friends closer still who wanted the best for her in the new year.

Like Angie, she, too, was loved and was all the more thankful for it. Such a small thing, really, a greeting card, but it could make all the difference. Somehow, along the way, dear Angie lost sight of it before losing it all.

A soft whine diverted Shelley's attention. Rory sat with rapt attention at her feet, eyes transfixed on the side table with its small brown bag. "I bet you're wanting something," Shelley said while bending down to scratch the dog's head. Rory responded with a lick of the lips along with an expression that said, "Oh, yes! Please!"

Shelley opened the bag, pulled out a doggie treat, and held it out to her Spaniel. The treat disappeared in an instant. Rewarded and content, Rory settled herself on the floor, but with eyes still focused upward in case another treat might materialize.

Shelley set the cards aside, now reaching the moment she had planned. She took the card for her former lover, and using the nearby book as a makeshift surface to write on, laid the card open. She took the pen in hand, and after collecting her thoughts, she transferred them to the paper.

She began on the upper left corner of the card, and she filled the entire page. Then she moved to the right side of the card and continued. When it was filled, she moved to the back, all the while writing smaller and smaller in order to put every last thought she had onto paper.

She bore her soul to him, her rage, her philosophy, her affection, and her contempt. Then at the very end, with only a little space left, she signed her name and put the card back into its envelope. Then gently, but with much focus, she placed the card on the fire.

She sat back in her chair, wine in hand, and watched as the card took to the flames, released into the world.

She sat for a while, feeling all the better, and then reached for another card on the table, the other one she had bought the previous day, the one that did not fall out of her bag.

After taking pen in hand again, she addressed the envelope to herself, then moved onto the card, again starting in the upper left corner. This time, she wrote of hopes and dreams, of the possibilities of all that was yet to come, and of pigs with wings. Once completed, she placed the card into its envelope and then carefully put it at the base of her tree where it would be waiting for her the following morning.

Then came the final card, to which she addressed to Angie. She considered what to write, the many words that might sum up her feelings—but it all felt too trite. These emotions were not so easily put into words—so she simply drew a heart, signed her name, and slid the card into its envelope.

She stood and rose onto tiptoe to place the card as high up on the tree as she could reach, next to the star-shaped topper. The card seemed to glow from the lit star, and Shelley took several steps back to examine the tree in full, with thoughts of auld acquaintances never to be forgotten.

"Merry Christmas, Angie, wherever you are," she whispered to her star, to all the others in the night's sky, and to the universe that gave them comfort. She felt a chill and pulled in her shawl.

Having made her peace with pen and paper, she settled back in her chair after retrieving a crumpled napkin from her purse. She took another sip of wine, this time to steady her nervousness a bit, and then tapped in the number on her phone.

Hopefully, he'd have a few minutes to spare on Christmas Eve just to talk.

After that?

Well, who knew what the future might bring?

Patrick picked up his cell phone on the second ring. He didn't recognize the number on the screen. It could've been anyone, most likely spam, but he had a premonition of who it might be. He excused himself from the room, leaving his family to their Christmas Eve activities while thinking that this Christmas was shaping up to be a very good one.

AN INTRODUCTION

FLASHLIGHT PERILOUS

This is the first of the stories that feature the Neuwirth family. At the time, I had no idea they would stick around. Martin, Bettye, and the family continue to reappear in other stories over the years, and whenever they do, I know things will never go as planned.

FLASHLIGHT PERILOUS

THIS MAY NOT HAVE been such a good idea, Bettye Neuwirth thought as Matthew ran ahead of her with his new toy. It seemed to be a smart move at the time—to buy him a little something to play with while they shopped, thus keeping him pacified. However, the toy had the opposite effect.

The upper concourse of the shopping mall bustled with a mass of people, their holiday packages in tow. Seasonal décor adorned every shop and kiosk while the motif carried overhead with brightly lit garland adorned with bows.

The visual bombardment equaled the cacophony of voices which overpowered the generic festive music. Welcome one, welcome all, to the busiest mall in town during the busiest week of the year.

This point made Bettye cringe even more. By attempting to finish her Christmas shopping here, she had joined the ranks of the frazzled mid-December shoppers. Her original inclination was for a more intimate marketplace, smaller, less traveled, and less commercial. If not for those several items that could only be found in this zoo, she would have stayed miles away. Now with less than a week to go until Christmas, she felt the pressure to get all the final presents off her list. Procrastination never worked well during the holidays.

The simple act of finding a parking spot became an ordeal, taking a good twenty minutes. Equally challenging was navigating the crowds, both inside the stores and out in the mall proper. Long lines materialized wherever she went.

The biggest frustration arrived when the two items that brought her to the mall in the first place were sold out. Most likely, they would not be restocked until the end of the week, requiring another visit to the mall at its absolute worst time—the mad rush of the last-minute shopper. In short, not a quality Christmas moment.

And she had Matthew in tow.

Let it be noted that the attention span of a five-year-old boy was equal to the entertainment surrounding him. A playground, a city park, a room full of toys, or that oft-used media babysitter—the TV—all worked for the same reasons that the clothing section of a department store did not.

Without a good diversion to keep him occupied, odds were that the child would find his own means of entertainment, and at the expense of Mom's patience. During their time, Bettye had repeatedly pulled Matthew away from the breakable items on display, twice lost him while he played hide-and-seek in the clothing racks, scolded him for not using his "indoor voice" which only made him want to shout even louder—and she panicked each time he ran out of her sight despite her strict orders not to do so. For his part, he did what any normal child his age would do—but it left her a nervous wreck. Some drastic measure was now in order.

Thus the toy store, a perfect solution for her problem. He could spend a few quality minutes having his kind of fun while looking at the toys and games he had asked Santa for (and many more to be included as an addendum to his wish list).

This allowed Bettye to chill. Most importantly, she set the bait for Matthew—a means to finish her shopping without concern about him climbing another shelf.

"You can pick out one toy," she told him, "on the condition that you behave while I finish our shopping." This was a no-brainer for a child when offered the toy of their choice.

"Yes, Mommy," he replied enthusiastically. "I'll be good." Of course, good in the mind of a five-year-old was relative.

Matthew spent the next fifteen minutes looking over the vast array of toys, wholly aware of the weight and enormity of such an important decision.

With choices endless, he ran from aisle to aisle, examining every toy within his three-and-a-half-foot reach: the transforming robots with the bionic battle cry, the helicopter with motion sounds, the multitude of comic book action figures, handheld electronic game packs, the super rescue soldier, the dragon hand puppet, the rocket ranger power glove, and the three shelves of spy stuff (including the night-vision stealth glasses, the super-secret hideaway camera, and mystery decoder watch).

Following this, he spent a good five minutes on the car aisle where any and all vehicles with four wheels were to be found, from the small metal cars to the multi-task dirt-digger construction vehicle.

But it was Cosmo Millennium, Galaxy Explorer, who won out in the end.

To be precise, this was the Cosmo Millennium ray gun, a glorified flashlight disguised as a sci-fi pistol. The silver plastic gun sported a retro fifties space-age style, with dark blue lightning bolts accenting either side.

The rear flashlight end contained a circular piece of transparent yellow plastic which could be turned on by pulling the upper section of the dual trigger. The lower trigger activated the light-up front propeller, a major appeal to the toy.

Extending from the front was a pair of two-inch cords with bright red light-up ends. When activated, the cables spun around like a propeller with the two red lights creating the illusion of a wheel of flame. Atop the whole assembly was a miniature replica of Cosmo Millennium with his arms wrapped around the barrel as if ready for takeoff. Matthew fell in love with the toy immediately and would have nothing else.

At least it doesn't make noise, Bettye thought as she made the purchase.

The problems inherent with such a device began almost immediately. At first, Matthew was content to pull the trigger and watch the light-up propellers spin. It then dawned on him that the true responsibility of the wielder of such an instrument was clear and single-fold: the arrest and destruction of extraterrestrials, monsters, master criminals, and other bad guys.

With this realization, he took immediate action, running up to everyone in his path with the single-minded intent of saving the universe. "You're dead! Hands up!" he cried before firing his blaster at the unsuspecting holiday shopper.

A few took this in stride, those being parents themselves, but several others were less accepting about being ray-gunned while searching for that elusive gift for Uncle Al.

When an elderly lady let out an alarmed shriek, Bettye figured her boy had done enough world-saving for the day. She patiently explained to Matthew how the spirit of Christmas meant clemency for space aliens.

They made their way to the clothing store where Matthew hid under the racks of coats, turning it into his super-secret hideaway. Occasionally, he peered through the suits, took careful aim, and blasted an incoming battle cruiser. Bettye picked out several men's shirts and checked out.

"Matthew, time to go," she said to the coat rack.

Silence.

"Now, Matthew," she repeated, this time with that well-used parental tone.

"You can't get me" came the voice behind the double-breasted forty-twos. "I'm Cosmo Millennium in my secret headquarters."

"All right, Cosmo, you tell Matthew that he has to go, right now."

The response was the sudden appearance of the ray gun through the coats. It blasted her then disappeared back into the secret hideaway. Behind Bettye, the department cashier watched with mild amusement having seen this type of thing more times than she could count.

After an extended standoff, Bettye launched a surprise attack from the rear, dragging the galaxy explorer from his lair, and ushered him briskly from the store.

Following the epic battle of the apparel rack, Bettye drew up a cessation of hostilities for a lunch break. They strode into the food court and decided on hamburgers, one of the few things Matthew might eat.

She placed their order: a fully loaded burger for her and a plain hamburger with mayonnaise for Matthew along with fries and milk. She nearly ordered an iced tea when she spied a Mexican food vendor—the one with the frozen margarita machine.

"Oh, yeah," she said to herself, figuring that the tequila would take the edge off her rattled disposition. Minutes later, they sat in the courtyard with their burgers, fries, and beverages of choice.

Matthew promptly removed the meat from the bun, transforming his burger into a mayonnaise sandwich. Only when she threatened to take his toy away did he reluctantly take a few small bites of the meat.

The Cosmo Millennium ray gun rarely strayed from Matthew's hand. When not in use, it lay on the table beside him. More often—between bites of his bread and condiment—he waved it around the table, and Bettye kept shifting the cups and ketchup bottle out of range of the spinning propeller cord. As she considered a second margarita, the spinning propeller went for the kill and sent the ceramic sugar tray flying from the table.

Bettye experienced a unique distortion of time as she saw it all take place. She moved her hand to intercept the sugar tray, but it flew past her before she could fully react. Then came that lo-o-o-ong period of silence before the tray hit the floor, shattering into hundreds of pieces and sending sugar packets and ceramic shrapnel across the room.

Dozens of eyes in the court descended upon her. A hole to hide in would have been welcome. Instead, she made a speedy exit with her son and his blaster in tow, passing by an annoyed courtyard worker now faced with a lengthy cleanup.

As they walked along the upper concourse, Bettye considered how her best intentions failed her. Matthew stood at the edge, overlooking the skating rink below, with both hands thrust through the metal guardrail. Like a junior sniper in training, he systematically blasted the ice skaters below, who obviously were nothing more than interstellar creatures in disguise.

"Blam! Blam!" he shouted as he picked them off one at a time. "Got you now!"

Bettye stood behind him and watched the activity on the rink while considering an alternate diversion—one that might be less prone to random destruction. The solution presented itself at the far end of the rink just outside the skate area.

"Matthew, look over there." She bent down to talk to him. "Do you see what I see?" He stopped shooting the gun long enough to stare where she pointed. "Why, it's Santa," she continued. "Let's go see him. You need to tell him what you want for Christmas."

His eyes widened. Visions of toys of mass destruction surely danced in his head as they made their way to the lower concourse and Santa's magic village. To Bettye's surprise, the waiting line was short with only a few children in front of them.

During the wait, she considered how Matthew would fare this year with the bearded guy. In the past, he'd been too scared to get anywhere near Santa and had let loose a flood of tears to prove his point. Despite the red suit, fluffy beard, and jovial personality, Santa could be an intimidating presence.

Ever the good mom, Bettye had acted as a liaison, scribbling down Matthew's list on a piece of paper and delivering it personally to either Santa or one of his holiday helpers.

These last twelve months must have boosted Matthew's courage because as soon as his turn came, he boldly walked up to Santa and plopped himself on the red velvet lap.

"Well, ho! Ho! Ho!" Santa exclaimed in a boisterous voice. "What is your name?"

"Matthew," he replied with no hesitation.

"And have you been a good boy this year?"

He nodded emphatically. "Oh, yes."

"So, what would you like Santa to bring you this year?"

Matthew wasted no time running down his list of highly desirable toys and games.

"That sounds like a good list. Ah, but I see you already have a toy with you," Santa said, noticing the flashlight gun in his hand. "So tell me, Matthew, what do you have there?"

"Oh, this is my Cosmo Millennium Galaxy Explorer ray gun. I fight bad guys with it. Here, let me show you."

In an instant, he lifted the blaster forth, pulled the trigger, and pushed the spinning propeller straight into Santa's beard. As a horrible sound of a clogged motor sounded, Bettye put her hand to her face, unable to watch anymore.

At that moment, surrounded by other parents, children, and holiday elves, she wondered how this would affect Matthew's ranking on the Naughty or Nice list. She had her doubts as Santa exclaimed something quite out of character, words that would have made Mrs. Claus blush.

AN INTRODUCTION

1.25 MILES

Yes, a story based on actual events. My father did run out of gas halfway between two towns and had to walk a few miles to the nearest service station while my mother and I patiently waited. He was furious, partially because he had done the math beforehand in his head and thought that we could make it home before needing to refill. Never second-guess the E when the needle gets close.

1.25 MILES

FAMOUS LAST WORDS: "I can make it to the next gas station."

With the first cough of the engine, Joel realized his folly. In an almost—but not quite—comical fashion, he tried to nurse their SUV as far as possible, gaining a few hundred yards before the vehicle rolled to a stop along the side of the road, well past the last town. Without a building in sight, this was hardly an ideal place to be on Christmas Eve.

Joel's reaction came off as neither parentally responsible nor festive, letting forth a series of expletives normally shielded from his son Paulie.

"Dad, you're not supposed to talk like that," the boy said.

In the passenger seat, Melinda simply glared, not having to say a thing. They'd already covered the subject earlier when he passed the first station. "It's on the other side of the highway," he'd answered. "Anyway, I can still get another fifteen miles after I hit E." So he drove past the station, figuring he had plenty of time, followed by another station five miles farther down the road, and another after that. Then they exited the highway, gas forgotten—until now.

Joel spent the next few minutes evaluating the situation, mapping out a strategy, and considering options, which were few. For months, Melinda had badgered him to join AAA, and he took the path of optimum procrastination. Now regret swept in, as once more, she proved herself right.

At length, she spoke softly and with more than a trace of irritation. "We're going to be late." This translated as shorthand for a) Why weren't you paying attention since you need to be the responsible one? b) This wouldn't have happened if we were going to see *your* family, c) You've royally screwed up Christmas, and I'm damned angry with you, but I won't say it, and d) Etc., etc., etc.

The way Joel figured, they'd lost themselves in idle conversation as he drove, so she should accept some responsibility for his distraction. He drummed his fingers against the steering wheel. "I'm going to find a service station."

"Where? There's nothing around here."

He pulled his phone from his pocket, tapping the screen with more force than necessary. The map app answered with location and distance. "Looks like the next town is about three miles ahead."

Melinda folded her arms. "I'm not walking that far."

"I didn't ask you to. You stay here. Paulie and I are going."

"Da-a-ad," Paulie whined, drawing out the vowel through his nose.

Melinda shook her head. "The boy doesn't need to go."

"No, he's going," countered Joel. "I might need some help. You'll be fine here. Anyway, we always talk about him not getting enough exercise. Case closed."

"I don't want to be left alone. It's dark."

"If we had left Stillwater earlier as I wanted, we'd be in Todd Mission by now. It's an eight-hour drive without traffic. We could have gotten up early, had lunch in Dallas, and reached your brother's place by evening."

She crossed her arms, her ire matching his. "But we didn't. Now you've stranded us."

"So you gonna walk to the next town with me?" he snapped back.

"No."

He took in a deep, calming breath, then let it out. "Mel, you'll be safe here," he said, placing his hand on hers. "Keep the doors locked. You have your cell phone and I have mine in case you need me."

Joel had no overriding reason to take Paulie. True, the boy spent way too much of his free time in front of the television. Nor would he be of any help. If anything, he'd slow down Joel. No, the reason had to do with mutual suffering. Joel may have created their current problem, but he refused to endure the consequences alone. Lucky Paulie. For the moment, the spirit of Christmas generosity eluded Joel's judgment.

They took to the road. Within minutes, their car faded into the darkness, while before them, the road stretched into an equally rich, deep black.

"Daddy, how far do we need to go?"

"I don't know. Just keep walking."

He should have anticipated the inevitable repeat, which came five minutes later—or four. Possibly even three. "How much farther, Daddy?"

"Paulie, we'll get there when we get there." His response spilled out as sour wassail void of holiday cheer.

"But my legs are tired. Can we stop for a minute?"

"No."

"But, Dad, I'm really—"

"I said no."

That put a lid on the conversation. Paulie should've known better when his dad was upset.

Joel had every right to be pissed, mostly at himself, for not paying attention. Now he reaped the consequences in the middle of a deserted Texas nowhere. Not a single car passed by since they took to foot. That, in itself, was unusual. Even the county roads had occasional traffic. The thought further sunk his mood.

A sign came into view marking the distance to the next town: one mile. All things considered, their predicament could have been far worse—five miles, ten, or fifteen. Once there, they could warm up a bit while Paulie rested his feet. Most importantly, he could buy the necessary can of gas. If Lady Luck decided to be extra generous, they might even find a ride back to their car.

A mile and a quarter perhaps, not too bad.

Except for two things. First, they had the cold to deal with, a point that Paulie kept bringing up. In truth, the temperature fell somewhere in the upper forties, but the associated wind made it worse. Joel's bigger concern had to do with a pointless trip. Not a single light could be seen ahead, leading him to an unpleasant conclusion of a town zipped tight for Christmas Eve.

This might be another bad call on Joel's part, not a new thing. He'd made them before and could relate to the joke of a rain cloud hovering over his head. For some reason, he managed to invite life's small unpleasantries on a regular basis. Tonight fell into place as another in a long line.

"Dad, I'm cold."

"Right." Joel stopped and took off his jacket. Paulie eagerly accepted the extra layer of clothing. "Is that better?"

"Yes, Dad. Thanks."

Joel now earned the right to feel the chill, so he walked all the faster. Big legs can do that in a way small legs can't.

"Dad, slow down."

Right. He eased the pace to Paulie's speed and rubbed his arms to generate some warmth. Looking ahead, he saw a light for the first time, there on the left side of the road. He hadn't seen it before. Regardless, there appeared to be at least one lit building in town.

"Dad?"

He looked over his shoulder to see his son farther back than before, now looking up at the sky. "Let's go, Paulie."

The boy pointed toward the night sky. "Dad, is that the star?"

"What star?"

"You know, the Christmas star. The one the smart men followed."

"Wise men," Joel corrected.

"Right. Wise men. Is that the one?"

Joel took a moment to look at the sky, letting his eyes adjust to the points of light overhead. He kneeled next to Paulie, pulling his son closer. "No, that's Mars, the red planet. That's where Martians come from."

Paulie responded with the *don't-BS-me* attitude that kids learn all too soon when the initial mysteries of the world were resolved and new ones arose in their place. "Dad, there are no such things as Martians."

"How do you know?" Joel grinned. "There could be a UFO with little green men zipping above our heads right now. Maybe they're Santa's helpers."

"I'm serious. Which star is it?"

He took a minute to look over the sky before giving up. "I'm not sure, Paulie. Maybe your Mommy would know. We'll ask her when we get back, okay?"

"Okay."

They resumed their pace, now with a lit destination in sight. As one footstep led to the next, Joel considered how they came to this point. Melinda's brother generously invited them to stay over for the holidays, which she immediately accepted. The siblings hardly saw one another now that their parents had died, and knowing this, Joel agreed. He waited too long to get plane tickets, so travel by car made the most sense even with the distance from Stillwater.

Her brother lived in Todd Mission, just north of Houston, meaning they would spend most of the day in the car. Had they left early, they might have enjoyed a leisurely Christmas Eve with her family. Instead, they left at noon.

Joel checked his watch: nine seventeen. Even in the best scenario, it would be another hour before they got the car on the road again. The remaining distance diminished—not quickly, but with slow consistency.

The light ahead revealed an aged gas station preserved straight out of the fifties when attendants in uniform pumped the gas and checked the oil as part of standard service. It wore well the passage of years, from the sign positioned near the roadway to the two pumps, likely of the same age as the station, lacking credit card slots and touch screens. He figured them to be for decoration, not function.

A lone exterior light located on the side of the building flickered on and off, indicating its weariness to the dark.

As they drew nearer, Joel realized his accuracy. The town appeared to be locked up for the night. Even this one building might be closed; the lights to the sign and above the pumps were off, and only as they drew nearer did he see a light in the building—along with movement.

"Thankyouthankyouthankyou," Joel said softly for the small miracle.

They crossed the lot, a finish line of sorts, but without the ceremonial ribbon to break through or the cheering crowds. Positioned in the station's window, through glass that might not have been cleaned in years too numerous to count, hung an OPEN sign with handwriting below which read WELCOME Y'ALL.

Joel opened the door, and a gust of warmth hit them both in the face. The interior of the station appeared much like the exterior, vintage in design and showing an abundance of wear. Dust settled in every corner as long-standing friends, and the related smell, a mixture of oil and age, reeled in the events of a thousand yesterdays. Behind the counter sat a man who matched the years of the building around him, arms crossed and legs propped up on a nearby stool. He eyed them both with mild interest.

Joel broke the silence. "You open?"

At this, the man gave up a grin that displayed an absence of dental care, teeth darkened and at odds with one another. For what the man lacked in appearance, the sparkle in his eyes compensated in full. "Was last time I checked," he said, voice coarse but friendly enough. "What can I do you for?"

"We ran out of gas up the road. Looks like the rest of the town is closed for the night."

"I reckon it is 'cept for me. Folks here are with family." The man paused for effect then added, "It's Christmas Eve, you know?"

Behind Joel, Paulie wandered the narrow aisles between metal racks filled with potato chips, peanuts, and other snacks. His small footsteps echoed in the stillness.

"So—out of gas, eh?" the man said once more, now setting his feet on the ground. "Heck of night to get stuck. Too bad. We're out of gas here too."

The man stared at Joel's reaction, one of abject misery, then let forth a roughened cackle. "Just kidding. Yeah, we got gas." His chuckle ended with a loud snort followed by a sigh. "That's why I'm here. Gotta peddle the petrol to those in need."

Joel feigned an unconvincing laugh. "Do you have any gas cans here?"

The man sniffed and pointed to the rear of the store. "Back wall, bottom shelf, nine ninety-nine plus tax."

As directed, Joel found a metal three-gallon can on the shelf. Judging by the layer of dust on the top, it had occupied that spot for years. He carried it to the counter and pulled out his wallet.

"That'll be ten seventy-eight, plus the gas, of course," the man said while ringing it up on a register of the same vintage as the building. It let out a *ca-ching* as the drawer popped out.

Joel cast a glance toward the entrance. "What about the pumps? They look sort of... out of date."

"Now don'cha judge a book by its cover. They never failed me yet." He sniffed again before running his index finger across his moistened nose. "By the way, the name's Elmer. Glad to be of help." He extended his hand, fortunately not the one used as a tissue moments earlier.

Appropriate name, Joel thought, shaking the man's hand while picturing the cartoon character and rabbit hunting. "I'm glad you're open. I don't know what I would have done otherwise."

"How far up the road are ya?"

"About a mile and a quarter. My wife's waiting on us."

At this, Elmer made a soft sound of reproach. "Shouldn't be leaving the lady all by herself even on Christmas Eve."

Joel slapped a twenty on the counter. "I didn't have much choice now, did I?"

"Now, now, didn't mean to get you all in a tizzy. She'll be fine. Ya got far to go?"

"Just past the next town. We've got family there."

"That's what it's all about. Family. Friends. It's the time for taking stock of the little things, ya know what I mean?" Elmer cocked his head. "You should expect the unexpected on nights like tonight. How come you run outta gas?"

Joel paused, not anticipating the directness of the question. "Because I didn't stop at the last station."

"Because..." Elmer's eyes twinkled.

"Because I forgot."

"Because..."

"I didn't pay attention. Happy?" Joel snapped.

"Ahh," Elmer replied, stretching out the sound. "Ya gotta slow down. Smell the roses. We get so caught up in where we're going, we don't think about where we are, or more important, them folks around us."

"You a preacher or something?"

Elmer offered up another toothy grin. "Nah. Jes' dime-store advice from an old geezer."

"Oh, cool!" came a voice from the rear. "Dad, check this out!"

Joel turned to see Paulie nearby, standing in complete rapture. The object of his attention rested on top of the ice machine. A bright yellow toy dump truck, large by adult standards and gargantuan to the eyes of a child, loomed above Paulie like the Holy Grail with wheels—or as Elmer might describe it, "the cat's meow."

No mere plastic cheapo, the truck stretched nearly two feet in length, solid metal, moving parts, doors that opened, and battery-operated headlights (with the batteries actually included, so said the cardboard packaging).

"Dad, can I have that? I really want it, really, really bad!"

Parental conditioning kicked in, and Joel nearly uttered the standard response—No—given that wherever they went, be it the grocery store, pharmacy, or any place of retail, the inevitable "I want this" line arose. Then he paused, opting instead for a more effective answer.

"Paulie, why don't we wait? It's Christmas and Santa will be bringing a bunch of toys."

"But Da-a-ad."

"I know. Do you remember what Mommy and I have told you about patience? Anyway, we would have to carry it all the way back to the car."

"I can do it, Dad. Please, please, please. I will be extra good today, tomorrow too, and I can use the truck to clean my room, and put all my things in its back, and move them, and, and, oh, please!"

Ahead of Joel lay two futures, one including the truck and one without. He stared at his boy, who now exhibited the classic wide-eyed wistfulness of a sad-faced orphan painting. He knew the outcome that accompanied choice A. For all his enthusiasm, Paulie might carry the truck for a block, two max, before complaining of it being too heavy and leaving Joel to drag it along with a full three-gallon gas can for the remaining distance. The alternative, the future sans truck, transformed Paulie into a miniature zombie, slumped shoulders, dragging feet—and walking dejectedly slow for the entire distance back. This alternative would stretch the return trip to twice the time.

Joel saw this as a no-brainer.

"All right, son, we can get it." At this, Paulie's face lit up brighter than any of the decorated houses they had passed on the trip from Stillwater. "Are you sure you can carry it back?"

"Oh, yes! Thanks!"

"Ya done good," said Elmer as Joel placed the oversized truck on the counter. "Mark my words... No matter what he gets for Christmas, this here truck's gonna be his favorite."

Joel pulled his wallet out once more. "So what do I owe you?"

Elmer eyed the truck, then leaned back into his chair. "Take it."

"Uh... I can't do that. Let me pay you for it."

Elmer looked Joel squarely in the eyes. "Listen here. I saw the look on that boy's face. That there truck's as much my property as the man in the moon. It belongs to him, always has. It was simply waiting for him to stop by and pick it up. So consider this a Christmas gift and think no more of it."

Reluctantly, Joel agreed and handed the truck to his son, who in turn struggled with the weight. "You got it, Paulie?"

The boy nodded.

"This is awfully kind of you," Joel said as he picked up the gas can.

"It's the little things, you know what I'm sayin'? Makes life worth living. Not a day goes by where I don't think about it." Elmer studied the boy, then added, "Ya got a ways to go. If you like, I can hold the truck for you until you gas up the car. Come back by and I'll have it waiting for you."

Joel let out a sigh of relief. "That's great. It's a long walk."

"Do I have to leave it?" Paulie worked his best pout.

Joel got to his knees, hands resting on his son's shoulders. "I know you're excited, but we need to get to the car first. I promise we will come straight back here for your truck. Deal?"

"Deal." The answer came with little enthusiasm. He turned and held the truck out to Elmer. "Thank you, mister."

Elmer showcased his row of crooked teeth. "You're kindly welcome."

Joel carried the can outside to the aged pump, accompanied by Paulie, and examined the relic. He lifted the nozzle, expecting it to cough air or remain dormant, but true to Elmer's word, gas flowed into the can without a problem. Once full, he returned for his change.

Elmer winked as he slid a couple of bills and coins across the counter. "You and your family have a merry Christmas."

Soon enough, the two began their trek back to the car. Paulie kept casting glances at the station behind them, its lights getting smaller the farther they walked.

The return journey played out differently from the first. Joel's disposition improved, having the gas can in hand. Despite the cold, he enjoyed the walk, taking in the quiet of the surroundings. Trees rustled as the wind swept past leaves and branches, this being the only sound aside from the steady *crunch, crunch, crunch* of feet against gravel. Silent night, indeed.

And for the first time this evening, he paid closer attention to the night sky. True, he'd looked it over earlier when trying to find Paulie's star, but now, the macrocosm spread out before him, each light a separate beacon. Such a simple thing to take for granted, this tapestry. In the city, stars vanished, washed out by the metropolitan lights. Out here, their luminescence held dominion.

They made better time on the return trip, helped by Paulie's brisk step. Joel understood his motivation: the sooner they reached the car, the quicker they'd return to the station and his new truck. At length, the faint outline of their SUV appeared in the distance. Paulie increased his pace as they drew near, and in the last few dozen yards, broke into a run.

"Mommy, Mommy, wait until I tell you!" he shouted before she had time to open the door. He leaped inside, telling her all the minute details of their adventure and of the truck that awaited him on their return. Melinda looked from Paulie to Joel, who remained outside with can in hand. Her raised eyebrow suggested *as if all the wrapped presents in the back aren't enough?* Joel offered her a smile, then stepped to the rear of the car to feed gas to a bone-dry tank.

Starting the engine proved to be a momentary challenge. Dry heaves and sputters ensued before the gas flowed freely through automotive veins, engine running. "Yay!" Paulie cheered, arms raised, as they pulled onto the road. "How long till we get there?"

"Hours," Joel teased. "Two or three, at least."

The boy knew better. Still, Joel figured that the mile-plus drive would stretch out far longer in the boy's mind than the entire time spent on foot.

As they drew nearer to town, Joel failed to see any lights. A block short of the station, and with no light apparent, he realized that Elmer might have shut down for the night. After all, this was Christmas Eve. In the final block, the station came into view, lights off. He pulled into the station lot. "Wait here," he said and stepped out of the car.

"Does Daddy have it?" he heard Paulie ask after a few scant moments. Of course, the boy had limited visibility from his vantage point in the rear seat.

A minute later, Joel opened the back door. "Here's your truck," he said, setting the toy on the seat alongside the boy. He returned to his spot behind the steering wheel and let out a sigh. Once more, wheels took to motion, and the SUV sped on to their Christmas destination, leaving the station far behind.

Paulie gave rapt attention to his monster truck, making little "*vroom, vroom*" sounds and repeatedly switching the headlights on and off, on and off. The strobe light effect transformed the interior into a miniature disco.

Melinda leaned toward Joel, speaking softly. "I can tell him to stop if it distracts you."

He shook his head. "I'm okay."

"Joel," Melinda said after a few more miles had passed in uncomfortable silence, "There is something about this I don't quite understand."

He kept his eyes glued to the road before him. "Can we talk about it later?"

The weary travelers, after crossing town, county, and state, arrived at their destination, welcomed with the warmest of hugs, the comfort of family, food kept warm in the oven, a comfortable fire to sit by, and wine to take the edge from the day. Paulie wasted no time in showing off the truck to his cousins.

Due to the lateness of the hour, the evening ended all too soon. Melinda put Paulie to bed, his truck resting nearby, and he fell asleep within minutes to dream of the next morning, Christmas Day, and all its surprises. Joel and Melinda soon nestled under the sheets in the guest room bed, listening to all the little sounds of the house. "Hon," she said at length, "what about the truck? You never told me."

"What's to tell? The guy closed for the night and left the toy for us next to the gas pump."

"But the station. It looked…"

"I know how it looked."

Melinda said nothing else, pulled the sheets tighter, and angled her body against him. Joel stared at the ceiling, his mind replaying the events of the evening and the return trip to the gas station. Melinda had every right to question its appearance. He had as well, for the building they returned to was one of long-standing abandonment: windows broken and partially boarded, a side wall and portions of the roof charred with black from a fire long before, signs askew or missing, and the whole unkempt, covered with the dirt of neglect. No telling how long the structure had been abandoned.

Joel had stepped closer to look inside, but could only see darkness. He told himself that he returned to the wrong place. There must be another station down the road—except for the evidence. Before him on a crumbled cement slab near one of the broken pumps rested the toy dump truck. It stood out in its sparkling newness against the age of its surroundings, awaiting the playfulness of a young boy.

Joel moved closer to his wife, bed sheets rustling softly. "Mel, I'm sorry… about earlier tonight. I shouldn't have taken it out on you and Paulie. I'm a jerk sometimes." She gave no response. When he looked at her, he saw she had already fallen asleep. Too bad—she would have relished the *I told you so* moment.

His mind returned to the boy's truck and the hows and whys, but no, he had no way to explain the unexplainable. Then, when logic exhausted itself, he considered the lesser details of the evening—that which gave him cause, moments in time, as well as the numerous transgressions in his own life. It all came down to that, not the great acts but the little things, words spoken kindly or not so kindly, actions with intent for good or ill, a thousand variables that made life worth living.

Pulling himself closer to Melinda, he drifted off, warm against her on the cold winter's night.

AN INTRODUCTION

CAPRA HAD IT WRONG

I love the idea of turning a story on its head. Every year, I pull out the holiday movies and we work our way through our favorites: *Love Actually*, *Remember the Night*, *White Christmas*, and one of the many versions of *A Christmas Carol*.

Two of the mainstays are *It's a Wonderful Life* and *The Bishop's Wife*. It got me thinking about what it takes to become an angel. Within the Pearly Gates, might there be a school for basic angel-work? And if so, might there be the A–students as well as those that... well, the term "slacker" comes to mind. Listen for the bell. It's bound to mean something.

CAPRA HAD IT WRONG

LEONARD FELT THE TAPE as soon as it made contact. He ruffled his feathers slightly, aware of the tacky adhesive stuck to them.

Instinctively, he raised his arms a bit, stretching shoulder muscles forward. Still, the effort failed to dislodge the strip while drawing attention from several students nearby. One of them, seated behind him and a little to the right, barely stifled a giggle.

He reached his arm behind him, finding the tape to be in that elusive area of the back well out of reach. With his thumb and forefinger, he barely managed to touch the piece of paper attached to the tape.

An initial tug did little to dislodge the sheet, only pulling against the feathers. Now irritated, Leonard gave it a good yank. This time, the sheet came free, leaving the tape in place firmly stuck against the feathers.

"Jesus H. Christ," he muttered.

"Leonard," said a voice from the front of the room, "did you say something you would like to share with the rest of us?" It was a low authoritative voice, one well-seasoned to governing the slings and arrows of a classroom.

"No, Miss Agatha," Leonard responded while moving the paper out of sight under his desk. He waited for further admonishing, but none came. She'd made her point. Once sure he was no longer the focus of attention, he glanced at the paper.

Written on it in big blue letters were the words *Bite Me!*

He leaned back and whispered to the person in the chair directly behind him, "Very funny, jerk."

"You weren't supposed to find it so fast," came the reply.

"Right. Now, how about taking the tape off my back?"

"Sorry, pal, but I can't get to it now."

"You stuck in there in the first place," Leonard snapped.

"Don't bother me. I'm busy doing my homework. Maybe later, I can—"

"Jeffrey!" came the voice of authority from the front, now addressing the person behind Leonard.

"Yes, Miss Agatha?"

"Jeffrey, our topic is *The Bishop's Wife*. Please tell me what Dudley's motivations were to help Julia."

Jeffrey appeared to shrink several inches in his chair, a remarkable feat for someone who stood five-foot-eleven and weighed two hundred thirty-seven pounds at the time of his death. "I think I missed that part."

Leonard covered his mouth and whispered loud enough for Jeffrey to hear, "Because he wanted to get laid."

Miss Agatha, the class instructor, held her pointer in one hand and tapped it impatiently against the palm of the other. She took several steps from the front of the classroom, her attention firmly on the two.

"I heard that, Leonard," she snipped. "By now, I think you would know better. My hearing is just as good as when I was a teen. I expect you to pay attention with the proper respect and decorum. I also expect you to learn this material. This is why you both are still in my class, and until the time comes that you retain the lessons, you will remain here. Do I make myself clear?"

"Yes, Miss Agatha," they both answered. Leonard sighed while Jeffrey put his hand over his mouth to mute a chuckle. If the instructor noticed, she gave no indication. Instead, she returned to the front of the room.

"As for your crass remark, Leonard, Dudley did not want to get laid. Angels don't *get* laid. Angels don't have sex." She paused momentarily flustered at the subject before continuing. "At least not in the corporeal manner you were inferring. Such things are for the living and the material world, so I would appreciate it if you keep your lewd observations to yourself."

She faced the class once more. Visually, she fit the proper school-teacher stereotype discounting, of course, the white robe, the feathery wings, and the glow that seemed to emanate from around her head.

She wore her gray hair pulled into a bun, framing a face lined with wrinkles. Thick, black plastic-rimmed glasses camouflaged those lines around her eyes. These she'd remove on occasion either to wave about or to emphasize a point before putting them back on.

In truth, it made no difference whether she wore them. Since passing over, her vision reverted to her youthful twenty-twenty. Still, having worn them much of her life, she was reluctant to give up the prop.

Her mannerism suggested she had been teaching for decades. By actual count, it was more like one hundred seventy-two, estimating by Earth time. The whole space-time continuum didn't apply here except as a reference point.

"As I stated," she continued, "Dudley is an ideal role model for your consideration. Pay attention to how he handles each situation. His confidence and dedication carry him through. He knows that his is a divine mission—that he is there only to serve, but he is always in control."

She paused for a moment either for the information to sink in or dramatic effect. "Some of you might consider *The Bishop's Wife* to be Heavenly propaganda, and in that observation, you are not far from the truth.

"Consider which muse might have fueled the scriptwriter's pen for the story. This is but another Earthly manifestation of angelic wisdom, of which, the writer was given a helping hand. This inspiration can also be found in song, literature, and art.

"However, today, we focus on this particular story which has dual purpose. For mortals, it is an entertaining diversion with a message. For our needs, it is a tutorial just like the Capra film we watched in our last class.

"Now, before I start the moving picture, I should like you to pay attention to the contrast between Dudley and the angel in the photoplay we saw in our last class. Note how Clarence, who so desperately wanted to get his wings, went about helping George Bailey."

Jeffrey leaned forward and whispered to Leonard, "They're both wussies."

"I guess," Leonard replied hesitantly. Cary Grant hardly seemed like the wuss type.

Jeffrey gave a snort. "And the 'earning your wings' line. Everybody knows you get your wings as soon as you croak. It's automatic. You sign in, get your wings, your glowy head-thing, and your instrument of choice. Even that is bull. I wanted a Fender Strat. Was told they don't allow electric guitars here. What a bunch of—"

"Shh," hissed Jessica, a new girl from the next row, obviously intent on listening to the teacher. Jeffrey responded with a nasty look but complied and closed his mouth into a forced pucker.

"Could have been worse," Leonard whispered to Jeffrey. "You could have been given an accordion. Anyway, I was never musical before. Now I am. Is that cool or what?"

"AC/CD just ain't the same on a harp, though," Jeffrey answered.

The room around them—not a tangible room of hard walls but a visual manifestation—grew darker as a projection screen appeared, rolling down the front wall. Nothing supported the upper framework of the screen—hardly a miracle in the larger scheme of things.

Miss Agatha strode down the center aisle to an empty spot midway. The space shimmered as a squarish shape took form, at first, barely visible like misty breath on a cold day.

Soon the chimera let go of its transparency as sides met corners and the whole became fully solid. The object hovering in midair was an old sixteen-millimeter projector, something that might have been commonplace in a schoolroom from the 1960s.

The front arm bore a full reel of film already threaded into the projector with its leader attached to the take-up reel in the back. An electrical cord extended from the projector's rear, stretching down to the ground where it faded from sight into some ethereal wall plug.

Miss Agatha stepped alongside the projector and switched it on, causing a loud racket as the film immediately lost its loop. Without hesitation, she whacked the projector gear mechanism with her pointer.

Her gesture was fluid and precise as if she had done it countless times (which most likely she had). Thusly reprimanded, the obedient projector purred, sending a beam of light onto the screen in front. Showtime, folks.

"How archaic can you get?" Jeffrey whispered. "You would think she'd have the latest tech."

"What is current, anyway?" Leonard replied. Good point. In a place where seconds can measure years and eons flit by in an instant, trends and technologies were a moot issue. Leonard's point of reference, pre-crossing, was VHS tapes and basic cable television.

For Miss Agatha, the projector served as a personal preference much like her glasses. Here, intention equaled manifestation, no projector needed. She simply liked the sound. Her own point of reference, pre-transition, was of the candle-powered magic lantern.

"I get really tired of this flick," Jeffrey griped. "I've seen it to death."

His comment brought another shush from Jessica. "If you'd pipe down, you might learn something."

"Relax, hon," he responded. "It's only the opening credits. Cary hasn't even appeared yet." He topped it off with a curt smile in her direction, which earned him no points. No matter.

Jeffrey had no reason to impress her. He swung the other way romantically in life and saw no reason to change—but either from some sense of decorum or slight embarrassment from being shushed again, he zipped it for a while.

Leonard shifted uncomfortably in his seat. By comparison, he found Jessica to be absolutely worth a healthy degree of attention. No, he'd never seen her before. People came and went, not a surprise. Most of the time, he gave it no mind.

Yet she was a vision of loveliness even without the soft glow about her head. The light only accentuated the positive—definitely angel material.

Onscreen, the landscape of a teeming metropolis appeared, fading into a street scene filled with holiday shoppers, carolers, and children.

So the story began: The children crowd around a store window in rapt attention, watching the mechanical toys on the other side of the glass. One figure appears, inspecting his surroundings with a keen eye—the sounds of cheer, the excitement in the air, the wonder of the children. This is good—exactly as it should be for the season. Cary smiles.

Someone in the classroom sighed with infatuation. Leonard looked momentarily for its source, then back at Jessica. Light reflected off the screen cast a soft luminescence across her face.

She appeared to be engrossed in the movie as much as the tykes at the store window. He noticed the slight upturn of her lips as she watched.

The movie continued: Grant goes about his angelic duties, offering help wherever possible. He spots Julia on the street corner, staring at a much-desired hat in a store window. But such extravagances are beyond the means of a bishop's wife, so she opts for a simple Christmas tree, a symbol of the season.

As one of her friends observes, "It's disgraceful. However, it gives me the illusion of peace on earth, goodwill toward men." Julia is oblivious to Dudley's presence.

"You're right, dude," Jeffrey whispered. "He does have a true love boner for her."

A muffled snicker caused Leonard to look to his left. Jessica had overheard, apparently thought it funny, and failed to keep a straight face. Then realizing she'd been heard, she looked at Leonard and offered a quick smile before turning her attention to the movie. Leonard returned the smile.

The image onscreen froze with Cary Grant in a cinematic close-up. Moments earlier, he'd met the bishop, Henry Brougham, for the first time.

"Let us consider the approach used here," began Miss Agatha, "in redirecting mortals to their spirituality. As with all things, there must be freedom of choice, free will. All we do is point the way.

"Dudley uses his gifts—words, deeds, and charm, not to make people change their ways but to allow them to choose it for themselves. This decision must come from inside. This is a good lesson that bears repeating for you will find it helpful in your efforts.

"Now, let us look at Clarence. Given, he is no Cary Grant."

"No sh--xmtplnz, Sherlock," Jeffrey mumbled, his favorite word dissolving into indecipherable gibberish. "Da--xzplfng. I hate it when that happens. You can't even swear in this place. My favorite words get censored."

"His path is not so clear cut," Miss Agatha continued. "Clarence knows what needs to be done, but the methodology is vague. As in life, there are no road maps..."

A hand rose from the back of the class. "You," addressed Miss Agatha to the student. "You have a question?"

"Yes," replied a youthful dark-haired girl with intense eyes. "In the story, we are led to believe that Clarence is a bumbler. He tried to get his wings before but failed. Judging from his character, it's not from lack of trying. Isn't wisdom supposed to be one aspect of divinity, and if so, how can we believe he is so inept?"

"Good observation. Despite his fumbling nature, Clarence means well and tries his best. That is the key. He keeps his target in sight. Of course, his tactics are considerably different than Dudley's, and he does not have the same amount of confidence. The end result is the same. In his case, wisdom comes from the heart, not the mind. So learn by example. Now, let us continue."

As the soft clatter of the projector resumed, so came movement to Cary's oversized image. Left to arrange the bishop's files, Dudley waves his hand and the cards rise of their own accord, darting past one another in the air before finding their proper place in the file holder.

The scene changes to the city park where Julia's daughter, Debby, has been rejected from the snowball fight. "She's too young. She's a girl," the boys argue. Dudley appears and offers her a guiding hand in throwing a snowball, smacking a boy on the opposing side. The lads immediately recruit her. First an outsider, Debby is now part of the battle.

"Leonard," whispered Jeffrey, "ain't angels supposed to be passive?"

"What do you mean?"

"This dude just aided and abetted one side in armed combat. Not only is he a proponent of warfare, but he also gave an unfair advantage. Something's wrong with this picture."

"It's only a snow fight."

"Yeah, well, that's how Napoleon started out. Look what happened there."

"Krisna did the same for Arjuno," Jessica whispered from the next row.

After a long pause, Jeffrey said, "Who?"

Jessica shook her head in dismay. "You need to pay more attention in your Comparative Godhead class."

"She has a point," Leonard agreed, perhaps too quickly.

"What for? I didn't ask for this. I just want to bum around on the fluffy clouds, not sit in a classroom and watch trite holiday movies."

"That's why you keep repeating Ascension 101. If you don't learn the stuff, you flunk and have to do it all over again. How many times have you sat in this class?"

Jeffrey didn't answer the question, but instead snapped back, "You're here too. So what's your excuse?"

"I'm stuck in the desk next to you, that's what. I'm always assigned to the seat next to you. Every time."

"Sorry," Jeffrey said.

"How do you think I feel?"

Miss Agatha cleared her throat—loudly and with a singular purpose. Both Jeffrey and Leonard got the message and piped down. "Some angel," Leonard muttered under his breath.

Irritation was hardly a heavenly virtue. As Leonard neared the end of his patience, he noticed he was not alone. Onscreen, Bishop Brougham encounters his inner frustrations. "I don't believe you're an angel," he states to Dudley. "I think you're a demon right out of h—"

His sentence is halted by Dudley, who cautions, "Oh, Henry, don't say that."

The irony was not lost on Leonard. He and Jeffrey were so radically different. He could not fathom why they were consistently paired. What glorious kind of message was that?

He leaned back and watched the rest of the movie. Under the helping hand of the divine Dudley, the bishop's goal of a majestic cathedral comes to pass.

More importantly, the bishop rediscovers the worth of friendship and his love for Julia. Just as quickly, an angelic mind wash takes place. He, along with his wife and friends, remembers nothing of Dudley, but their lives are all the richer for his visitation.

This, of course, was the way of things in Heaven and Hollywood, complete with a happy ending.

"That is all for today, class," Miss Agatha said. "Please review what we have covered so far. Our next class will delve into the role of a historian and how we can use a person's past deeds to institute change. We will examine the past, present, and future methodology in *A Christmas Carol*. Good day."

Leonard rose from his desk, eager to stretch his legs and wings—and speak to the "girl next door"—except Jessica's desk now sat empty.

He scanned the classroom, looking past the other students working their way to the exit. There, at the doorway, he saw her. She looked back at him with a generous smile and waved–the type of gesture that involved the wiggling of each finger. Then she disappeared from sight.

Not fast enough, he thought, but there was always the next class. A line of dialogue from the film ran through his mind: "Sometimes, Henry, angels must rush in where fools fear to tread." Words to live by for the living, as well as for the… well, everything else.

Since his homecoming, he realized once more how the macrocosm was in a constant state of flux. Never-ending change to a larger whole. It made little difference whether one was of a physical state since existence was more than the sum of such trivialities. Existence simply was.

At this, Leonard smiled. As with all things, once two elements meet, they are forever bound no matter how great the distance. She smiled at him. Yes, they would meet again.

Of course, they had already met and would again, over and over, a dance of energy replayed in limitless permutations. She smiled, a smile not of a moment but for all time. A smile was forever.

"Yo, dude," said a voice from behind, reminding him that Jeffrey was still there. "I'm off for some quality cloud time. Are you game?"

"I don't think so," Leonard replied as they made their way out. "There's someone I'm looking for."

"Suit yourself."

In the distance, a bell rang, softly tinkling.

"Hear that?" Leonard asked.

"Yeah. Yeah. Teacher says every time a bell rings, a mortal couple falls in love. Do you really buy that?"

"Sure," he replied. "Why not? There are far worse things to believe in. Is it any more of a stretch than the 'angel gets his wings' line?"

"It's bunk. The universe is not that magical."

"Yes, it is," Leonard said softly more to himself than anyone else. It was that magical. "Jeffrey, you've got a bit of a negative streak," Leonard added, louder now. "Anyone ever tell you that?"

"Yeah, as a matter of fact. Funny thing that I ended up here."

"How is that?"

"There was this house fire, you see. A couple of kids inside. I don't know what came over me, but I ran in to get them out. They escaped. I didn't. Serves me right for a good deed. Wham-bam-boom, I end up here being force-fed Jimmy Stewart films."

"Some angel," Leonard said again.

"Right," Jeffrey answered. "We're some angels. I'm outta here. Catch you later." With that, he left through the crowd, growing more transparent until he vanished.

Leonard made his way into the open, considering his own path to eternity. Even without flesh and blood, bone and muscle, and reduced to divine particles of light, he found himself still saddled with the same issues he had in tangible form.

One thing was certain: the universe was one of infinite variations with each and every particle distinctly unique. The dance of the cosmos changed with every turn, never constant, never the same.

Predictability was not part of the equation. In this, Heaven and Earth were one and the same. What brought the macrocosm together? What was the sacred glue—its singular variety?

As Grant noted in the film, "We all come from our own little planets. That's why we're all different. That's what makes life interesting."

Leonard tensed his back muscles and again felt the tape still adhered to his back. He tried once more to remove it, this time reaching his arm over his shoulder. His fingers could just touch the tape. He stretched his arm farther, and after a few tries, managed to get the tape between two of his fingers. With a quick pull, he dislodged the strip along with several feathers.

The accompanying memory of pain coursed down his back, making him wince. Maybe *jerk* was too kind a word for Jeffrey. After removing the plucked feather, Leonard wadded up the tape and cast it away where it faded into littered nothingness before even hitting the ground.

AN INTRODUCTION

MY LIFE OF SO MANY WINTERS

Some characters never die, but merely get recycled. While this is a stand-alone story, it served as a great way to bring in some minor players from another unrelated tale.

Christine Mauskopf is both a minor and major player here—minor in that she exits the story within the first few pages. But it is in the backstory where she gains importance, as discovered by her grandniece, Anna.

As mentioned before, I love return engagements for my characters. They are family. Oftentimes, they drop by unannounced. When they do, I simply put new sheets on the bed and make sure they have fresh towels. There's no telling how long they will stay.

The other major player here is the snow globe—or rather the collection. This is the common link that ties together the generations as well as.... Well, I can't say more without entering spoiler territory.

There is a lovely underlying story here and I feel that I only scratched the surface. I may return someday to fully explore Christine's past and give her the time and affection she deserves. Until then, the mystery remains.

And, yes, I couldn't resist the nod to *Citizen Kane*. The openings are similar but Christine could not be more different than Charles Foster Kane. In the end, she had a life of riches that he'd never comprehend.

MY LIFE OF SO MANY WINTERS

A BLIZZARD in miniature.

Flakes of snow swirled about in their descent, each reflecting the light and falling atop other specks of white, layering the ground and buildings.

Towering skyscrapers stood in distorted proportions beside smaller structures of a few stories, with the latter nearly half the height. No street or walkway separated the buildings.

Next to a miniature red Chinese theatre ran the waterfront with a cruise ship near a sailboat of the same dimensions. If this diorama had been actual size, the result would appear ludicrous.

All this fit within the confines of a globe mere inches in width.

With each shift of the globe's position, the snow took life, agitated into movement around the buildings while an occasional chiming note sounded from the internal music box. Had the key underneath been turned and the mechanism allowed to play, the full succession of notes would have resurrected George and Ira's "Someone to Watch Over Me."

The globe tipped again, this time slightly to the left, caused by the aged hand that held it, making the snow take flight once more.

Fingers curled against the wood inlay of the globe's base, partially covering the words *Visit sunny Los Angeles*. A finger brushed against the base, feeling the lines formed by a small, almost indistinguishable covering.

Christine Mauskopf studied the globe through half-closed eyes, watching the powdery spirals mimic that of the macrocosm outside her window. There, real snow fell, cold crystalline formations that would eventually melt to make way for yet another season.

Comparing the two flurries served as an exercise in similarities and contrasts: one real and one not, both in motion with a similar purpose, the temperature outside vastly different from the globe kept warm by her hand. Most notable was that of age and location.

The memento she held originated in a region unfamiliar with the white stuff, quite different from the falling Tulsa snow visible from her window. Above all, Christine recognized the difference in time: the globe was of her past, a relic of a younger self and of special, even secretive, significance.

But that was then, and this was now at the end of her days. As each breath brought her closer to the inevitable, she held tighter to the snowfall of youthful times.

There were thoughts, a lifetime of them, flooding back in quick succession, some of them lingering. Flashes from childhood, moments of happiness and despair, people long gone.

In the mix were her two sisters, both younger than she, arriving into the world later and exiting sooner; her husband of so many years, now also gone; her grandniece, the one fascinated with the snowy globes when she came to visit. And there was the one who got away, but who had always been close to her heart. He, the secret one.

So many secrets, but she came from a family full of hidden agendas.

The globe kept her company much like Charles Foster Kane at his end. The breathing turned shallow and labored until a deep one became the last. There were no final words, no thoughts of "Rosebud."

Her hand slackened, and as in the movie, the globe fell. It rolled from the sheets onto the floor where it landed safely on a soft cushion of carpet. Unlike the continuing fall of the snow outside, all motion inside the globe settled to stillness.

"Anna, it's about your Great-Aunt Christine."

Anna held the phone close to her ear. "Yes, Mom?"

"She passed away the day before yesterday."

Silence.

Not the awkward silence that falls into the lulls of a conversation, the kind that begs for one or the other to speak. No, this came as a beat in measure.

"I thought she already died." Anna shifted the phone in her hand. "A couple of years ago."

"No, that was Great-Aunt Sarah."

"The one in California?"

"Right," her mother said over the phone. "She died about the same time as your grandmother, Belinda. They were all sisters. Christine was the oldest."

"Sorry to hear it," Anna said distractedly while looking around the front room of her apartment. She might have sounded more convincing, but *eh*, at least she gave a proper response. In the train wreck of her personal life, the passing of a distant aunt hardly registered on her empathy scale.

The flagrant neglect of her surroundings showcased that upheaval. Dishes piled up in the kitchen sink, clothes meant for the washer were strewn about the floor alongside a random collection of magazines, and a single wine glass, still partially full and marked with yesterday's lipstick, rested on the end table near the TV.

On one side of the room stood the Christmas tree, halfway decorated with a strand of lights still dangling to the floor. Nearby sat a box of ornaments along with a former glass ball now smashed on the floor. She'd get around to cleaning the mess eventually.

Underneath the tree rested a single wrapped present, never to be given to its intended recipient.

It could always be returned, she figured, and good riddance. That is if it wasn't broken. She'd thrown it against the wall a couple of times.

"Well, her death was expected," her mother answered. "A good thing, actually. She had not been in good health as of late."

"Bad timing this close to Christmas."

"Yes, it does complicate matters."

"Oh?" Anna sensed the repercussions even before her mother spoke the words.

"We've been talking this over with your Uncle Tyler." A pause came before the payoff line. "So what do you have planned for the holidays?"

Anna stifled a laugh. A big nothing loomed in her immediate plans, this being a complete change from a few weeks back. At that time, she still had a hot boyfriend in her life before she found out what a total asswipe he was.

Not that he would have affected Christmas Day, which she always spent with family—her mom, dad, and two younger sisters. But prior to the big dump, she had seriously considered taking Ted home for holiday dinner.

"There are some details involving Aunt Christine that require us to be there," continued her mother, "and while the timing can't be helped, Tyler suggested we spend the holidays in Tulsa with them.

"You and I can fly up tomorrow and stay for a few days. We celebrate Christmas there, and if you need to get back early for your job, you can leave when you need to. Can you take off from work, hon?"

Not an issue. Her job went down in flames at the same time as her man. Always remember—never sleep with the boss. Not a good idea.

Her folks knew none of this, just like a great many other aspects of her life. She preferred to keep her affairs to herself—always had—and from the time she moved off to college six years earlier, she kept Mom and Dad informed of her comings and goings on a need-to-know basis.

Most of her boyfriends were unknown to them. She liked the simplicity with no questions or expectations. Ted, her most recent boyfriend/lover/boss/creep, was no different, making it all the more ironic that she even considered inviting him home.

"Just us? What about Dad? Alex and Robin?"

"Dad can't break away that soon, so they will take a later flight—but I'd like it if you could go with me. So how about your job?"

"I think I can arrange it, Mom," she answered, less said, the better. She should have mentioned the whole lack of employment part earlier. They'd had multiple opportunities, but she really didn't want to deal. Yes, she'd landed a few interviews, one looked promising, but nothing defi-nite.

After all, who hired during the holiday season? Instead, attention was centered on peace, goodwill to fellow man, and completing the gift-giving for the least amount possible.

So Merry Christmas, Ted. Hope you die.

Of course, there was also the whole comeuppance thing to deal with, considering she had dumped her previous boyfriend, Jeremy, to make the migration to Ted. In retrospect, it was not the most brilliant move on her part, either in the way that she handled it or her motivations in the leap from one bed to another.

Way to go, Anna. Always doing the wrong thing.

Some of it had to do with commitment—all right, a lot of it—and while she kept telling herself that Ted was what she really wanted, there was something deeper that touched on her shortcomings.

Did she end it with Jeremy because she grew too comfortable or found him too dull? Either way, she did the walking out without much consideration for his feelings. As far as burning bridges go, she torched that one in bonfire glory. On a karmic scale, she deserved the Ted treat-ment and more.

"I know this isn't how you planned to spend the holidays."

No kidding. I figured to wallow in holiday self-pity and up my drinking quota.

"But the change of scenery could be nice," her mother rambled on. "Tyler said it snowed the other night, and the ground cover might still be intact when we get there. Now how often do we see snow around these parts?"

"Fine, Mom. I'm already in."

Anna needed no arm twisting. Instead, she needed a break, away from her day-to-day life, lack of a job, lack of a guy, and far removed from her apartment with its pitiful, half-adorned tree. And the guilt.

"Wonderful," Mom said, exuding her usual, grating cheeriness. "I'll tell your dad. We'll get the flight arranged, and I will let you know the details. Despite the unfortunate circumstances, this might be fun."

Yeah. Right.

Anna stumbled into the kitchen in search of much-needed coffee. Along the way, she mumbled something that sounded like "Gmurn" in response to those she encountered, and that was forced at best.

Never the morning person, she.

Anna and her mom arrived in Tulsa the night before, after suffering through the expected holiday crowds—and delays—at both airports. Uncle Tyler greeted them at the terminal.

Funny, Anna thought as he walked alongside him, how he bore an interesting resemblance to a balding Alec Baldwin with about fifty extra pounds around the waist. She wondered if he did any good impressions. His wife, Aunt Beth, would have joined them as well, he explained, but she was playing Suzy Homemaker at the house, whoever the hell that was.

Anna pulled her coat tightly around her as they made their way to the car. While she despised cold weather, she found solace in the white that surrounded them. Rarely did she see snow, therefore, it held some attraction for her.

They made the short drive to Tyler and Beth's home, a fairly large house in a posh Tulsa neighborhood. After unpacking and a round of warm-up drinks, dinner was served and the discussion evolved from general catch-up talk to the reason for their stay.

The final days of Christine Matilda Haggarty Mauskopf came with a speedy decline for one who had been in good health for so long. Given the alternative, a drawn-out walk to the exit, this was more favorable—not that death was ever a pleasant experience.

For her part, Christine was ready and took it all in good grace as she had other aspects of her life. For her last days, she had been confined to bed, and when death finally arrived, no one was surprised. Sad, emotional, even nostalgic, but not surprised.

The service was arranged for the day after Christmas, still a few days off. They'd spend tomorrow—Christmas Eve—going over aspects of her estate that needed to be dealt with. The details of her will were already known, and Anna's mom offered to help in sorting through the belongings. This appeared to be a monumental job as Great-Aunt Christine apparently held on to everything. They would begin the next morning.

So after more small talk and a second bottle of wine drained of its contents, they all retired to bed. Anna felt flushed, no doubt from the excess wine, and found the bed in the guest room to be incredibly comfortable.

At first, she shivered from the cold, but once she pulled up the duvet and her body warmed the sheets, sleep swept over her.

So came the morning, and the zombie march to the kitchen. Everyone else was awake and in obscenely good spirits, reinforcing her opinion that early morning pleasantries should be terminated with extreme prejudice. The fact that the clock showed the time to be well past nine a.m. was beside the point.

Several cups of dark roast and breakfast helped to take the edge off, and an hour later, Anna reverted to her normal self, more or less.

By eleven, they crammed into the SUV and headed across town to Great-Aunt Christine's house where the rest of the day would be spent, followed by Christmas Eve at Uncle Tyler's. By that time, her dad and sisters would have arrived.

As they drove, Anna took in the landscape with its covering of white. She embraced the surreal quality of it all, having not grown up around the regularity of snowfall.

Yes, she'd seen movies, especially the seasonal ones: Jimmy Stewart shouting "Merry Christmas, emporium! Merry Christmas, you wonderful old Building and Loan!" as he ran through downtown Bedford Falls; the Grinch and Max racing into Whoville in an over-packed sled; Charlie Brown with his dismal twig of a tree with a jazzy piano tinkling in the background; numerous retellings of Scrooge shouting "Bah! Humbug!" as he trudged through the snow to his chilly dwelling, and countless other programs that embraced the wonder of winter while ignoring its more uncomfortable aspects.

Ah, but to see it firsthand—now, that was another matter. Something about the coldness around her seemed to warm the insides even more.

At length, they came to a side road, traveled a short distance, and pulled into a drive partially obscured by trees. Then the house came into view. Mansion, more like.

"Damn," Anna whispered to herself causing her mom to look at her with curiosity. Half-buried memories rose of the few times she had been here before, usually for family gatherings in her youth. She recalled playing around the house and at a creek nearby and climbing the trees in the back. All those memories were of warmer months without the ice and snow.

This was a grand house, one that spoke of old money, old generations, and history, a multiple-story structure built sometime in the early part of the last century. It had since weathered the change of the times and seasons with the elegance in which it was first built. Christine had married well.

Wheels crunched against gravel as they came to a stop at the side of the house. Before Anna even unbuckled her seat belt, Tyler and Beth were out of the car and walking to the porch.

Her mom turned to her. "Are you okay?"

"Yes. Fine. Just... things I've not thought about in a long time."

"You remember being here, don't you?"

"Bits," Anna nodded. "It's been a while, though."

"Well, we were never as close a family as we should have been, otherwise, there probably would have been more. There were... issues between Auntie Christine and her two sisters."

"Oh?" Anna replied, still not taking her eyes off the house as she stepped from the car.

"Actually, Christine was the peacekeeper of sorts. She was the one with the level head, or as level as one might expect. As skeletons in the closet go, there are bones aplenty in this family."

"Like what?" Anna asked, mesmerized by the turn in the conversation as well as her surroundings.

Her mother smiled. "Later."

The memories of the past can be elusive, especially when buried in childhood when everything seems overblown in proportion. Those intangibles need only a trigger to rise to the surface, and even then, possessing a haziness broken into jigsaw puzzle fragments of sight, sound, and even smell. Once resurrected, they are hard to dismiss as if each memory is looking for its proper space to reside.

If the brief flashes Anna initially encountered gave her pause, it was nothing compared to what awaited her inside the house. As the elder generation set about their work, Anna wandered the halls and corridors, room after room, allowing experiences from so many years earlier to surface in disjointed bursts: running across a room in search of a toy, sitting in the living room watching TV, a family dinner with food she didn't like.

In the den, she remembered an uncle who held her upside down by her legs, thinking it was fun despite her cries to the contrary. She hated the uncle, thereafter, and avoided him as much as possible.

And there were the globes. She remembered the snow globes all lined up on a shelf, each with a different landscape inside. She spent hours captivated by them.

Now they were nowhere to be seen.

Already, many of the belongings had been boxed up. The contents of this house, that which made up a lifetime of experiences, had lost much of their meaning. Its benefactor had left the building, and for those now in charge, this became a matter of reconnaissance, sorting and eliminating things without monetary or sentimental value.

The day progressed with Anna helping to move stuff around and put clothes into boxes destined for charity. At other times, she wandered alone or camped out in the library examining a collection of books older than even her great-aunt. Exploration became an ideal time waster, and she managed to inspect almost every corner and closet, even the storage attic and its collection of dusty artifacts from the past.

The evening drew near. Once more, Anna holed up in the library, spread out on the sofa, oblivious to the outside world, instead plugged into her iPhone and classic Alanis Morissette. "You Oughta Know." Thinking of Ted. Mr. Duplicity. Bad enough to be dumped so unceremoniously, but not to even be told.

She knew who his new girl was, which made it all the more irritating because she could not fathom the attraction. And the crowning blow of a pink slip on top of that. Okay, maybe she shouldn't have slapped him so hard. Not very professional.

Like hell, if I'm happy for you both. I hope you feel it.

There was a nudge on her shoulder, bringing her back to the present. Uncle Tyler. She removed the earbuds.

"Christine left something for you," he said, indicating a large box he had brought in and set on the floor nearby. "She was very specific that you should have them."

"What is it?"

Tyler answered with a knowing shrug and stepped back as she crossed to the box.

Inside were objects, all wrapped in tissue paper and bubble wrap, each one measuring about six inches in size. Kneeling, she took one in hand, and a soft gasp slipped from her mouth as she removed the packing.

A snow globe.

She looked down at the box with its many other wrapped objects all similar in size and shape.

"Her globe collection?" she asked Tyler. He answered with a smile and a nod.

"Oh, I remember these," she said as she examined the glass ball. "They were my favorite thing here. I must have been seven... eight years old." Her eyes glazed over as memories of another time swept over her.

"Christine remembered that as well," said Tyler. "I think that's why she wanted you to have them. She believed in gifts for those who truly might appreciate them."

Anna tipped the globe slightly to one side, sending the flakes into motion around the miniature houses inside. They swirled about and ever so slowly floated back home to the bottom.

Uncle Tyler scratched his head, an action so casual, he probably did so a thousand times a day. "We're nearly done for the afternoon. We'll be heading home in about thirty minutes." With that, he left her to go through the contents of the box.

Anna looked closer at the first globe with its miniature Currier & Ives diorama, a horse-drawn carriage crossing over an icy bridge. The date—1954—accented the wooden base along with the small brass key located on the opposite side.

She wound it, and the movement came into play, producing a familiar melody, the name of which she could not remember. After another shake, she placed it on the nearby table and watched as the flakes danced inside the small sphere.

At length, the music slowed and came to a stop. She gave her attention to the next shape in the box, unwrapping it and laying the packaging to one side. This one depicted a holiday scene with two dancing figures in Victorian garb in front of a festive tree accented by ornaments, candles, and an angel on top. Again, a date marked the base—1961.

She gave the key a turn and the globe's mechanism came to life, this time producing a song she recognized: "Deck the Halls."

One by one, she took out each globe, carefully unwrapping them, listening to the music of the spheres, and noting the variety of dates, ranging from 1947 to 1973.

A knock came from the doorway. She looked up to find Uncle Tyler watching her intently. "I have something else for you." He stepped forward with yet another globe in his hands. It appeared more weathered than the rest, the glass in need of a good cleaning.

He stared at the globe for some moments. "This was separate from the rest. She was holding it when she died."

"Eww." Her response came automatically, slipping out before she had a chance to retract it. Not the thing to say to a mother's son. Her face flushed as her uncle gave her a look of—well, it was a look.

"I'm sorry," she managed to say under his gaze. "That was not very..." She took the globe in her hands, feeling his reluctance to let go. It felt heavier than the others. "Thank you."

"It's what my mother wanted," he said with a pause as if considering other responses. "It's about time to leave."

"I'll gather my things."

Tyler nodded, then turned to leave. Anna watched him as he exited the room, feeling smaller than she had in years, smaller than she had been the last time she had wandered the rooms of this house. With another look at the globe in her hands, she noted the date. 1946.

First, she placed it on a nearby table, then returned her attention to the globes scattered across the floor. Carefully, she rewrapped each globe, setting them in the box, the last one being the sphere that Tyler had brought in.

Once they were all neatly packed away, she stooped down to pick up the box and nearly doubled over from the weight. It was heavier than she expected. Getting a better position, she took a firm grip on the sides and lifted. For leverage, she leaned back, feeling the weight work against her spine. *God, anything for a dolly right about now.*

Then the bottom of the box gave way.

She felt the sudden shift of weight as a lower flap broke loose, even as she attempted to reposition her hands to hold it into place. Already, the contents began to fall from the opening with the first one hitting the carpeted floor with a loud thud followed by a second.

Anna dropped to her knees, setting the box on the ground, her eyes set on the two globes that fell. One had slipped from the packing, its snowy contents an agitated blur of motion. She picked it up, looking for damage. No cracks from what she could see.

Good fortune and a plush rug had been on her side. She examined the base. Like the others she had looked at, this was dated 1963. To her disappointment, she found that the impact had taken its toll after all. A small panel roughly an inch square on the underneath side of the globe had come loose.

Far from broken, it appeared to be a door built into the base with the covering held into place by a means of tabs on one side that could slide back to open. She pushed the panel over, releasing it from the base, expecting to see the music-producing mechanism within, but the gleam of metal was absent when the door was removed. Instead, she found a small compartment, half an inch deep.

Inside rested a folded piece of paper.

Anna used her fingernails to pry the paper free and unfold it. She found handwriting, half-printed, half-cursive, in blue ink.

Dearest Christine,
In my life of so many winters,
Always made warm with thoughts of you.
Always, my love. Always.
— Allen

Whoa.

Anna read the note several times, letting the meaning wash over her. *Always, my love.*

This was no casual greeting between friends but something much, much more. It spoke of passion. Longing. Always.

Except that Christine's late husband's name was Stan, not Allen. Unless he went by a middle or nickname, this note came from someone else, suggesting that...

She stared at the words, realizing the implications.

One, a safe interpretation: this came from someone who had known Christine prior to her marriage, whenever that was. The forties she figured. That meant that the note's storage was arbitrary and placed inside well after the fact with no significance to the globe itself.

Possible, but not likely.

Two: the globe and note were related in date and meaning. Stan and Christine had been together for ages, well before the date on the snow globe, so the note would imply...

Anna laughed at the thought. Great-Aunt Christine was a frisky one. But, no, that was being presumptuous. Already, her mind had gravitated to scenes of steamy trysts; this could be entirely innocent, a fond friendship for another with nothing more implied than that.

Yeah, right.

And somewhere in the middle of this, her rash dismissal of Jeremy came to mind. Any humor to the situation melted like microwaved chocolate.

"Anna, time to go." Uncle Tyler stood at the door once more.

"Uncle, could you help me with this box? The bottom came apart."

"Sure." He picked up the box with arms positioned underneath to hold the flaps in place, and then nodded to the wrapped globe that still lay on the floor—the other one that had fallen free earlier. "You missed one."

With her attention on the globe with the note, she forgot about the other. She picked it up and examined it, peeling away the packing for a better view; it was unharmed. She tucked it in the box Tyler held. "Is this too heavy?"

"Not at all. I'll need to get you a sturdier box. Better yet, two smaller ones. Easier to carry. Ready?"

"Yes. Thanks." She held tightly to the 1963 globe with its hidden compartment and scrap of paper, the note of untold mystery, and held it close.

By chance or by intention, she had now been entrusted with something personal, something secret. She was still unsure what to make of it, but she knew that for the moment, it was meant for her alone.

"I'm ready."

Christmas Eve arrived along with Anna's dad and sisters gathered with Tyler, Beth, and a few distant cousins. Dinner was served, a delicious brisket that Aunt Beth started earlier in the day.

It cooked slowly throughout the afternoon, filling the entire house with its aroma. With this came a variety of steamed vegetables, salad, couscous, and home-baked bread, followed by a wonderful pumpkin pie (most likely store-bought). They washed the feast down with a delicious cabernet.

The conversation lasted long after dinner, then everyone chipped in to get the kitchen back in order. Anna's mom breezed up to her, holding a stack of dirty plates. "You hardly said a word all evening. Is everything okay?"

"Fine." Anna avoided eye contact by gathering the stray silverware. "Just stuff on my mind."

"Like what?"

She paused, aware of the crossroads she stood at and the many directions the paths might lead. But tonight was not the time for deep conversation. Ted, her job, her suck-ass choices, as well as her great-aunt, and the choices that might have shaped her life. No, all this must wait.

"Just... stuff. Nothing to worry about." She smiled and escaped to the kitchen with knives and forks in hand.

The clock in the hall—an old grandfatherly sort with chimes that echoed throughout the house—showed the time to be a little past eleven. As if set to a timer, a fresh round of snow began to fall, luring everyone to the porch.

It came initially in a few flurries, random spots of white against the night sky, and then multiplied in its numbers. True, Tulsa got its fair share most every year, but for it to fall tonight of all nights, yes, that was special.

After a while, each person in their turn left for home or went inside in preparation for bed and the following day. Christmas Day. Anna was the last to go in.

The last to retire.

For the longest time, she sat next to the window in the guest room watching the snow outside—and the snow globe in her hands, the one with the secret compartment. She alternated, staring first at the flakes of white floating inside the glass, then at the night sky accented by snowfall.

There were questions, as many as the flakes that fell, and the more she thought about it, the more intricate the questions became. The whos, whys, wheres, and hows all formed a point of collision far more detailed than the simple note which lay on the nearby table.

Most of these questions were historical: what happened when? Amid these was the more personal one. Was this discovery mere happenstance, or did her aunt want to be found out?

One after another, she removed each of the globes from the box and placed them in order by date. In all, there were twenty-seven, beginning in 1946 and ending in 1973. One a year, each year, every year.

Anna took the first globe, the weathered one from 1946, which her great-aunt had clung to with her dying breath. She turned it over to inspect the base, running her hands over its surface, searching for something that might reveal more than what was immediately visible.

But no, there was nothing, no compartment, only the key for winding up the music mechanism. She obliged, giving the key several turns, and thereby bringing the inner workings into motion.

The resulting song, at first unfamiliar, soon gained an element of recognition. The song played through once, twice, and a third, before slowing to a stop. The singular final note echoed into silence.

Disheartened, she placed the orb on the floor and nearly moved on to the next when she noticed an ever so slight separation on the side of the base.

"Maybe," she whispered to herself as she examined it closely. Sure enough, she found a small rectangular indention on the side like the front of a drawer but without any handles. It was smooth to the touch, blending in nearly perfectly with the wood grain around it.

After a minute of playing with the panel, she pushed it in, thereby releasing a spring, and the cover came off.

Just inside, barely visible, was the outer edge of another note.

She removed the paper and unfolded it, finding the same half-print/half-cursive writing. She read the words, revealing another clue to a life now past.

> *My Dearest Christine,*
>
> *I am so sorry about all that has happened between us, but if I could go back and change things, I would not alter a moment. More than ever, my feelings are for you.*
>
> *You, who surround my every thought, my entire being, and consume me whole like a snowstorm. But you have your life to return to. I understand. So I send you this globe, which you admired so much before. Think kindly of me. I will love you always. Allen.*

A chill ran across Anna's shoulders. In an instant, a lineage became clear, and she looked down at the row of globes, neatly arranged in chronological order, from the earliest date to the last.

And she knew.

Even without looking any further, she recognized each of those globes for their true purpose: love letters. They served as a reminder of a time passed from someone very important in Christine's life.

She also grasped the other key point, that all of the people who knew Christine—including the man she married and had spent her life with—probably knew nothing of this.

Every year for twenty-seven years, Christine received these globes. She might even have sent presents in return. She left an impression on another person so deep and so profound that it brought about this yearly tribute.

It spoke of ritual, of going to a place of worship and making an offering. It spoke of a connection unbroken by time and distance, or by two lives lived in their different worlds. It spoke of her meaning to him–and possibly the reverse in equal measure.

For all his devotion, was this a torch that blazed just as strongly on her part as well? What was it they shared that made their connection test the passage of time?

More questions arose, as many as those that had been answered. She looked over the line of snow globes, knowing that in good time, she would work her way through each one, slowly deciphering a part of Christine's life.

Was this her great-aunt's intention? Anna preferred to think of it as such. This was a gift of trust. Because, in the end, Anna had been bequeathed a portion of Christine's life–and that of another.

The fact that this bonding between generations came mere days after Christine's death added yet another twist; less than a week earlier, they could have talked and shared details with one another. That line of communication was now closed. But it took Christine's passing and her final wishes to reopen this connection.

Christine, who Anna had only known vaguely, was now more tangible than she had been in life. If this was a love that died with Christine, then the embers had now been rekindled secondhand.

Anna knew there must be a larger meaning to it all—and she'd unravel it in her own time.

Somewhere in the mix was Jeremy. Maybe she would call him tomorrow and wish him a Merry Christmas.

A Happy New Year.

An apology.

She expected nothing in return. That time had regretfully passed. She screwed up on a massive scale and nothing could remedy her shortcomings.

She picked up a globe and shook it, watching the dance of the flakes reflecting the light. Then outside, and its duplicate, life-size and real, cold and tangible.

Anna recognized the randomness of events and how they might steer a life. Each flake that fell was unpredictable in its descent. It might shift to the left or the right but held tightly to the whims of the fates around it. And in knowing its purpose, it held true, moving with the wind to find its spot to rest and call its own.

Anna felt the nudge of devotion, and in a moment of perfect clarity, accepted it.

AN INTRODUCTION

THE NAUGHTY LIST

A warning in advance: This story deals with family ties, human frailties, separation, and new beginnings. It also includes nudity, seduction, pornography, and masturbation. If you don't feel that a good, healthy f**k belongs in a Christmas story, you might want to skip over this entry before things get steamy.

If, on the other hand, you love a sexy misadventure, read on. Also, be careful what you do with your cell phone.

THE NAUGHTY LIST

IT WAS THAT SPLIT MOMENT right after she hit the email send button with her homemade porn video that Ellen realized she had made a terrible, terrible mistake.

It was not the video itself; she was actually quite pleased with the results. It was suggestive and sexy and sure to get Joel way excited. For the last week, she had been planning to make it as an early holiday present to imply what the two of them would be doing on Christmas Eve once her son, Sammy, had gone to bed. True, the video might not win any Oscars, but she was anticipating a much more physical kind of award.

The setup was easy, nothing more than propping up her smartphone on the dresser in front of the bed and hitting the record button. She took her place at the footboard facing the camera, a medium shot of her head and upper torso.

"Hi, baby," she began with a sly sparkle in her eyes, mirrored by a knowing smile—that of a cat about to eat the canary. "I've been missing you so much, and I've been thinking about when you get back into town. I hope you've been thinking of me as well. So let me tell you what you can expect this Christmas. I've prepared a very special Naughty list for us..."

As she spoke, she played around with the buttons of her blouse, allowing her words to set up the scene. Then she undid the topmost button before working her hand down to the next, slowly unfastening her shirt and finally letting it fall open, revealing all beneath.

"I hope you like what you see," she added before removing her shirt and scooting back onto the bed. Only then was it evident that the blouse was the only article of clothing she had been wearing, and with the position of the camera, there was nothing left to the imagination.

Ellen leaned back against the pillows, allowing her hand to travel southward, even as she narrated in full detail what the two of them would be doing to each other. Words synced with action, all in clear view of the camera lens. Her hands first caressed her breasts before moving down, stopping momentarily at her navel. As she went lower, she raised her legs into a more inviting position. Then she reached that sweet spot, and it was bliss. Ellen let her fingers do the talking, slowly working herself up to the inevitable crescendo, all the while expressing her desire in a series of gasps and moans. The finale was indeed cinematic, and for all that was lacking in finesse, she made up for in enthusiasm.

"Merry Christmas, baby," she cooed after it was over. She turned the phone recorder off, slid on her robe, and after pouring herself a glass of wine, sat on the sofa to watch her acting debut.

Holiday music played in the background from one of the classic rock radio stations, but it was otherwise quiet. Had Sammy been home, he would have been fast asleep by now. As it was, he was with Pete, her ex, who had custody of their only child this week. Ellen had the house to herself, which had made making the video all the easier. Sammy would be back for the weekend and the last few days leading up to Christmas. Joel would be back in town as well, and she was missing him, big time. Whether the feeling was mutual was still questionable. This was, after all, her first steady guy since the divorce, and she could not help but wonder if he was nothing more than the man picked up on the rebound. She had been doing the bulk of the pursuing throughout the relationship.

She took a sip of wine, allowing the subtleties of its flavor to pass over her tongue and warm her insides, a delicious counterpart to that post-orgasm glow.

After making herself comfortable on the sofa, she hit replay on her phone and watched her performance. It was something of a revelation having never seen herself like this before. Sex was always something internalized, experienced from within. Seeing herself go through the motions was a surreal experience, both exciting and demeaning.

Actually, it was a bit sleazy, but that was the inherent nature of porn.

"Christ, do I really sound like that?" she whispered, and that little voice inside replied, *Yes, you do.*

It was hardly the erotic exhibition she had hoped for, but then again, this was for Joel's benefit, not hers. There was also that underlying question of whether this was even a good idea. Probably not, but even the safest of sex was a risky business. She had never made an X-rated video before. And—dare she admit, she got quite a thrill from it. Oh, she was a naughty little girl.

Before she could second think her motives, she selected the forward button on the screen, pulled up the email address, and hit send.

It was in that split second as her finger touched the surface, just beyond the point of pulling back, that she recognized the error in the plan. By then, it was too late. Even as the bits of electronic information flew out from her phone and into the world, she felt a wash of cold sweep across her, quickly eradicating her inner glow.

She had just sent the video to the wrong address.

"NoNoNoNoNo," she blurted as she searched for some impossible way to recall that which had been sent. Email functioned as a one-way street; once out the door, there was no retraction. The rational part of her mind knew this, but that did not stop her from quickly looking for any way to bring it back. Time travel would have been an excellent option, to step back a few scant seconds and undo her actions. With this not being a possibility, she took her phone and tried throttling it, but choking an electronic device was no more productive than time shifting. Only after coming to terms with the fact that what was done was done, she looked closer at the recipient's name, and noticed the small but highly significant detail. "Oh my god," she groaned as she saw the tragic error of her ways.

The trouble was a simple matter of similar names. Joel's last name was Hanson with an email address of jhanson@. It was easy to see how the slip-up occurred where she instead selected jhammon@.

Jeffrey Hammon. Sammy's elementary school teacher.

Any lingering erotic thoughts dwindled to nothingness as she pondered the ramifications. She had just sent her son's schoolteacher a porno. Could it get any worse?

Oh yeah, it could.

Parent/teacher conferences were coming up the following Monday. She stared at the half-empty wine glass, and then at the bottle on the nearby table, and suspected that it might not be enough to get her through the night.

⟋◎⟍

The downward spiral continued the next day with a text from Joel:

> Ellen, I think we should call it quits. Sorry, but you are just too needy for me. I can't handle it. My problem, not yours. Merry Christmas. – Joel

Her sometime boyfriend had just demonstrated his true colors, yellow being one of them. It was a pretty shitty thing to do, resorting to the safety of email rather than a direct confrontation. Not only did he do so via long-distance—during the holidays—but then indirectly stated that it was her fault.

Fortunately, he had not seen the video she had initially intended for him. After the debacle of the initial misdirect, she had decided not to send it to him, at least not electronically. Once burned, twice shy, as the saying goes, especially when it includes masturbation. Had he seen it, would it have swayed him to stick around? Probably not, certainly not for the long haul. Oh, he might have postponed his exit through the holidays just to get a final lay out of the deal, but he would have pulled the plug thereafter.

Suddenly, the fact that he had not received her home movie seemed more like a blessing. At the bare minimum, he could've had the decency to have broken up with her before she made her sex recording and sent it out; it would have saved her a great deal of embarrassment.

Okay, so he was an asshole. Creep. Scumbag. Dick. The descriptors could go on. After her initial shock and subsequent outrage, she attempted to be philosophic about it. If that was the kind of man he was, it was a far preferable thing that she be free of him. Deep down inside, she knew she could do better. Still, it was of little consolation at the moment. No one liked to be dumped even under the best of times.

"Really?" she asked herself as she reread his cancelation notice. "And I am not needy. I just… like things my way."

She thought of something her ex-husband, Pete, had said to her once during one of their many spats. "The problem with you is that you want your life to be perfect—but it never will be because life isn't perfect. You need to accept that and move on."

He was not entirely correct on that assumption. Yes, she would have liked to have her world rose-colored, and she tried to make it that way. That was different from expecting it to be idyllic. Her marriage was ample proof of that, and it came crashing down for a variety of reasons with blame laid equally on both sides. The irony was that she and Pete now got along better than during their marriage.

While the custody of Sammy was joint, they tried to spend time with him together as Mom and Dad for his benefit. Divorce could be rough on a child, so they made an effort to smooth the edges as much as possible, considering they now lived separate lives. He had wasted no time finding another partner to shack up with, which only added to her insecurities. What had become clear was that they made better acquaintances than a married couple.

So what would Pete think if he knew about her bit of screen acting? She cringed at the thought of him ever finding out. In retrospect, it was a pretty stupid thing to do and something that could not easily be taken back. It certainly could not be recalled from the inbox of the teacher's email.

There would be repercussions. How could there not be? It might not be immediate, but be it later in the day or tomorrow—or at the parent/teacher meeting—there would be hell to pay. Prone to having an active imagination as it was, Ellen's brain began to play out a variety of scenarios that might occur. She kept checking her phone as the hours passed, both dreading and expecting some sort of response from jhammon—even something as dry as "Please check your address line." Of course, this was a ridiculous train of thought. More likely, she would be reported to Child Protective Services as being an unfit mother. After all, teachers were required to look out for anything that would suggest a harmful home life.

There it was. The weight of it fell heavily upon her shoulders.

Oh, my God, I'm a horrible mother. I'm a bad influence on my own child.

In Christmas terms, she was a prime candidate for the real Naughty list, or even the ultra-naughty list, if there was such a thing. If defining what constituted naughtiness, one would most certainly be a mom who self-pleasured herself in front of a camera.

Any thoughts of an immediate response turned out to be ungrounded. Throughout the subsequent day, she heard nothing from either Jeffrey Hammon, the school, or any child advocacy groups. No phone calls. No emails. No knock on the door. The end result was that it only made her more anxious as one day led to the next, all drawing nearer to what was bound to be a very uncomfortable parent/teacher conference.

Even worse was that she would not be alone. Pete would be there. The scenario was ripe for extreme embarrassment should Mr. Hammon decide to mention the attachments to his recent emails. With this being one of those worst of times, a far better resting place might be a preferable option under those circumstances.

One day passed to the next, drawing ever closer to the conference, which would signal the end of the school quarter and the beginning of holiday break. As expected, Sammy was thrilled with the dual joys of no school and Christmas, and he kept adding to his lengthy Santa list. Ellen and Pete had already divided its contents in half so each could make sure the fat man delivered the goods. Ellen was taking even more care than usual in an effort to be a sound, responsible mother—because underneath it all was that little voice that reminded her of her folly.

You're a very bad mom! Bad! Bad!

Soon enough, Monday came around, and she stood at Sammy's elementary school entrance, steeling herself to pay the piper. She hoped for the best. She expected the worst. She reminded herself that this meeting was supposed to be all about Sammy, and she should walk in with those expectations in place.

With a deep breath, she opened the door and stepped in.

Pete Downing was already inside the classroom seated at one of the miniature chair/desk combos designed for younger students. The proportion made him look a bit comical, and Ellen might have been more amused at her ex had she not been otherwise preoccupied. Facing the rows of desks was Sammy's teacher, Mr. Hammon, who sat behind a desk of proper scale for an adult. He offered a professional smile and gestured for her to take a seat. She could feel his eyes following her all the way to her desk. For her, it took an eternity.

"Hi, Ellen," Pete said as she sat. He always seemed to be in a pleasant mood in the mornings, one of his traits that was simultaneously endearing and annoying. She returned the greeting while not feeling very happy about it.

"Good morning to you both," began Mr. Hammon. "Let's get down to it, shall we." He began to run down the specifics of Sammy's performance through the quarter, pointing out where he had excelled and where he needed work. Under other circumstances, Ellen would have been more engaged, asking pertinent questions as they arose. Instead, she found it hard to concentrate wholly on what was being said. For his part, Pete stepped in and quizzed the teacher about details. On the whole, Sammy was doing reasonably well in class, making the conference mostly a ritual courtesy.

Through it all, Ellen could feel Hammon's eyes on her, so she averted hers whenever possible. What must he think of her? she wondered, knowing he had seen her in the most revealing way imaginable. Did he find it disgusting? Worse yet, was he aroused? Might he be fantasizing about her even now?

It occurred to her that the circumstances still could have been far more disastrous. No YouTube postings that she knew of. She could not speak of Mr. Hammon's character, but he didn't seem to be the viral posting type—not a prude or a letch. On the contrary, he came off as quite ordinary.

He might have been in his late twenties or early thirties, with medium-length brown hair and a matching shade of eyes. His body seemed well structured. He probably took pretty good care of himself, eating right and with moderate exercise. Yeah, he was reasonably attractive. Not drop-dead model handsome, but quite pleasant to the eyes. Instinctively, she glanced at his hand, an old impulse from her pre-marriage days that had recently resurrected itself. No ring, possibly eligible. With this, the little voice inside her head erupted.

What are you thinking, woman? Are you seriously checking out your son's schoolteacher? And you call yourself a mother? You might as well just strip and jump him right here.

In the midst of this inner dialogue, Jeffrey Hammon turned to her, their eyes met, and she quickly looked downward again, feeling her face flush. How evident was it? If he noticed, he kept it to himself and continued talking about Sammy's reading progress. She zeroed in on his voice, noticing the consistent quality, the slight intonation from one word to the next, and the occasional pauses for breath. It was a pleasant voice, one that fit the face, not that she was staring. The desk was a far better place to keep her eyes focused.

Pete asked another question, Hammon responded in kind, and Ellen wondered how long the conference would take. She had been too distracted to pay attention to everything he had said. Still, it was clear that there were no immediate issues with Sammy's education. She could at least count that as a positive and she could use as many of those as possible.

There was still the remote chance that her email had somehow not reached its destination, and she was blowing this all out of proportion. Emails were lost all the time for any number of reasons. For all she knew, Jeffrey Hammon might still think of her as an upstanding mother and member of the community rather than her sleazy true identity.

Not likely, though.

"Do you have any other questions?"

With a jolt, Ellen realized that Jeffrey Hammon was addressing her directly.

"I'm sorry," she managed to say, flustered. "What did you ask?"

"Do you have any other questions, Mrs. Downing?"

"Please, it's Geyser. Downing was my married name."

Now, Hammon seemed nonplussed as he examined the paperwork on his desk. "I'm sorry. According to the sheets here, you are both listed as Downing."

Ellen took some comfort in his confusion. "No worries. It probably was never updated in your records, and the divorce was somewhat recent."

"Six months," added Pete, whose voice suggested some irritation at the change in topic. "Can we continue?"

"Yes, of course. Do either of you have any other concerns?" After exchanging brief, uncomfortable glances, both Pete and Ellen shook their heads. "Then I guess we're done. If you have any questions later—need to talk about *anything*—please don't hesitate to call me. I'm available."

With that, the meeting concluded. Pete and Ellen said their good-byes and made their way to the door with him moving at a brisk step. "I'm late for work. Bye, Ellen," he called out as he was halfway down the corridor. It was clear by his actions that the subject of their divorce was not something he liked bringing up at school. In a flash, he vanished from the building.

By comparison, her pace had slowed as she replayed the last few minutes in her head. As awkward as it might be, she had fully considered confronting Mr. Hammon and asking him if he had received her email. Such an option led to all sorts of uncomfortable scenarios even though it would resolve all doubts in her mind. If nothing else, it would give her a chance to explain.

Uh-huh. Explain what?

Why she sent a video doing herself in front of a camera? Any answer to that would be a real doozy.

Yet the thing that caused her to stop was what he had said at the very end. "If you need to talk about anything—please don't hesitate to call me." What did he mean by "anything"? Could he have been directing the question specifically to her—or was she reading far more into his words than was intended? And there were his last two words... "I'm available." That was wide open to interpretation.

Before she could back out, she turned and walked back to Mr. Hammon's classroom.

He stood behind the desk, collecting papers into a file, and looked up as she appeared in the doorway. If she knew what she would say, the words now vanished in her throat.

"Yes, Miss Geyser?"

With too many thoughts scrambling through her brain, she stood at the door and said nothing. The flush she had experienced earlier returned with a vengeance, turning her face bright pink. He responded first with a quizzical expression, waiting for her to say something, and then he offered up a smile.

Shit. What kind of smile was that? Was he just being courteous while waiting for her to talk? Was it a professional smile, a gentlemanly smile, or a knowing smile?

Somehow, she managed to mumble "Never mind" loud enough for him to hear, and then fled from the doorway, making her exit as quickly as possible. Only after she reached the outside could she regain her composure and then threw a mini-tantrum, stamping both feet in quick succession. Her actions offered only momentary relief, but she felt even more dismal when she looked up and saw that Pete had not yet left the school grounds. He sat in his car, watching her with a look of perplexed dismay on his face.

"Just kill me now, please," she groaned and walked to her own car, choosing to ignore her ex. For his part, he made no attempt to get out and see what was troubling her. He sat and watched as she reached her SUV, climbed inside, and drove off. Only then did he shake his head and leave the campus.

The funny thing about coincidence is that in retrospect, it never seems like it could be simply coincidental. By nature of the odds, the mind grasps for some higher order manipulating the events, or some plausible explanation for the occurrence. Chalking it up to random chance is far too easy. Fate has a way of always mucking up the simple structure of things, and sometimes with unexpected results.

This is especially true during the holiday season when life is in general chaos, and everyone looks for that extra bit of magic—which is at the core of the season. This is summed up in almost every feel-good Christmas movie from George Bailey and Bedford Falls to the countless made-for-TV shows that appear like clockwork every year.

Ellen had already had her fair share of the unexpected, much of it spawned from her specific actions. Christmas was still a week away. There remained plenty of time for further mishaps, which was what she worried about.

The countdown to December 25th continued. Homes and retail stores alike were decorated in lights and garland, and images of Saint Nick could be found at every turn. Large plastic snowflakes brightly lit with LED bulbs suggested a winter wonderland, a contrast to the actual sixty-plus-degree weather. Christmas carols pumped through the speakers of every store and restaurant. Even if a person desired to escape the holiday festivities, there was little chance of that happening. Christmas was everywhere.

Ellen managed to consume herself with the rituals of the season. There were presents to buy for family and friends, preparations for the pot-luck-food office party which she had been assigned to coordinate, and, of course, Sammy. She was determined that he'd have a wonderful Christmas. The days grew increasingly busy, but through it all, there was not an hour that went by when she did not think of the stupid things that people do and her own contribution to that phenomenon. The passage of time did little to lessen the self-abuse she gave herself over her little stunt.

Then came the epiphany. She had wandered into a corner lot filled with Christmas trees and wreaths for sale, along with mistletoe at the checkout counter strategically placed as a holiday season impulse buy. She thought back to her own experiences under the mistletoe, the times and places, who she had been there with, and how it had felt—and in a sudden wave of awareness, she realized what had been missing from her current life.

It was romance.

Pure and simple, it was the swept-off-her-feet feeling that had been absent for so long, even during the latter part of her marriage. Yet, deep down, she needed to fan the flames of love and affection.

That was what she was trying to get from Joel, who turned out to have nary a romantic bone in his body. Yes, the sex had been fantastic from day one, but never had he sent her flowers or made any other similar gesture. It was not in his nature. There had been no hand-in-hand walks in the park, no candle-lit dinners, or sweet whispers in her ear. From day one, their relationship had been more motivated by mutual attraction and lust than hearts and roses.

All this was what she had wanted, especially since her divorce—the feeling of being loved. It was not that she was asking for a lot, but flowers would have been nice—or an unexpected card—or just a few words. Was that too much?

This was why she had stripped down and made the video, a desperate attempt to lure a response out of Joel, even if it catered to his more basic instincts. If he could not bring her a bouquet, at least he could deliver her a blooming-hot orgasm.

Now he was gone, and she was stuck with resignation for whatever might come her way. Being single was always the worst during the holidays, so any feelings about romance were only a concept without an actual person to help manifest them.

Instead, she had the additional baggage of an errant email and the consequences it might bring. So far, nothing had happened, even though she played out a barrage of equally possible scenarios. Then again, nothing might come of it. She had no way of predicting the future. All she could do was play the waiting game.

Of all the possibilities, what she could not have expected was to run into Jeffrey Hammon at a nearby department store. Quite literally run into, as in collision. Enter coincidence stage left.

It happened like this: Ellen stopped off for a few presents for Sammy and a bottle of wine for herself. She turned an aisle corner. He came around the opposite corner. She had orange juice and the merlot in hand, en route to the toy department. He had paper towels and his cell phone. The impact caused her to lose her balance, along with the juice and wine. She fell to the ground, the sound of her landing overpowered by the shattering of the bottle and the ensuing spillage.

Deep maroon mixed with orange in a swirl of color across the floor, as well as her skirt, creating an irregular tie-dye pattern against the light fabric. His cell phone also hit the floor where it slid through the purple/orange combo, coming to a stop a few feet away. The paper towels came through unscathed. It was a prime example of Sir Isaac Newton's third law of physics in action.

Their initial shock from the impact doubled when they realized who the other person was.

"Oh my God," Jeffrey said while extending his hand to help her up. "I am so sorry, Miss Geyser. Are you hurt?"

She allowed him to pull her to her feet while checking to see if the broken glass had cut her. "Only my pride," she replied and then shook her head at the deeper double meaning of what she had just said. She glanced at him, but he did not indicate if he caught the reference.

"It's all my fault," he said as he studied the sad state of her clothes and the mess across the floor. "Are you sure you're not hurt?" He tore the plastic wrapping from his paper towels and handed her a length to wipe herself. It was a noble gesture, but the damage was already down to her skirt, and the towels only caused the stains to smear. After several attempts, she wadded up the toweling and let it fall to the floor.

She shook her head again. "Of all the people to bump into."

He looked around for his phone, and they both spotted it at the same time, following its wet path after it slid through the spilled liquid. The black protective case, glistening from the wine, had served its purpose well with no apparent harm done to the phone. He quickly picked up the phone before she could reach for it and inspected the screen for cracks.

"Is it damaged?"

He wiped it down with a paper towel after turning the screen off.

"Doesn't appear to be," he said as he pocketed the phone, "but your clothing is not as lucky. There's a coffee shop at the entrance. They should have some water so you can clean yourself up."

"I think I'd be better off with the ladies' room."

"Of course," he answered. "I should have thought of that."

"But I could use a cup of coffee," she quickly added as a sudden impulse overtook her. "Would you mind waiting?"

They made their way to the front of the store, and she excused herself to the ladies' room where she was able to inspect the damage in a mirror. Oh, she was a mess. There was little chance the skirt would ever be the same again. True, it was not one of her favorites, so she could easily part with it.

Then she noticed a small amount of red on her arm where an errant piece of glass had cut her. She washed the area in the sink and then tried to make herself as presentable as possible—a mostly hopeless case. She'd not expected to meet anyone at the store and was hardly wearing anything becoming. She didn't even bother with makeup this morning, so she already started off looking like a slob. The spilled wine and juice combo only reinforced the fact. Knowing that her appearance was a lost cause, she smirked at her mirror self and then walked out to the coffee shop.

"Better?" he asked when she returned.

"Not really."

"Let me get that cleaned for you at the very least. I am so sorry."

"Thanks, but it's not worth the effort. It was sweet of you to offer, though."

"Then allow me to get you some coffee," he replied with a smile. It was a nice smile, she thought.

"Deal."

They got their coffee and were soon sitting at a little table at the shop's perimeter separated from the department store by a fence-height wall. The conversation was a series of starts and stops with mostly generic questions followed by generic answers. Do you live in this area? How long have you been teaching? Naturally, Sammy came up as a topic. There were other questions that wanted to come out into the open, but

Ellen was not sure if or how they should be broached. Then Jeffrey created an opening.

"I've been thinking about contacting you."

"Oh?" Her attention piqued.

"At the parent conference. You gave me the impression you wanted to ask something."

So there it was. She knew where the conversation could go if she chose to pursue it. She had the opportunity that day when she stood speechless at the door to the classroom. At the time, she opted to walk away. Now the situation presented itself once more.

"It was..." she stammered, again feeling that loss for words before opting for the easy path of avoidance and redirection. "I don't remember exactly. Are you doing your holiday shopping?"

"I don't have much shopping to do. Except for my sister and her husband, the rest of my family live up north. I won't be making it up there this year, so it's a solo holiday for the teacher."

"But you'll see your sister at least?"

"I've been invited for Christmas dinner."

"That sounds very Dickensish."

"It does at that. No Tiny Tim, though," he laughed.

"So no one else? Wife? Girlfriend?" As soon as she said it, she caught herself. Not only did it sound as if she was prying, but it also reeked of political incorrectness, so she quickly added, "Partner? Significant other?"

"No to all of that," he replied, catching her alternative meaning. "Not married. No current relationship. And no, I'm not gay. Would you like my social security number next?"

She apologized for how it sounded.

"No need to apologize," he answered. "Actually, I like not being tied down to a set schedule at this time of year. There is so much craziness leading to Christmas that I can sidestep. I figure that I have plenty of time later for that madness. Anyway, I..."

There was a chirp that seemed to come from his pocket. He pulled out his phone, checked the screen, and set the phone down on the table.

"Just a text. No big deal," he said. "I assume that Sammy is looking forward to Christmas."

"What child isn't?" she replied after taking a sip of her coffee while being careful not to scald her mouth. She had always found it amazing how store-bought coffee seemed to be far hotter than anything she could make at home. As a result, she allowed it ample time for cooling. It was that Goldilocks part of her nature, wanting everything just right.

"Santa's going to be extra generous to him this Christmas," she continued. "It has not been an easy year for him. At least he does not blame himself for everything that has gone down."

"He's a good kid. Must be the upbringing."

"That's kind of you to say. We've tried—even harder now since the divorce. I know that Sammy still hopes we will get back together again."

"Any chance of that?"

"I don't think so. Paul has moved on, and—well, let's just say there's no going back."

"Sorry. I didn't mean to pry."

She smiled and returned his phrase. "No need to apologize."

He nodded even as another one of those uneasy silences fell upon them. "Will you pardon me for a minute? The men's room is calling." With that, he was up and away from the table, leaving Ellen to her coffee and her thoughts. Then she noticed he had left his cell phone there on the table.

She turned her head in the direction of the clothing department but was soon casting glances back at his phone. Already, an idea had come to mind—one that could likely get her into trouble.

She could not bring herself to ask him about her email, but if she acted quickly, she might be able to check his mail herself. It was quite possible that it could still be in the inbox on his phone. Then she would know for sure. Even as the thought crossed her mind, the ethics behind it appeared, creating the angel-versus-devil argument. Of course, it was such the wrong thing to do, snooping through his personal messages. Then again, it did concern her.

In the end, she reached for the phone, becoming one with Greek mythology. Whenever there was a box of mysteries, Pandora always won. Ellen was merely embracing her own inner goddess.

She touched the keypad, finding to her relief that there was no security password. The mail program loaded, and she scrolled backward through the contents while looking for her sender address. With each line, her nervousness grew, hoping against hope to find nothing while knowing she would only be sure if she found her name there.

Then she saw it. A weight descended in the pit of her stomach as she recognized the sender's address. There she was with a video attachment included in all her brazen, naked glory. There was no doubt now he had received the video and all too likely had watched it—possibly more than once. To his credit, he had been a gentleman the entire time they had spoken today as well as at the teacher/parent conference, and had made no reference to it.

Of course, what could he say? It would probably be just as embarrassing for him.

She clicked off the mail while still looking at the screen. There was a screensaver, one that in all probability he had loaded, of the school exterior right at dusk. It was a lovely picture with the remaining sunlight casting deep shadows across the buildings. If he had taken the shot himself, then he certainly had a flair for photography.

While knowing she should put the phone back on the table before he returned, her curiosity got the better of her. She clicked on the photo library, immediately bringing up an extensive archive of images. There were other shots of the school, all beautifully photographed, as well as a miscellany of landscape images, pictures of people, most likely colleagues or friends, and the usual array of random images.

Then she came to a stop, finding a photo of a woman's face.

Her face.

She clicked on it, allowing the image to fill the whole screen, and she realized exactly what she was looking at. The picture was a still shot from her video. Specifically, it was taken from the very beginning, prior to her full-frontal exhibition when she was still wearing her blouse. Despite the familiarity with the photo, there was also something distinctly different; the image appeared softer, yet better lit, with none of the discoloring from the overhead lighting. Even her hair seemed to be backlit on one side. It was almost as if...

A shadow fell across her and the phone. She looked up and into the face of Jeffrey Hammon. He, in turn, stared at Ellen and her image on his phone. In a moment that seemed to be an eternity, a pin drop would have been akin to thunder.

"Awkward," she squeaked as she set the phone back on the table. Any discomfort she felt was equally matched and raised by Jeffrey.

"Very awkward." His voice was likewise strained. He sat down, still looking at her with a quizzical expression—much like that of a boy with his hand in the cookie jar when caught by a fellow cookie thief.

"So who goes first?" she asked meekly.

"Ladies first?" he offered, ever the gentleman.

"You watched... it?" She didn't have to elaborate on what *it* was.

He nodded which was answer enough. When she made no further reply, he added, "It wasn't meant for me, was it?"

"No."

"I thought not."

A long pause followed, one that, if not pregnant, then was ripe for seeding.

"I hope he liked it," Jeffrey finally said when it was evident she had nothing else to add.

"He never saw it." Ellen took a deep breath, preparing herself for full disclosure. "I sent it to you by mistake. His address is very similar to yours. After that, I could not bring myself to trust email, so he never saw it." With a shrug of the shoulders, she added, "Anyway, we broke up the following day."

"His loss, then." Jeffrey's comment caused Ellen to blush again. Somehow, it came off as a rather sweet compliment. She reminded herself that he had seen her in a manner very few people had—and it was not by invitation. It had been extended to someone else— someone who turned out to be unworthy of her attentions.

Enough about her. What about him? "There's a picture of me on your phone—separate from the video." It was more of a statement of fact than a question but still demanded an answer.

"Yes."

"You took it from the video."

"Yes."

"And you saved it with your photos."

"Yes."

Ellen abruptly realized that this was enough information. She did not want to know any more, finding the whole situation beyond what she could handle. Without another word, she rose from the table and walked away. She needed to put as much distance as possible between her and Jeffrey Hammon. Not only did he watch her video, but he deliberately saved a frame of it into his photo library as if it were a picture to be added to a scrapbook. No, that was the wrong analogy.

It was more like a butterfly collector—or a trophy hunter with a head mounted on the wall. The trophy had no say in the matter; it was simply there. Why would he do such a thing? It was akin to an invasion of privacy, even though she could not define precisely why. It felt wrong and intrusive, and very, very creepy—leaving her with an icky feeling like she needed to take a shower.

But really, whose fault was that?

Just as she reached the store's front doors, she came to a complete stop as all her feelings came full circle. Anything he might have done was only due to her previous actions. Isaac Newton was right. Had she not made the video—had she not accidentally sent it to him—then he would not have followed through with his part. No matter how she played it through in her mind, he was only counteracting what she had already put into motion. She was the one who stripped down for the camera. She was the one who sent it to him. He simply reacted. So now who was the sicko?

Reluctantly, she turned and walked back into the store. Jeffrey was still sitting there where she had left him. Before she could say a word, he was on his feet, attempting to apologize.

Ellen raised her hands to make him stop. His words were unnecessary.

"No, please. Let me speak," she said once she had his attention. "This is very difficult for me. It's bad enough that you saw something you were never meant to see. And now I discover you are carrying me around in your phone like I was a casual snapshot from your summer vacation. We both know that this was not the case. That scares me. You scare me, which is too much because I'm already doing a fine job of scaring myself. So why is it that you kept a picture of me, especially since... since..."

Then it struck her what the core of it was. The photo of her that he chose to save was not of her in full-frontal glory, nor was it even slightly provocative. He selected an image from the very beginning of the video with her still properly dressed, at least from the waist up. It was a portrait shot, pure and simple. As racy as the video was, he picked the opposite to adorn his photo gallery, one that was downright respectable. She could hardly object to whatever he might have selected, given the circumstances of how he got the source material. Still, with the choice of either sleaze or style, he opted for the latter.

Her rant immediately lost steam, and she settled for a simple "Why?"

"You'll laugh at me."

"No. I assure you I won't."

"You're right," he replied after considering her answer. "You already think this is weird. And creepy. And not funny. Okay, so here it is." His eyes met hers as he spoke. "I was smitten."

Her immediate thought was did anyone still use the word *smitten*?

"What you sent came as a big surprise, as you can imagine. It's not the type of thing I usually receive. But then I couldn't get you out of my mind—but not for the reasons you might think. I thought you had this glow about you, a radiance... an inner beauty that was very apparent. And... I could not stop thinking of you. I know how this probably sounds."

"You did something to the photo."

He nodded. "My hobby is photography. I used some filters."

"You're very talented with a camera. I liked the photos of the school."

"Thank you."

"Still, I'm sorry. You should have never seen that video, and I'm not sure how I feel about you keeping that picture or what your intentions are. But it was my fault to begin with. So what does this mean? Are we nothing more than a couple of degenerates?"

"No. Just a couple of people ruled by their passions."

She thought about this for a few moments and realized she needed far more time to process it all. "I should be going. Thanks for the coffee. I can't say the same about the wine stains."

"Please let me cover the cost of getting it cleaned."

"No. It's not worth the effort, but thanks anyway."

"At least let me walk you to your car."

It was a reasonable enough offer. Ellen and Jeffrey rose and left the store into the unseasonal December weather outside. They walked in silence, unsure of what to say next. Despite their time together at the coffee shop, there was still a level of unease between them. Porn videos could do that sometimes. Jeffrey was first to break the quiet as they reached her car.

"Miss Geyser, would it be too forward of me to ask you out for dinner?"

"Ellen, please," she corrected. "And I sent you a sex tape. I don't think you can get more forward than that."

"Point taken," he laughed.

"Then yes," she answered. "I think I would like that." She reached for her keys and then paused as she considered the implications of a dinner. After all, he had already seen her in a very compromising position before they had even gone out. He might have the impression that she would be equally easy on a date. "Just so we're clear, I don't want you to have any preconceived ideas or expectations based on, well... you know. What I mean to say is..." She found herself unable to complete the sentence, so he did it for her.

"Don't expect to get laid on the first date, right?"

She responded with a smile.

"May I be forward with you?" he asked, causing her to laugh.

"As I said, we may be beyond that."

"Then let me express myself as best as possible. In a way, we have already done the sex part, even if it was not in the conventional sense. That is something a couple usually works up to, but in our case, we are going backward. It's like reading the ending of a book and then working to the beginning, chapter by chapter, and encountering all the wonderful things that culminated in that end.

"So here we are, two novels, with two lifetimes of experiences documented within their pages. I can't think of a better way to spend the evening than with a good book. I am looking forward to all the discoveries from this person that I would like to know more about. I want to find out who she really is because I find her very, very attractive, and I only hope that she feels the same way."

Ellen let his words sink in, considering them carefully before answering. "That may be the sweetest thing anyone has ever said to me."

And it was—sweet and thoughtful—and incredibly romantic. Of course, she would say yes. He was right; it had gone backward for them. Even though he had a distinct advantage, she still had to rely on her imagination.

A woman walked past them, several grocery sacks in hand, reaching her car a short distance away from them. They watched as she unlocked the car, and one of the flowers from the bouquet she was holding fell to the ground. She never noticed. After setting the bags in the back seat, she climbed into the car.

A gust of wind blew across the lot, picking up the lone flower and sending it across to Jeffrey's feet. It came to rest there as a faithful pet might to its master. He picked it up and handed it to Ellen.

"Flowers usually come later," she observed.

"Like I said, we seem to be working backward."

She accepted his offering, taking a quick sniff at the petals and noting the scent was at odds with the season, rich in the fragrance of cinnamon and nutmeg.

"You've not said anything about the video," she said, her voice now sounding meek. "Do you find me at all... alluring?" She meant to say *sexy* but could not bring herself to say it, at least not to him. Regardless, he knew exactly what she meant.

"I think you are the most alluring woman I have ever met."

Now she blushed the brightest of crimson. It was a tone well deserved.

"I should be going."

"Tonight? Seven?"

"You can pick me up at my house."

"What is your address?"

She leaned in and kissed him briefly on the cheek. "I'll email it to you."

Ellen got in her car and left the lot, giving a final wave to Jeffrey on her way out. This was not what she could ever have expected, yet it was everything she had been craving. She wasn't asking for much, just a little romance. Already, Jeffrey had said things far more romantic than anything Joel could have come up with, or her ex, for that matter.

And he gave her a flower. How sweet was that? As she passed by a corner tree lot, she began to hum along to a seasonal pop song on the radio, the one about mommy kissing Santa Claus, feeling much more in the spirit than she had in a while. The remainder of the holiday season had the promise to be something extraordinary, full of warmth and tenderness. Perhaps she had made the Nice list after all.

And she had a date tonight.

A date with a very charming man. Who could say what would come from it? As to taking it slow, she was already thinking of skipping that part. Given the circumstances, he had an advantage. She needed to even the score—and he might even teach her something new along the way.

AN INTRODUCTION

THE KONDO METHOD

Most people know who Marie Kondo is. If you've been hiding in a cluttered room and don't have a clue, then Google her. It ties indirectly to this tale. Cleaning house takes on many forms from the literal sense to those aspects of our past that need to be discarded. As to the latter, we all have those in our lives who have treated us less than respectfully. There comes a time when we do an inventory to address what is most important in our lives.

THE KONDO METHOD

BETHELLEN STANLEY LEANED BACK in her wheelchair while watching the steady fall of snow outside the window. She shivered from the chill that settled in her old bones. Without a thought, she pulled her shawl tight, even though her room temperature held at seventy-three degrees. Hardly a day went by when she felt comfortably warm. The cold had become an unwanted companion, and no amount of extra layering of clothing or hot herbal tea might drive it away.

Winter was part and parcel of her life; summer, fall, and spring were now relegated to her past as fond, bittersweet memories, a long stretch of time that far outnumbered the days she might have left.

The flakes fell softly, making not a sound, and formed a pattern across the backdrop of the night. Only the single light from the outdoor streetlamp cast a soft yellow gleam against the snow. Her window offered a limited view of the small yard alongside the parking lot, the trees and cars alike covered in white. It reminded her of how much she missed the lovely view she once had at her former home, one she had lived in since childhood.

That two-story house belonged to her parents before she inherited it, a wonderful home with its four bedrooms, tall ceilings, a spacious kitchen, and a real wood-burning fireplace that served as a social gathering spot in the front room during the December through February stretch.

The home sat on three acres of unspoiled land with its combination of pines and oaks and wildlife that ranged from squirrels and raccoons to an occasional deer. Having forged eight decades of memories under its roof, the house had become a part of her. Her children sold it last year, along with most of her possessions accumulated throughout a lifetime. Now she had a single room to call her own.

She reminded herself that things might be worse. Care facility residents often were forced to share a space, listening to their roommate gripe, cough, snore, and pass gas. Some managed to get along. Many hated each other, that is if they could remember who and where they were.

BethEllen had that much going for her. She had her wits and humor – sharp as a tack, as the expression went. Ditto with eyesight, except the reading glasses, a tool she'd needed since she hit her fifties. Her hearing had slipped a bit, but not worth complaining about. Mobility presented the big problem.

Arthritis had done its corrosive work through her body, making it all but impossible to move easily, hence the wheelchair, another unwanted companion. Ironically, it had partially spared her writing hand, all the better for her current project.

She cast a glance at the nearby table with the stack of cards and envelopes. She'd get to it soon enough. That's all she had now, borrowed time. This evening, she'd spend it by writing a few holiday cards.

Cards to family. To friends. Acquaintances. Those who deserved her words.

Movement caught her attention outside the window. A bird landed in a nearby tree, its feathers a stark contrast to the surrounding snow. It held its position, looking from one side to another. She wondered if it had lost its way, separated from the rest of its flock. For a second, it looked straight at her. *Where are you going this late at night, little bird? How many more miles do you have ahead of you? How many adventures?*

Then the moment broke. The bird let go and took to the sky.

BethEllen gave a heavy sigh at the desertion. It merely reinforced the loneliness she already felt. With the tree barren once more, she turned from the window. The snow would continue to fall, regardless of whether she watched it or not. Her cards waited.

She wheeled her chair to the table and picked up a pen. Where to begin? To the side rested a small organizer book opened to a set of names, phone numbers, and mailing addresses. Best to start with the ones that mattered most. After all, she had planned to prepare these cards as a way of getting so much off her chest. What better way to do so than at Christmas with its countdown to the new year?

She addressed the first envelope: Morris Stanley.

Her son.

After a moment to collect her thoughts, she took the card in hand and began to write. The words came quickly. In her mind, she'd already written it many times over.

Morris,

I hope you and your family are doing well. We never see each other now since you live so far away. I assume it will be the same this Christmas. Please know that I love you, even though what I have to say suggests otherwise.

You've treated me badly. After so many years of looking after you, bathing you, making sure you had something to eat, nursing your wounds when you were hurt or ill, and watching you take your first steps from the house in search of your independence, I had hoped for more. I was always there. You found your life and never looked behind.

Only after your father died and my life became difficult did you step back in. I believe you only acted out of obligation, a job that must be done. You and your sister packed me away. Then you left again. I can only assume that it will remain this way until I pass, and then you will return for your duties again unless you talk your sister into doing it all for you.

I know this sounds harsh, but I know you far better than you know yourself. You need reminding – not everything revolves around you. I hope you learn this before you are where I am and see the world in hindsight.

I expect this card will make you angry. You will fume and rage and call me all sorts of names. You will consider me unapprecia- tive. You might even call me senile, although we both know that's far from true. Regardless, that was not my intention. But I hope it makes you feel guilty, as it should. I gave you everything. Now, you've taken all I had left. That's not how a son should behave.

Somewhere inside is that little boy I nursed when he needed it. I wish you could have returned the same amount of care.
With more love than you know,
Mom

BethEllen read her words, then did so again. The card failed to say everything she wanted. To do so would take a full journal, but it captured the essence. Even as a child, Morris had been an enigma, able to win over the most hardened heart with his smile while remaining totally absorbed in himself.

For the longest time, she bore the guilt so familiar in motherhood that it was all her fault. Somehow, she must have been responsible for his lack of empathy. Only in recent years had she accepted the fact that he could have been raised by Mother Teresa and still cared not for the world. Upbringing could only do so much.

She set the card and envelope to one side and moved on to a fresh one.

Dear Sara,

Merry Christmas to you and your family. I had hoped we might see each other for the holidays. It's been a while since we've been together in person. You had been so regular in your weekly visits until recently. I understand the reasons, with the flu, viruses, and lockdowns. One can't be too careful, but isolation has its price.

Talking over the phone or computer is not the same. I miss our regular chats in person, your humor, and your personality. And, yes, your home cooking that you brought to me. I dream of your chicken carrot stew (even though you got the recipe from me).

I must say something and I hope you take it well. You're a caring, dutiful daughter, and I love you all the more for it. You know this has not been easy for me. I've given you an earful on numerous occasions, and you listened to me as a thoughtful person would. But I think you need to face up to facts.

You're a pushover. Always have been, ever since you were a child. That's not bad, but sometimes it's important to stand up for what you want. I've watched as you gave in to your friends, to those you work with, your husband, even your children. One by one, you let go of your fondest dreams. Most of all, you always buckled to your brother. I doubt he'd do the same for you.

I know he was the one who made the decision about me. You caved. That's more than spineless. You allowed him to sell off everything I had while you stood by and did nothing.

I'm still furious with him for it.

I try every day not to blame you too. I know that you meant well.

Sara, you have a good heart. Please try to do what's right for a change.

With love, my dearest one,

Mom

The letters blurred on the page. She paused to wipe the wetness from her eyes. That had been far harder than she expected. Still, words must be said.

She moved to the next blank card, took a deep breath as she collected her thoughts, then set ink to the page.

Dear Margo,

I hope you and your family are well. I think back to the times when the four of us would go out, you and John, me and my Mike. I always found it wonderful how good we were as friends. I even considered you to be my very best friend.

Of course, it took me a while to find out that you and Mike were having an affair. Three years. That's a long time to keep such a secret, but I did eventually figure it out. I never said a word to Mike and hoped that he'd eventually lose interest. Eventually, he did.

For the longest time, I despised you. I still don't respect you, but have accepted it all as part of the past. Perhaps you gave my Mike something I could not.

Or maybe you were nothing more than a slut in the bedroom.

Regardless, I want you to know that I know who and what you are. You probably won't want to talk to me again after this.

It doesn't matter anymore. I don't care.

Sincerely,

BethEllen

Three cards down, more to go. She worked her way through the address book, finding the names of those she needed. One by one, she wrote what must be said. With each one, she grew confident in her thoughts. Words could indeed cut deep. She allowed herself to be merciless. The envelopes piled up, each made out in clean, legible handwriting.

Tim Hines, Mike's attorney. He handed all their business details while Mike was alive. When her husband died, he served as executor. He'd been skimming off the top for years. No telling how much he had embezzled from them. He also saw to the liquidation of her home and belongings. He and Morris fell from the same tree.

Shelley, Mike's secretary. After Margo, he found his way into her bed. Again, BethEllen remained silent for better and worse and all that. Shelley eventually quit for another job and moved away. They'd never been friends. She saw no value in starting now but wanted to have the last word.

Bob and Kellie Stanley, Mike's brother and his wife. For some reason, Bob never approved of her and made his feelings known even before the wedding. His attitude never changed. Kellie mirrored his feelings and attitude, most likely based on whatever he told her. A pity too; she seemed nice enough. The last time BethEllen saw them was at Mike's funeral.

She considered a card for Hester McBride, a resident a few doors down from her at the retirement home. Hester always screamed at her and called her all sorts of names: nasty, horrible, a communist, a whore, a liar, a heathen, a pickaninny lover (whatever that was), and a Democrat. BethEllen stilled her pen in compassion. It wasn't Hester's fault, just the baggage that came with old age. There but for the grace of God, go I.

She moved to the final letter, one never to be mailed.

Dearest Mike,

    I have so much to thank you for. The way you caught my eye that first night at the skating rink, your smile, and bad jokes. The wonderful life you gave me. The children we brought into this world. How you stayed with me to the very end.

    But you never stayed true to me. You've disappointed me so often over the years, but most of all, for the countless times you came home with the stink of another woman on you. I'm not naïve or stupid. Never was.

    I know how many affairs you had, from the one-nighters to the ones that lasted longer. Margo. Shelley. The others. Perhaps I wasn't as adventuresome as you wanted. Or boring. Or possibly you just wanted variety. What's done is done. You're gone now. You were my one and only, so I have no way to compare. I'd tell you to live with that, but you can't now, can you? But you were my husband and you loved me in your own way.
Rest easy.
Bethee

The stack piled up, well over a dozen by the time BethEllen finished with her husband's letter set to the side. She considered the stack before her. Already, she felt better even without sending them. The act of writing served as a means of purging one's soul. Impure thoughts must find a release in one manner or another. She'd kept these for a lifetime.

Now, she felt lighter, even carefree. This might be the best Christmas present she'd ever given herself. She counted the cards, a total of fourteen. Then she counted out another set of blanks of the same number. On the first, she wrote:

> *Dearest Morris,*
> *   Best wishes to you and your family for a holiday full of light and affection.*
> *I love you, son.*
> *Mom*

She wrote similar greetings to the remaining thirteen, all full of cheer, love, and goodwill. Then she leaned back into her wheelchair, needing a good stretch. Her fingers ached from all the writing, but she felt satisfied. Before her sat two stacks of cards, identical in all respects except for distinctly different messages.

She'd only send one stack.

BethEllen rested her hand on a set, her eyes closed as if feeling its intention, predicting outcomes. After a time, she moved her hand to the other and repeated the process. With a smile, she selected a pile, then began to stuff each one into its associated envelope. Licking and sealing the first came easy, even the second and third. Her mouth grew dry with the fourth. The remaining envelopes took more time, but at length, she had them ready for mailing. All they needed now were stamps and Godspeed to them. One card remained apart, that for her Mike.

For the longest time, she sat still, examining the other stack. The room seemed especially quiet now, perhaps matching the aftermath of her restless thoughts. Somehow, the stillness offered comfort. She took the remaining set of cards and set them on her lap, along with Mike's card, and a plastic bowl from her bedside table. She turned the chair and rolled out of her room.

She found no activity in the hallway. By nine, most tenants had retired to their rooms, leaving the nurses and attendants free to walk the halls. The corridor bore its solitude as markedly as the somber wallpaper, stretching from one end to the other. Even with the garland and Christmas decorations that accented the walls, she found it lacking holiday spirit. Instead, she thought of an old movie from the '80s about a haunted hotel in the dead of winter—another kind of holiday spirit.

She worked her chair slowly toward the front office, expecting to find a night security guard at the desk. A shrill, repetitive squeak from her wheels echoed against the walls of the hallway, broadcasting her arrival well before she reached the front. Sure enough, as she turned the corner, the night attendant gave her a smile. A small radio on the desk offset the silence with a soft melody of festive country music.

"Good evening, Mr. Taylor," BethEllen said as she pulled herself close to the desk.

"Shouldn't you be in your room?" Taylor asked, his smile intact. She figured him to be somewhere in his forties, but with streaks of gray in his hair, he could be older. The twinkle in his eyes was ageless. A few more decades and he could be a resident as well.

"I couldn't sleep, so I wrote out some Christmas cards."

"I usually read when I can't sleep."

She nodded. Reading books. Counting sheep. Whatever works. "Mr. Taylor, would you be a dear and do me a favor?"

"Anything for you, sweetheart." Land sakes, what a charmer.

"Do you have a paper shredder in the office?"

He gave her a perplexed look. "Whatever for?"

She held up the cards. "These are my extras."

"You can just put them in the wastebasket."

"I know but..." she offered a shy grin. "If you would indulge me just a little. Think of it as goodwill for the season."

He nodded, rose, and disappeared into the neighboring room. A minute later, he returned with a small tabletop shredder. "I'm afraid I have to help you with this. House rules, you understand."

"Aren't you the sweetest thing? I'd love the help. Can you put the scraps back in this bowl?"

Taylor stared at the bowl as if calculating her intention. In this place, that surely came as second nature to the staff. Fact and fiction blended under this roof. He took the bowl and positioned it in the receptacle bin.

One by one, she handed him the cards, and he ran them through the shredder. Each time, the sound of metal blades striking paper countered the twangy holiday music in the background. Within a minute, the deed was done, and he handed her the bowl now filled with confetti. Unlike the old-style shredders that sliced in only one direction, this machine cut horizontally and vertically, reducing the paper into perfect tiny squares.

She held out a final card, the one for Mike. It transformed into shreds, along with the others.

She stared at the bowl. "This is wonderful."

"Will that be all?" he asked.

"Just one more thing." She looked at him, returning his sparkle. "I need to go outside for a minute."

He gave her *the look*. "Doors are locked, Mrs. Stanley, like they are every night. And it's too cold to be going out."

"Just for a minute? It's important."

Taylor stared at her for an extended moment, letting his gaze wander from her imploring eyes to the bowl of shredded paper in her lap. She remained attentive, returning his stare. She watched his expression change to understanding as he did the math.

"I'm sure you have your reasons." When she nodded, he asked, "Special delivery?"

"You might say that."

Taylor laughed. "Postal service always was too slow." He reached into his pocket and pulled out a set of keys, then paused to study her as one might an impetuous child. "You know, I could get fired for this."

"I'll only be a minute. You can stand right behind me if you want."

He rose from his desk. "I plan to." After pulling on his jacket, he stepped into the adjoining room and returned with a small blanket, placing it over her shoulders. "I can't let you go catching a cold, can I?"

"I suspect you're a treasure," she cooed.

He wheeled her to the nearby door and unlocked it. "I'm not leaving your side. Understood?"

"In this world, we all do what we must do. That's our blessing and our curse."

He paused, apparently considering her words, before opening the door and guiding her out. The cold hit them both, and she slid her hand over the bowl to keep its contents intact. She felt the falling snow strike her face, and she thought back to her childhood, so long ago, of making angels on the ground. As she had then, she stuck her tongue out, letting a few flakes make contact. It tasted of magic, youth, and possibilities.

"Is this good enough?" Taylor asked.

She pointed to the corner of the driveway where the sea of white began, the green lawn covered by the snow, and the lone tree in the middle, its leaves bravely putting up a fight against the oncoming winter. He pushed the chair to its edge. "This is as far as we go. You have one minute, Mrs. Stanley."

"Make it two." She heard him take a few steps back, giving her space to collect her thoughts. The cold dug into her skin even with the blanket, but she gave her attention to the landscape before her, the falling flakes, the single tree in the center, the white below, and the night sky above.

Had she been in the countryside, there would be more twinkling dots of white above, the stars visible in the heavens. Most here were obscured by the city light. It all came to this, her life at this moment, one of so many before.

She said some words to herself but meant for others, thoughts best kept in check. Then the wind kicked up, causing the falling snow to change direction to a steeper angle. The time had come.

She took a handful of confetti and tossed it in the air. The paper took flight, mixing with the wind and the flakes, and set sail across the lawn. She repeated the process several more times until the bowl had been emptied, and the shredded remnants of her thoughts blew away, as well they should. Some things were never meant to be shared. It's not proper. Anger and hatred should blow away like the wind.

"Are you done, Mrs. Stanley?"

She heaved a sigh. "Done."

Taylor wheeled her back into the facility, down the corridor, and to her room. She handed him the remaining set of sealed envelopes. "Will you see that these go out in the mail tomorrow?"

"I'll do that." He turned to go back to his post.

"Oh, Mr. Taylor..."

"Yes?"

She looked him over from head to toe. "Are you good to your folks?"

He grinned. "I try to be. They may outlive me."

"You do them right. And your wife too. It's important."

He cast a glance around the empty hallway before looking back at her. "I know."

She nodded. "I know you do."

He walked back to his desk, and she readied herself for bed, a day closer to Christmas and a day shorter in all other respects. Outside, a multitude of tiny paper squares found their way onward. Some settled on the ground, growing soft from the wetness of the snow. Others, those scraps with a sense of freedom, clung to the wind and floated on to farther destinations, each carrying part of a larger intended message meant to be spoken but never heard.

Words have power. Consequences. Resolve.

Sometimes, it's not the listening that's important, but the act of speaking aloud, even when there's no one around to hear.

BethEllen slept the best night of her eighty-plus years.

AN INTRODUCTION

THE NORTH POLE PAPERS

What is a Christmas collection without Santa? Like many of us, I grew up watching the Rankin–Bass animated special, *Rudolph, the Red-nosed Reindeer.* The first time I saw it, the Bumble scared the hell out of me. Of course, we can all relate to Hermey, the misfit elf with dreams of becoming a dentist—but what if an elf became a whistle-blower for factory injustice?

The inspiration for this story came from the news reports of the time and the activities of Julian Assange. If you look for trouble, you are bound to find it, even at the North Pole.

THE NORTH POLE PAPERS

"THIS IS BAD."

Santa furrowed his brow in concern as he looked at the computer monitor. "Bad. Bad. Bad. Definitely not nice."

The words served as a mantra, repeated over and over as if to reach some inner mystical calm. But there was no transcendence to be found, neither with the words nor with the content on the screen before him.

"Bad. Bad. Bad. Definitely naughty."

In days of old before technology redefined how lists were made, he'd spent long hours poring over lengths of parchment, feather quill in hand, examining name after name. Next to each, he'd made notes, added checks, crossed out some names, or drawn small coal icons. That was tradition, the way it had been done throughout the ages, and it proved to be a tried-and-true method.

Then dawned the computer age with its hardware, software, internet, keyboards, constant updates, and occasional crashes—bringing an end to the era of hand-written communication. His quill sat on the upper shelf collecting dust, and he could scarcely remember the last time he had pulled it down.

It took him a while to embrace the new technology, and at first, he'd steadfastly refused to consider the switch. Why convert? Ink and paper had been good enough for centuries, so why change now? But the pressure on him from his chief advisors, accountants, and the factory elves always eager for the latest toy trends and fads was overwhelming. Even dear Mrs. Claus egged him on, ever so gently, suggesting how it would free up his schedule. Of course, she simply desired more quality time for them to be together.

So out went the parchment and in came the computer along with a strenuous learning curve. Santa quickly realized this was a medium for the young, not the old. Still, he muddled through somehow to get a handle on the various databases, e-mail addresses, BCCs, and mail merge commands needed to do his work.

And lo and behold, the process did become more manageable. Santa found additional time for himself along with a very appreciative Mrs. Claus.

The master Naughty and Nice List was the first to change, and maintaining it became a cinch. Instead of copious notes, he perused multiple categories with the standard "Naughty" and "Nice" columns accompanied by "Absolute Angel," "Passable," and "Evil Incarnate." To his delight, additional columns included note fields for pet preferences (and pet allergies), favorite colors, clothing size, and other notations.

What could he say? They had been right all along.

Other changes followed, including his method of correspondence. One time beautifully scripted longhand on decorative parchment fell victim to the great electronic usurpers: e-mail and texting. These messages were quick, efficient, and easy to archive. Santa refused to budge on fonts; he kept a decorative script typeface as a nod to his earlier exquisite penmanship.

Texting became the standard operating procedure, an effective way of communicating with his advisors and accountants, toy manufacturers, various world charities, top management of multiple companies, and world diplomats in arranging clearances and protocols, as well as the elf managers and directors here at the pole. Indeed, the electronic age had arrived.

Which was why he was now in deep reindeer dung, shaking his head and muttering, "Bad. Bad. Bad."

The Naughty or Nice List on the monitor screen was not a current document but excerpts from a list a few years prior. Yellow highlights marked names here and there, and many had notations of their goodness or badness. The list included not only children but grownups along with details of their activities. The charitable ones who had earned nice marks were credited with their humanitarian efforts. The naughtiest had their own rap sheet of offenses in another column. The listing ran the whole gamut of unscrupulous deeds. As always, Santa had been thorough in his evaluation of each and every person, and only a select few, aside from himself and Mrs. Claus, ever saw this master list.

So the fact that Santa was reading this list on the internet was a very, very bad thing. The internet. The public internet for all the world to see.

There was going to be a backlash to this; he knew it. Important names were of world leaders, well-known movers and shakers in commerce and global leadership, celebrities, and with each one, a list of all their laundry (both clean and dirty).

The offenses were many and varied; lying, embezzlement, cruelty, ego, and sloth were just the tip of the iceberg. Attacks on neighboring countries, nuclear experiments, terrorist acts and the support and funding for mass violence, financial misdealing to cheat others of their investments and retirement... the list ran on and on and on.

The Naughty or Nice List was top security information, never to be seen by anyone outside of the North Pole, but here it was. Even worse, the N&N list was only one of many pages of lists, reports, letters, and e-mails, totaling in the thousands, all leaked to the public and listed on a website headed by a singular, disturbing name:

WinkiLeaks

"Ah, but he's a nasty piece of work, isn't he?" said a voice directly over his shoulder.

Santa nodded but kept his eyes on the screen. "I thought you had someone keeping tabs on Winki. You're my key advisor. I expect you to keep up with everything going on around here."

Santa's advisor, Persnicketi, took a step back and nodded in agreement. Like all of Santa's other employees, Persnicketi was an elf. Unlike the others who dressed in festive outfits of green accented with red collars and boots, he wore a traditional suit and tie. His only allowance for elf attire was the splash of red on his tie.

"Unfortunately, Winki seems to have dropped off the map. I have my people working on it, but he has managed to disappear."

"I can't believe he has stooped to this," Santa said with a groan. "Yes, I know he was a disgruntled elf, but this..." He waved his hand at the screen before him. "This is too much."

"Winki is a troublemaker. He did everything he could to gum up the works. I'm not surprised he would try using this tactic."

True, Winki was one to clog the system. Whereas most elves lived for conformity and joy, Winki lived for chaos. This behavior was evident from his first day of employment. He challenged every order, tried to change processes, and retaliated when things did not go his way. During his stay in the toy factory, he attempted to unionize the workforce, unsuccessfully incited his fellow elves to strike, changed work orders behind his manager's back, posted rude signs about management on the walls, took to graffiti on the factory exterior, and did just about everything he could to keep things from running smoothly.

Prior to his expulsion, he reprogrammed all the talking girl dollies. Instead of saying "Hello, Mommy" or "I love you," they spouted off sexually lewd phrases that made even Mrs. Claus, who had been around the world a few times herself, blush.

Disgruntled was putting it lightly. Winki was a bad elf.

Now he was a bad *missing* elf.

Santa examined the web page with increasing alarm. The masthead bore the name WINKILEAKS in large red letters. Set to its left was a silhouette drawing of an elf head dripping liquid onto a world map below. Underneath were the words *Keeping Elfdom Strong and the North Pole Open*

The page fell into different sections with their individual headings: Reindeergate, The Santa Diaries, Elf Equality, Leaks and Logs, About, Media, and the N&N List.

"For once in my life, I am at a loss on what to do," Santa said. "This entire operation has been built on the principle of secrecy. Everyone knows and respects that. Without discretion, we could never manage to do our work. All those secrets are here on the screen for all to see."

"We're trying to put a lid on it, but no sooner we close down one site than a mirror of it pops up in his place. Our best IT elf, Techi, has been on it nonstop, but so far, he's been in reactive mode."

Santa clicked to another page. A listing of documents and e-mails came up. Some were innocuous—requests for clearance in country airspace, permits, supply updates for parts and equipment, and the like. Others were more concerning, including the directive to the British Prime Minister where Santa complained about not gaining access to certain countries due to their internal politics and the egos of those in charge.

True, he had been pushed to his wit's end when he wrote the e-mail, but there was still no excuse for him to have called that country's president the names he used; oh, what would the children say if they had heard him use such language?

Santa opened one at random and began to read.

> *Dear Presidente,*
>
> *Ho, ho, ho, and the merriest of Christmases to you. I hope you and the family are doing well.*
>
> *As per my previous e-mail to you, I still am at a roadblock regarding your neighbor to the south. As such, I have concluded that as long as its current administration is in charge, there will be no revision in its policy to my efforts. This, of course, will not do.*
>
> *Perhaps a change in its regime could be considered? Please let me know your thoughts on this matter.*
> *Sincerely,*
> *Santa*

This was bound to raise eyebrows. How he yearned for those simpler times when he could transverse the globe without concern for the peculiarities of each country. The world seemed to be a much happier place then. Now, society acted as a global community, interconnected by immediate, wireless communication.

"There has been some expected backlash," Persnicketi said. "Naturally, we've received inquiries from adults and children worldwide. The official stance of the North Pole has been that this was an irresponsible joke in poor taste and that we know nothing about it. So far, that line has been accepted."

"Good, but for how long? Unless the site is removed, there will be more questions. People want to know who did this."

"That's pretty easy to find. Click on the About tab."

Santa clicked, bringing up a biography page with a small headshot of an elf. The professionally taken photograph displayed the elf in a contemplative pose, hand placed below his chin as if weighing a serious decision. Instead of the red/green outfit, he wore a tailored black shirt with a forest-green tie. To the right of the photo was a bio:

WinkiLeaks is a not-for-profit organization with no ties to Santa Claus and his operations. Our goal is to bring important news and information about Santa's stranglehold on the season to the public. We provide a secure and anonymous way for sources to leak information to our journalists in order to keep the North Pole free and open.

This site's spokesman and founder, Winki, is a North Pole journalist, publisher, and activist, as well as a former slave of Santa's dictatorial workshop. Winki speaks out for various causes, including freedom of the press, censorship, investigative journalism, equal rights for Elven people, and fair trade for toymakers.

"He's a smug little prat, isn't he?" Persnicketi said.

"Perhaps he has reason to be," Santa replied. "He wanted to upset the toy cart. Obviously, he has done so. My concern is how he is getting his information. Surely, he did not amass all this by himself."

"We believe he is not working alone. Once he left, he would not have access to any of this information. There must be someone else feeding him the documents."

Santa shook his head in dismay. "I can't believe anyone here would stoop to that. We have a trusted family. To do so would be a betrayal to all we have worked for."

"That may be so, but keep in mind, Winki is an elf, and elves stick together."

Santa looked him straight in the eye. "You're an elf. Where are your loyalties?"

Persnicketi straightened his tie. "I think my past record speaks for itself. Unlike others here, I see a bigger picture. You needn't worry about my allegiances."

"My apologies," replied Santa. "I did not mean to accuse, but this whole affair is wearing me quite thin."

"It may be the only thing about you that is thin," Persnicketi quipped. Santa shot him an unhappy glance. "Sorry, just kidding."

Santa pulled up another page from the site—an internal memo from him to the head of toy operations.

> *To: Rolli-Polli*
> *From: Santa Claus*
>
> *It has come to my attention that in the early months of the year, there has been a lessening of efforts in the factory. While we are still many months from delivery day, there seems to be an attitude that we have plenty of time. This will not do. The preceding months are our best time to get ahead of the game. I expect you to drive the force harder than you have in the past. Due to the global economic downturn, it is all the more pressing. Still, it also means there cannot be any additional compensation for those efforts. If these changes cannot be enacted, we may need to evaluate a shortening or elimination of vacation time to reach our quota.*
>
> *Please do what you must.*

"I sound like a Scrooge here," Santa mumbled.

"Poppycock. It was meant to get the product line moving, and you didn't do anything rash. You even gave out extra vacation time that year. I remember the e-mail."

"Yes, except that particular memo seems to be conveniently missing here."

Persnicketi nodded. "Winki is trying to paint an unfavorable picture of you. I don't think he will put up anything that shows your better nature."

"So what about accomplices?"

Persnicketi shook his head. "Nothing. Whoever is leaking the papers to Winki is very good. We found no trail. I wish I could tell you otherwise."

"What is the general elf attitude to Winki and his cause?"

"As to be expected, he has his admirers and his detractors. Some see him as a hero fighting for the common elf. Mostly, they keep quiet about it. As you might guess, open support for Winki does not bode well for job security."

Santa considered this for a moment. "Should we launch a counter-campaign? Show how his actions are reckless and dangerous. Brand him as a terrorist?"

"No," Persnicketi answered. "My advice would be to try to shut the site down. As to Winki, let him shout all he wants. If we show through our actions that we are not what he says, then it will all fade away soon enough. Elves have a short memory."

"And what about the rest of the world?"

"The key is to bring down the site."

Santa scrolled over to the Video tab and clicked. A listing appeared.

    Santa and the Missus #1
    Santa and the Missus #2
    Santa and the Missus #3 – Hot Chocolate
    Santa and the Missus #4 – Leather and Lace
    Santa and the Missus #5 – You gotta see this!

He clicked on the last link, and a video appeared onscreen showing the dimly lit Claus bedroom. In the video, soft holiday music set the mood while Santa and Mrs. Clause were deep in the revelry of doing...

"How the Hell did he get this footage," Santa shouted, clicking off the video just as Mrs. Claus's squeal of ecstasy rang through the speakers. "I want a lid put on this. What are the children going to think when they see this?" He then turned another shade of red as he saw the next video category: Santa and Rudolph – Reindeer games. "I'm really beginning to hate that little pipsqueak," he growled.

"Now, Santa, remember that hate is not a holiday virtue," Mrs. Claus said, entering with a plate of milk and cookies. "You don't want to end up on your own naughty list."

Santa quickly clicked to another, less personal page before she reached the desk.

"Good evening, Persnicketi," she continued. "Would you like some refreshment?"

"Thank you, but no. I'm good."

"Hard at work, I see. Are you going over this year's list?"

"Checking it twice," Santa replied with a smile.

She laid down the tray, gave Santa a quick peck on the cheek, and left the room.

"That had to be the quickest mouse click I've ever seen."

Santa agreed. "No sense in letting her know she may become a favorite on YouTube. At least, not yet."

"Damage control?"

"I think we are up to our necks in it," Santa sighed. "So give me your thoughts on containment."

"We are beyond containment. The information is already out there and cannot be retracted. The best we can do is try to keep any more from being released while we look for a way to shut it down completely."

"And Winki?"

"He's already gone public about another massive dump of documents in two days' time. He said it would include top-secret details about the inner circle of our operations, as well as..." Persnicketi found the words caught in his throat, knowing that things could get far worse.

"Go on," said Santa.

"More videos. This time including underage elves."

Santa lowered his head to the table. "Is there any good news in all of this?" he asked softly.

"Er, no, sir, I don't think there is."

"And all because of one bad elf," Santa growled. "How does he sleep with himself at night."

"Beg your pardon, but he doesn't. Remember, elves don't require sleep. That's why we make such a good workforce. You know that."

"It's a blasted figure of speech, Persnicketi! I know elves don't slumber!"

"Right," Persnickety answered with a sheepish expression. He fumbled with his tie for a few minutes as Santa continued to browse the website. The tension had been great before, but it was far worse in the silence. The elf cleared his throat.

"Um, sir, there might be another option. Winki could simply... disappear."

Santa raised his eyebrow. "I thought you said he had vanished."

"I mean disappear for good. We do have ways... of dealing with things. Some favors are owed to us. All we would need to do is make a request to the right people."

Santa scrutinized him for what seemed to be a minute before answering. "Although tempting, we must live by our principles. What you suggest goes way beyond mere naughtiness. It is reprehensible, and I cannot in any way endorse even the thought of it. Sorry, Persnicketi, but the moment we cross that line, we are no better than Winki."

"I understand, sir."

"But I sure would love to see the little turd get his comeuppance if nothing else than to teach him a good lesson."

A clamoring came outside the door, the sound of running feet growing closer. Santa and Persnicketi rose to see what was the matter. Techi burst through the door, out of breath but also clearly excited.

"Santa, I've got it! I've solved the problem!"

"Calm down," Santa replied, his demeanor instantly upgrading a few notches. "Take a deep breath, and then tell me what you have come up with."

"It's a special program I've just finished writing. It works like a virus. It automatically corrupts all the files within designated parameters based on programmer descriptions and rules. It replaces those files with alternate data and file commands."

"Can you put that in plain English?" Santa asked.

"Of course. We send this virus to Winki. It pulls all files related to Santa's operation and replaces them with page after page of Christmas carols. As an added feature, it also plays a children's choir humming those carols. I call it the Hum-Bug Virus. Think of it as our own very special Christmas present to Winki."

Santa nodded with satisfaction. "Very impressive, Techi. Very inventive. But what about new additions to the site?"

"The virus is both ex post facto. Any new additions are immediately corrupted. The virus will not remove the site, but it will render it harmless."

Santa patted him on the shoulder. "You have exceeded yourself. Thank you very much, not only from myself, but all the children of the world."

"Oh, and one other thing, sort of like a final touch. I hope you don't mind. I left one of the reindeer videos intact but with some… alterations. Now it features Winki making naughty with the reindeer. I got a little carried away with the editing, but it has some additional scenes that are… Well, it's a pretty steamy video, if I do say so myself. Also, it could lay the groundwork for possible prosecution from animal rights groups. They tend to frown on these sorts of things."

Santa managed to stifle a laugh. "Santa would never endorse such a thing… but let's pretend I never saw it."

"Shall we begin then?" Persnicketi asked.

Techi sat at the computer. His fingers turned into a blur as he typed in code and commands. Within a minute, a new screen came up on the monitor – a simple green background with a red button and the words PRESS ENTER TO LAUNCH below it. He rose from the chair and gestured for Santa to take his place.

Santa sat in front of the computer, looked at Techi and Persnickety with a grin, and then turned back to the screen. He raised his finger and held it aloft directly over the ENTER key.

"Merry Christmas, Winki," he said as he pushed the key.

AN INTRODUCTION

ORPHANS

Benjamin Franklin is generally credited with the quote that nothing is certain but death and taxes. This story is not about taxes. Nor is it about death, not directly—but for many of us, we do become orphans, even if it is late in life.

This story is a direct result of my joining the club. The landmark in the story does exist in Houston exactly as described, and it is a site that draws onlookers every evening, especially in the months when the weather is neither too hot nor cold.

Some might find the premise of the story a bit creepy, but beauty is in the eye of the beholder. I believe that magic is all around us and can be found if only you open your eyes.

ORPHANS

"I WANT a Christmas with wings."

Mandy cast a quick glance at her boyfriend, then back to the street scene around her. Reminders of the season surrounded them, the retail vendors selling their holiday wares, the popular carols piped through multiple speakers, the colored-light strands glowing well before dark, and the hustle-bustle of shoppers making their last-minute purchases. Within a few hours, the stores along Nineteenth Street would close in preparation for Christmas Eve.

"Like angels?" Hank asked, his hands crammed in his pockets as he walked alongside her.

Mandy answered with a sigh ending in an annoyed rumble of the lips. "I dunno." She came to a stop as a woman passed by loaded with shopping bags and wearing earrings in the shape of tree lights, one green and one red—both lit.

"I can tell you what I don't want tonight: mass-produced, superficial tripe. Give me something meaningful and real." She shot a disparaging look at a nearby shop window full of holiday glitz. "Christmas Eve should be intimate, genuine. Time spent with those you love the most. I don't want television with those silly holiday movies. I don't want crowds of strangers. I don't want to be sold a bag of commercialism with a red bow." Again, she waved her hands in exasperation. "What I want is a reminder of the world at peace." She reached for his hand, pulling it from his pocket and taking it in hers. "I need this. Something tangible."

Hank let his fingers slide between hers. "You're thinking about your parents, aren't you?"

Even with a smile, her face caved a little, weighed down by memories. "Yeah. It's hard not to. They were always there for me—especially this time of year. To lose both of them so close together... I'm still struggling." She cast a shy glance at him. "But you know all about that."

Hank looked upward at the blue December sky dotted with clouds. "Mine passed away when I was a teenager. It seems a long time ago now, old history. You've been fortunate to grow into adulthood with yours."

Mandy wiped at her nose, it taking on a reddened tinge. "It's not enough. There are the things they'll never see. Meeting the man of my dreams, seeing me getting married, having kids. All the old traditions are gone forever."

"Time to make some new ones."

"It's not that easy."

He gave her hand a gentle squeeze. "No one said it was."

A soft breeze kicked up, adding the slightest chill to the otherwise warm weather. Unlike the climates of the northern states, Houston's December temperature ranged anywhere from the upper twenties to the seventies, with a typical Christmas being anything but white. With it currently in the high sixties, Hank and Mandy had no need for coats, scarves, or mittens, and hot cocoa offered little medicinal value to warm the body, only sweeten the tongue.

They crossed Nineteenth Street with the pedestrian light counting down the seconds, heading toward another set of shops and a corner cafe.

"Coffee?" he asked.

"I'm good. Thanks." She paused, her thoughts evident on her face. "They would have liked you, I think. Mom once said that you can trust a person by the color and depth of their eyes."

"I wish I could have met them. Too bad we didn't meet a year ago."

Mandy took in a deep breath, held it for sustenance, and released it back into the world. "And time moves on." She stopped abruptly, turning to him with the look of a child on Santa's lap, fearful to ask for her dearest desire. "I need something tonight to ground me to the world, without the stupid jingle bells and fa-la-las, without the frivolous crap. I want..."

"Angels?"

She shook her head. "Not exactly. But something to remind me that I'm part of a larger world, a place with meaning—and that we are merely a small section of it." A laugh escaped, a soft, melodic sound that had enraptured Hank the very first time he had heard it. "I'm being foolish, of course."

He ran his hand across her cheek, relishing the warmth that spread over his fingers. "Not even." She leaned her face into his palm, letting the moment take hold.

"Eventually, we all become orphans," he said. "I can't replace your folks. Nothing can. But we do have each other. Can that be enough for you tonight?"

She slid her arm around his waist. "For us both. No one should be alone on Christmas Eve."

They had planned the evening to be just the two of them, beginning with her fixing dinner and him promising to clean up. The previous day, he had picked up a bottle of wine, one more expensive than he might have typically bought, but he wanted the night to be special. She deserved it.

Already, he had several presents for her, wrapped, labeled, and nestled under the tree she had set up in her apartment. Until now, he figured his shopping to be complete, but her request shifted his mind to problem-solving mode.

Something real.

Something capable of taking flight.

The idea came to him without warning as they made their way down Heights Boulevard, causing him to stumble, both literally and figuratively.

"What?" she asked, noting his distraction.

"Nothing," he replied, not yet prepared to share.

The notion was everything true and nontraditional, unique but bonded to the world with no tie to the holiday season—and even a bit weird. But he understood the connection to the spinning wheel of life about them.

And as requested, it came with wings.

He checked the time, nearly five in the afternoon, just early enough for them to reach the destination. "I have an idea."

"What?"

He offered a grin, one very similar to the one she first saw months earlier, the same that convinced her to say yes to a date. She'd grown to love that smile.

"I'm not ready to say, not yet. It might require a step outside the box."

She studied his expression, both curious and dubious at his vagueness. "Okay... Is the box wrapped?"

"Not exactly, but we need to head back to my car."

Not long after, they sat in his vehicle, a compact, well-used Toyota, driving out of the Heights. Within ten minutes, they reached their destination. He pulled the car into an empty parking space alongside Allen Parkway bordering the park along Buffalo Bayou. Under normal conditions, the chances of finding a vacant spot fell into the negative numbers, it being a popular place for jogging, picnicking, walking the dog, and so forth. Tonight, being the eve of Christmas, most people had settled in their homes for their Christmas Day preludes.

"So why are we at the park?"

Hank gave her a wink before hopping out of the car. "You'll see."

Intrigued by the mystery, she stepped to the curb and shut the car door. Already, he had his hand outstretched, ready to lead her. "Come on. We don't have much time."

She took his hand, and together they followed the walkway, mostly vacant except for the occasional cyclist zipping by. The sun had begun its descent, shadows growing longer as the light dimmed. The sky erupted into a cascade of colors, deep blues turning to purples accented by the fading orange and red rays. In response, streetlights kicked on to counterbalance the dark.

As they approached the Waugh Drive bridge, Mandy's nose wrinkled. "What's that smell?"

Hank pointed to the street ahead of them. "It's from the bridge. Underneath, there is a colony of..."

Mandy yanked his arm as she laid on the brakes, now making the connection. "Bats? You're taking me to see bats on Christmas Eve?"

His amusement evenly matched her incredulous expression. "You did ask for wings. And doves are rather hard to come by right now."

"But... but... Yuck!" A sound emerged from deep in her throat, matching her disgust. "Can't we save this for Halloween?"

"Like I said, it's an out-of-the-box idea. Just roll with it."

"But it's creepy... and embarrassing."

He gave her arm a gentle tug. "It's Christmas Eve, so I doubt there will be a crowd. Come on."

Either his smile, or her trust, or the spirit of goodwill for the season, freed her feet from their anchor. She gave way, allowing him to lead her toward the bridge and the ever-increasing aroma, one definitely not of cinnamon and holly.

To the surprise of both, people gathered at the side of the bridge and on the platform with signage about the Mexican free-tailed bat. Though not a large crowd, perhaps a dozen, and far smaller than the daily attendance at other times of the year, Hank and Mandy found it unexpected for the evening at hand.

Several couples waited alongside their children who appeared excited about the outing. To one side, a musician in his twenties sat on the grass with a ukulele, plucking at the strings. Next to him, a goth girl clad in black swayed to the melody. A trio of cyclists stood with their bikes. Judging from their appearance, they rode every day, regardless of weather, season, or holiday.

Mandy edged up to Hank as they made themselves comfortable on the ground. "No people, right?"

He wrapped his arm around her. "Who woulda thunk."

"This is so not what I had in mind. You might as well have given me a live rat because it reminded you of the one in *The Nutcracker*." She punched him several times on the knee, the blow being just beyond playful but not full spite.

He gave her an out. "Forget it. It's still early enough to catch Handel's *Messiah*."

She rubbed her hand along his leg, massaging the area she had hit moments earlier. "No, we're already here, and I didn't want a commercial production. But I did ask for intimate, remember?" She let her eyes wander along the bayou, skimming the darkening silhouette of trees from the ebbing light, the bike trail in the foreground, and to the left, the looming bridge stretching across the waterline.

"Don't bats sleep during the winter?" she asked.

"Not here, apparently. I think it has to do with the breed as well as the climate. We have them year-round, although you get a better show in the warmer months."

The musician launched into a rendition of *Silent Night*, humming the melody as he played. His girl in black soon joined in, a soft, lilting voice that betrayed her dark exterior. Based on their clear harmonies, this was not a random, unpracticed event. Two children approached them and started to sing along, reminding Hank of the end of the Charlie Brown holiday cartoon.

Mandy laid her head on his lap, staring at the darkening sky. Already, a few stars had appeared even with the combating light from the city.

"This isn't too bad," she said as much to herself as him. He answered by running his fingers through her hair, feeling its soft texture. "In the grand scheme, we are really puny things, here for an instant and taking up a grain of space. So why is it that we make such a big deal of ourselves?"

He chuckled. "My, but we're getting heavy in our thoughts tonight."

"I'm not always this way."

"I know."

"Would you prefer me light and funny?"

"I'll take you just the way you are, no complaints."

"I just..." Her words trailed into thoughts far away and emotions jumbled from the time of year, and company both present and lost. "You might be better off without me tonight."

"On the contrary," he replied, leaning forward to kiss her. Her lips tasted of want and regret, tempered with a sweet sadness. "Anyway, you promised me dinner."

"Oh, yeah." She returned the kiss with affection. "You called us orphans earlier."

"I did." His hands moved to her shoulders, gently working the tense muscles.

"It sounds strange. I think of the homeless kids in the Dickens books standing out in the snow with nothing to eat. Not this."

"We were born to grow up and lose those who raised us, to have children of our own..."

She looked up at him. "And leave them?"

"That's the circle of life. Time moves on. For some, it's more abrupt."

"And here we are on the one night of the year to celebrate peace on earth, the sanctity of life, and we talk of death. Don't you think that's a bit gloomy?"

He squeezed her shoulders. "You're right. We should go to your place and watch one of those absurd Christmas movies."

Her snort matched a sideways glance. "Right."

"Just joking. We can cuddle on the sofa. A nice glass of wine. Just you and me, two souls without a family—spending our first Christmas together."

She pulled his ear close to her mouth, letting her breath tickle the lobe. "There are places more intimate than the sofa."

He responded in a falsetto voice, doing his best Oliver Twist. "Please, sir, I'd like some more."

She kissed his cheek and let her head fall back to his lap.

"So tell me again... What are we doing here?"

As if on cue, a distinct sound rose from the bridge, causing the musician to stop playing. The small group turned their attention to the structure as a few dark spots appeared from underneath, fluttering about, then up to the sky.

Then came the mass, dozens, hundreds of small shapes, backlit against the indigo sky, swarming upward for their nightly quest. They served as a counterpoint, black dots instead of white stars, moving, and shifting, and growing ever smaller as they made their way outward with no concept of the specialness of the day or their role in the world.

Then they were gone.

More than ever, a solitude descended upon those in attendance, now with the show over. A few stood in rapt attention, hoping for just one more creature to appear.

One by one, the small group dispersed. The musician packed his uke in a travel bag, took his girl in hand, and they wandered from the bridge. Perhaps he might play her another song that evening, something festive or something soft. She might sing along as she had earlier. Or she might not.

The bikers biked to parts unknown. Parents led excited children away, with the eve and their special rituals still ahead.

Hank and Mandy walked back to his car, fingers intertwined and lost in thought. She rubbed her thumb against his, appreciating the company on this night and his attempt to give her the gift of her most fervent desire. If only it were so simple. Some things could never come back, not as they were before.

A soft sound came from overhead, causing them to look up. Two black shapes, fluttering with wings outstretched, hovered way above their heads, moving about in circles.

"What do you make of that?" she asked.

He stared at the creatures as they escaped into the distance. "A message."

"Of what?"

"That we're not alone."

"Never?"

Again, that smile, and she fell for him as she had countless times since they met.

"Ever."

She considered his words and nodded before adding, "Just for the record—I still hate bats."

He kissed her on the cheek and led her onward, two orphans losing themselves to the night.

AN INTRODUCTION

THE GREEN TREE
AND ORNAMENT REBELLION

This is the second story I wrote with the Neuwirths. It came the same year, soon after the first. This came as a direct result of the yearly Christmas tree ritual and the hassle of pulling the boxes from the attic, assembly, and turning the house into a holiday wonderland—all the while knowing that within several months, I'll have to dismantle everything and sock it away for next year.

Of course, there is a sense of wonder about a lit tree. On one occasion, we have had multiple trees in the house: the primary family tree and a second-themed tree with ornaments ranging from nut-crackers to spaceships with robots. Our record is four trees at the same time. Still, wouldn't it be easier if one could just throw a switch and have the tree magically appear?

THE GREEN TREE
AND ORNAMENT REBELLION

THE NEUWIRTH GREEN TREE and Ornament Rebellion took place with surreptitious precision on Christmas Eve. The overthrow arrived quickly with nary a volley fired. Still, it forevermore changed the balance of power on all things with tinsel. The event went down like this…

It was immediately apparent when Martin Neuwirth returned home that something was afoot. First, there arose such a clatter—sounds of bumping and exertion as a large object was maneuvered through the front door. Hearing this, Bettye called from the kitchen, "That you, Martin?"

His reply came in a single word. "Yes."

"Did you pick up the Christmas tree?"

After a noticeable pause, he said, "Yes."

"Pick out a good one?"

"Yes."

Following this came the scampering of two sets of little feet, those belonging to Matthew and Elizabeth, ages three and five, and Lizzie eagerly shouting, "Oh, cool, Dad. What is that?"

The commotion brought Bettye to the front room prepared to see a fresh, unadorned tree of the Christmas variety. This was, after all, what she and Martin had discussed that morning before he left for work. With

Christmas fewer than two weeks away, the presents already piled up in the corner—brightly wrapped orphan boxes without a mother pine to rest underneath. This absence contrasted with the house fully decked in garland and ribbon, and the outside, likewise, lit with hundreds upon hundreds of twinkling lights.

But, alas, no tree.

True, this delay was due in part to the yearly real-versus-fake debate. Hardly a Christmas went by where they did not argue the pros and cons of buying an artificial tree. Real trees were a messy nuisance from the chore of going to a lot and spending an hour to find a decent one, to strapping it to the top of the car without scratching the paint. Once home, there came the tactical maneuvers of getting it inside, particularly through the doorway, while leaving the telltale trail of countless pine needles along the way.

Despite the proper tree-moving attire—a thick shirt with long sleeves and heavy-duty gloves—branches and needles still found a way to deliver a scratch or two. Maintenance followed with daily checks for adequate water in the base so the tree would not dry out; not that this diminished the continual shedding of more needles on the carpet. Finally, there was the matter of disposal after the holidays were over.

Whether it was recycled—which meant strapping it to the car once more and driving across town to a collection center or simply dragging it out to the street for pickup—the end remained the same. The tree became trash, a waste, considering the rising cost every year.

For Martin, the tree equaled a big chore, which was why an artificial one had such appeal: no travel, no mess, easy setup, and an equally quick tear-down for storage until the following year.

Only one factor worked against the fake tree—it was fake. No matter how good it might appear, it still wasn't the genuine artifact. It lacked the imperfections of a real tree. The branches were too orderly. The needles felt different. Just the knowing made a difference.

Most importantly, these impostors did not have the smell of a natural fir, a scent that evoked the very essence of the season. In addition, Bettye argued that selecting a tree was a special ritual in itself and one the kids would treasure as they grew up. This last point always rankled Martin's sensibilities since she usually sent him off to pick up the tree by himself.

This year followed the same pattern. Martin's after-work assignment was to stop off at the lot and find a suitably shaped tree, thus ending the debate for the current year. The Neuwirth home would have its Douglas fir, and Bettye would have her smell with Martin earning the random scratches as he moved the tree into place. No, it was time for a change, and Martin had already decided on what to do.

The idea took hold a week earlier during a visit to one of those high-dollar gadget stores he frequented. There, amid the numerous digital audio and video play toys, the voice-activated golf balls, the auto-reclining chairs with built-in heat and massage features, the hands-free remote talking thermometer, and the all-in-one travel grooming kits (with the combination nose and ear hair clippers), he stopped in his tracks, looking at the ideal solution. Yes, ideal. Christmas this year would be different with no needles to clean up afterward. Oh, how he loved new technology.

Martin returned a week later, bypassing the previously discussed tree lot. In a flash, the well-used Visa ran through the card reader. He tried not to dwell on the price—way high. For this one item, he could have bought trees, lights, and decorations for his entire neighborhood. Instead, he remained secure in the fact he'd never have to strap a pine to his car roof again. Ironically, getting the three-foot-square box out of the shopping mall and into his car presented twice the work than the live tree he would have otherwise bought.

This was the box that greeted Bettye when she entered the front room. Its packaging was simple, bearing the manufacturer logo and the words *Lumo-Brite Virtual Tree*. An accompanying image suggested a brightly lit Christmas tree glowing with an unreal quality as if transparent. Even before asking, she probably realized she would not be hanging ornaments tonight.

"Where is the tree?"

He beamed as brightly as an LED. "You are looking at it."

"Martin, I thought we agreed not to buy a put-together tree."

"You are correct," he replied, noting her choice of words. "This is not a put-together artificial tree. It is something much, much better. There's no assembly; all you do is plug it in, throw a switch, and—voilà! Instant tree!"

He said the last enthusiastically with arms outstretched, immediately causing the kids to jump up and down with shouts of "Yay!" Clearly underwhelmed, Bettye turned one hundred eighty degrees and stomped back to the kitchen.

With the prospect of a new gadget to assemble, away Martin flew like a flash to the task at hand. He tore open the box, tossed aside the Styrofoam packing, and lifted out his new diversion. The unit was a round metal shape some two feet in diameter like a spherical audio component with multiple controls on the front. A power cord hung from the back adjacent to several optional input and output jacks designed to connect to sound and computer devices. The top, which angled in like a squashed ice cream cone, had a circular glass plate about four inches wide at its center.

It only took a minute to get the unit out of the box and plugged into the wall socket. Then he spent the next hour entrenched on the sofa while reading the instruction manual from cover to cover. After an additional thirty minutes of hands-on tinkering, setting up the Wi-Fi to the nearby speakers, and rechecking the manual, he was ready for the unveiling.

Lizzie and Matt had long since become bored and had run off to jump on the living room sofa. They currently watched one of the oft-repeated holiday cartoons on TV, most likely the one with reindeer and the bumble. Bettye remained in the kitchen, refusing to acknowledge the presence of either Martin or the illegitimate tree.

"Okay, kids!" Martin called. "It's showtime." The announcement encouraged a fresh round of cheers. He then called Bettye while using the "considerate husband" voice all men use when they know they're in the doghouse. "Honey, would you like to come see?"

"Not really" came the reply, "but let's get it over with." She reappeared in the front room and leaned against the doorway, arms crossed, with an expression that matched her attitude.

"Come on, Dad. Let's go," chirped Lizzie.

Martin pressed the ON button, which started a low-pitched whirring sound. With a look at his captive audience, he flipped the projection switch, and the room was suddenly filled with a soft, ambient light emanating from the top of the equipment.

"Nice lamp, dear," Bettye quipped. "So, where's the tree?"

"Wait just a moment. Let me adjust the sharpening control."

With some additional fiddling, the light began to pull inward, taking on substance and forming a roughed shape as it came into focus. Then in a snap, the tree took shape with the minute details becoming crystal clear. Branch and needle alike were fully materialized in rich colors that were almost real—except for a haunting transparency to the visage.

Despite its realistic appearance, the back wall was clearly visible through the branches. In fact, it looked much like how Marley's ghost would have appeared if he were an evergreen. This was a minor detail to the kids, who "oohed" and "ahhed" at the overall effect. Bettye remained unconvinced.

"Okay, smart guy," she said. "How do you hang the lights and ornaments?"

"Ah, that's easy. It comes with over three thousand programmable settings for lights, ornaments, toppings, tinsel treatments, and base settings—plus the additional modes for sound and a whole buttload of special features."

"Daddy said butt," Matthew snickered.

"Whatever," Martin continued. "Here's the great thing. It links to the computer, so we can customize the ornaments we want and upload them into its internal memory. It's quite amazing. For example—"

He adjusted one of the controls. Immediately, the tree began to grow as he worked the height control. "No more worrying about getting the right size tree," he said as he raised it to a foot below the ceiling, allowing just enough room for the tree topper. "Now for the width. Honey, since you have a good view over there, will you tell me when it gets to the proper height?"

He cranked the control way over to the left, causing the tree to appear anorexic as it took on skeleton-thin proportions. He did this solely for the kid's amusement, and they loved it, laughing hysterically. He began to fatten the tree, and despite her initial disdain, Bettye found herself taking on a director role and saying, "Keep going. Keep going. Oh, too much. A little thinner. There! That's it!" She likely figured she was stuck with the damned thing, so she might as well make the best of the situation.

"Next, we do the lights," Martin said. "What color do we want?"

"White," she replied, immediately causing the kids to jump up and down in protest.

"No! Color! Color! We want color!" they screamed.

She nodded in defeat. "Fine. Color."

Suddenly, the tree exploded with lights (a paradox of sorts since the tree itself was nothing but) in a multitude of colors.

"Twinkling or non-twinkling?"

The two kids immediately voted for twinkling mode, but Mom pulled an overrule. "That's way too much," she said. "No twinkling lights." The kids whined in disappointment, but she stood firm.

Martin reached for another knob. "There may be a compromise here." After readjusting the settings, the lights began to pulse ever so softly, adding a touch of movement without being garish.

"I can live with that," she said and then stood in silence while examining the tree. "Martin, I miss my white lights." After reworking the controls, an undertone of white lights appeared, effectively diffusing the colors. "Much better," she nodded.

With the lights complete, it was now time for the ornaments. The ornament database offered five hundred preprogrammed choices, including a random setting. The Neuwirths spent the next half hour looking over the different options, ranging from traditional, country-style decorations to what amounted to a product placement mode—ornaments of famous cartoon characters (which the kids loved), select brand soda cans, and hot sauce bottles among them. They finally settled on a variety of plain glass-blown balls, carved angels, stars—and a few cartoon figures to appease Lizzie and Matt.

They repeated the process for the tree topper, the final selection being a beautiful ceramic-style Christmas angel with rich red and gold robes. This color theme extended throughout the tree by adding streamers of chiffon ribbon trailing down the branches from the topmost point to the bottom.

"Done," Martin said at last.

"If that's what you want," Bettye replied—hardly enthusiastic, but at least relenting.

Martin arranged the presents under the tree, then stood back to admire the overall effect with intense satisfaction. It would be hard to say who was more aglow, him or the tree. He continually popped back into the front room during the rest of the night to appreciate his handiwork. Bettye occasionally returned for another look before shaking her head in irritation.

So began the twelve days of the Neuwirth holographic tree, culminating in the inevitable coup and the reclaiming of all that was traditional, tangible, and non-programmable.

Day two became an open house for the Neuwirths. Martin invited the neighbors to see the tree, showing it off with the typical male bravado of a new sports car. He failed to consider that the house was not properly cleaned and vacuumed, which sent Bettye into a tizzy.

She quickly ran from room to room, picking up the lingerie hanging to dry on the doorknobs, the random unwashed cups and plates, and the multitude of kids' toys scattered around the house. Martin gave no mind to the clutter, figuring most neighbors were also parents, and therefore, used to such disarray. This, of course, represented a standard difference between the sexes.

Word spread quickly around the block, drawing more neighbors over to see the tree of light, and placing Bettye into hostess mode, hardly a way she had planned to spend the evening. She maintained a cheerful exterior but kept firing Martin glances that might melt a glacier.

Meanwhile, the children discovered a new activity to preoccupy their time, beginning when Lizzie took a running jump and leaped through the tree to the other side. Figuring that if she did so, it must be okay, Matt also began jumping back and forth over the tree base, with projected branches and ornaments appearing on his pajamas as he passed. This kept the two busy for a while, but after a near collision with the presents underneath, Mom put a stop to their Olympics.

For two days, Bettye kept her grievances to herself. On day three, it all poured forth. "The problem with your tree," she griped, "is the same with all artificial trees—it's not a living, growing thing. It has no fragrance, whereas a real one would smell, well—it would smell real."

He threw up his hands in dismay. "Oh, I completely forgot about that." In an instant, he disappeared, leaving a very perplexed wife behind. A minute later, he returned with a sack in hand. "I had this in the trunk the entire time. This should remedy the problem."

He pulled forth a bottle of clear liquid from the sack and a box with the same markings as the tree box but labeled *Lumo-Brite Scentual Plug-in*. A bad feeling settled in the pit of Bettye's stomach, much like the one fathers have on Christmas morning when faced with all the presents that required assembly. This would not end pleasantly.

She sat in stony silence as Martin went to work. He connected the plug-in unit to the main tree base and poured a liberal amount of the liquid pine fragrance into the intake opening—but paying no mind to the instruction sheet.

"This will take a few minutes to warm up," he noted while pushing several buttons in sequence. Once finished, he gave her a satisfied grin, and they waited for the scent of fresh-cut pine trees.

And they waited.

The fine mist finally sprayed forth into the air—but not the scent of an evergreen forest. The fragrance reminded them of cheaply-made air freshener in a public restroom. Martin's grin melted away as the full impact of the odor assaulted his nostrils. "I think I'd better turn it off," he said meekly. As for Bettye, she said not a word, a show of great restraint.

It would take several weeks for the smell to fully dissipate from the house.

By day four, Martin added personal touches to the tree. He pulled out their boxes of holiday ornaments, a random collection that had been growing each and every year. The best of these were hung against a white background, one at a time, and he carefully took digital pictures of each with his phone.

After several hours of conversions on the computer, he uploaded these images to the database on the tree hard drive. When Bettye came in, she was pleasantly surprised to find some of her favorite ornaments hanging in virtual light on the tree.

This was Martin's way of apologizing for the still omnipresent smell.

The gesture hardly got him out of the kennel, and day five did little to endear himself to Bettye's better graces. Thoroughly inspired by the previous night's image conversions, he decided to create a personalized tree mode just for himself. Bettye found the tree completely stripped of her heirloom ornaments and replaced with little revolving football helmets sporting Martin's favorite pro teams. "That's not very Christmasy, is it?" she commented.

"Ah, but I can remedy that," he replied and quickly reprogrammed the unit. The helmets remained, but the logos were immediately swapped out with little Santa faces.

"It's not quite the same," she said. Eventually, he relented and restored the tree to its former appearance.

On the sixth day, Martin activated the sound-reactive mode and cranked up the stereo with seventies-era disco music. The room transformed into a tacky dance club as the tree lights flashed to the boogie beat. This kept Lizzie and Matt entertained for a solid twenty-one minutes. Better taste soon prevailed, and the musical fare was switched to holiday tunes by Crosby and Sinatra.

The following night, Martin turned on the deluxe Elf option. This setting displayed a group of life-size holiday elves who waved their hands and ran around the tree. Matthew thought this was too cool, but it scared the bejesus out of Lizzie, who screamed incessantly for the next hour. "You probably scarred her for life. She'll never get near a tree again," scolded Bettye. Martin quickly switched off the monster elves, and he figured it best not to activate the eight-foot Santa projection in fear of further repercussions.

Day eight became a white Christmas for the family with the tree's Winter Wonderland mode. White snowflakes appeared out of nowhere above the tree and drifted to the floor. As an added touch, Martin changed the tree's appearance from plain green to a beautiful flocked white, and Bettye even admitted that the overall effect was quite enchanting.

Martin lit the fireplace, which created a contrasting illusion, the blazing fire being so close to the holographic snow nearby. After they put the kids to bed, he selected soft holiday music to fill the background, turned down the overhead lights, and joined Bettye on the sofa. They watched the snowflakes fall and the flames rise from the Yule log while enjoying that quiet period that comes only after the children were asleep.

"We have so little time between us now," she said, snuggling closer to him. "Between work, kids, housework, and everything else, there are no more hours in the day—and much as I love our children, I feel like I never see you anymore. Not like this. By the time Lizzie and Matt go to sleep, I am exhausted."

"You have me now."

"Yes, and I'm exhausted. I just wish things were less frantic sometimes."

He answered this with a soft kiss on the lips.

"I love you," she said. He responded in kind, and they remained on the sofa for a while longer, watching the dance of snow and flame.

Day nine allowed Martin to further experiment with the flocking functions. The tree went from white to blue, red, orange, and finally a bright purple. He'd never owned a purple tree before and thought it quite unique. "It is unique," replied Bettye with a tone not complimentary. Soon bored with the color, he found a genuinely outrageous combination: Flocked Candy Cane, with a thick red stripe spiraling down the length of the white tree, turning it into a massive evergreen confection.

He was back at the computer the next day, scanning photos of family and friends to add to the tree. Bettye concluded he must not have anything better to do with his time. Before long, he converted a wide array of family photos and mementos into ornaments. All went well until little Lizzie saw Mommy's face—more specifically, a spectral image of Mommy's severed head hovering amid the branches. The kid immediately lost it. They spent half the night convincing her that, no, Mommy's ghost did not live in the tree.

The final straw—that which led up to the holiday coup—took place at night on the eleventh day. While Martin bore the brunt of the previous misadventures, this last occurrence was not his fault. Instead, the blame rested solely on the unforgiving December weather.

The evening had been relatively calm; the kids played in their room, Bettye wrapped presents in the bedroom closet, and Martin was assigned kitchen duty. He'd just put the leftover rice in the microwave oven and set it to reheat when it unexpectedly shut down—along with the rest of the power in the house.

With the interior now in total darkness, several things happened in quick succession. First was the voice from the other room exclaiming, "Martin, I think the bulb's gone out in the closet." From another room came Matt's voice, but he was drowned out by Lizzie's high-pitched afraid-of-the-dark squeal.

As Martin felt his way across the room in search of a flashlight, his toe struck a hard, unmoving piece of furniture. He hobbled the remaining distance, using the most colorful of words, even in the pitch black. After finding a flashlight, and a separate search for batteries, he went forth to save the kids. Finding them was easy—all he had to do was follow Lizzie's ear-piercing shrieks.

Bettye had since figured out that the problem was more severe than a bad bulb and made her way to the front room. "Where were you?" she fumed.

"I went for the kids."

"You could have gotten me first."

"You weren't screaming as loud."

She lit several candles, adding a soft yellow cast to the room, and two additional flashlights gave the kids a means of entertainment during the outage. A glance down the street confirmed Martin's assumption; the cold, damp weather had caused a transformer to blow, thus affecting the whole block. It might take hours to restore the power.

Fifty-five minutes later, the lights came back on, but the resulting power surge caused the tree to reset to default mode. All the uploaded settings that Martin had labored over were wiped from its memory. Worse yet, a glitch somehow crossed the Nativity mode with Santa's Workshop.

A detailed Nativity scene, complete with Mary, Joseph, wise men, shepherds, donkeys, and cows, kept reappearing at the base of the tree, but instead of the baby Jesus in the manger, there rested a giggling Christmas elf. With its red suit, pointed ears, and maniacal laugh, it resembled Satan more than a happy elf. Despite Martin's attempts to turn the setting off, the surreal Nativity refused to vanish, and he finally shut it down for the night.

Bettye figured enough was enough, and by the time she went to bed, she'd hatched a plan with one single objective—death to the tree.

Day twelve—the day before Christmas—began much like any other day. Martin and Bettye rose at their usual six fifteen. She made coffee, then settled on the sofa with a magazine while he readied himself for work. With no school, the kids slept in. At ten after seven, he slammed back a bowl of cereal, kissed her goodbye, and was out the door. Bettye watched from the window as his car backed down the driveway and drove out of sight.

Then she went upstairs to wake and enlist her two co-conspirators.

Between breakfast waffles and morning cartoons, they carefully mapped out the scheme, and by nine, they were in the car heading for the closest tree market. Lizzie and Matt had a wonderful time at the lot, running and hiding between rows of trees while Mommy made her selection and paid for the tree. One of the attendants hauled the pine to the car, strapped it on the roof, and was given a generous tip for his efforts. So far, so good.

Once back at home, Bettye set to work on the great intruder, the Lumo-Brite Virtual Tree. Easier said than done. It proved to be heavier than she expected. She heaved. She hoed. Eventually, she maneuvered it into Martin's study. It still had a purpose—she'd see to that—but some things must wait.

Next came the real tree, cut from the car roof and carried inside with the help of a conspiratorial neighbor. Even so, the tree was heavy, hard to fit through the door, and a good half of the needles left a trail behind her. Not knowing from prior experience to wear gloves and a long-sleeve shirt, by the time she finished, scratches covered her arms. She thought of Martin, and of coal set in his stocking on Christmas morn.

Following this, they ventured into the attic in search of the multiple boxes of lights and ornaments. It took thirty minutes to find them. It took another fifteen to get them down the ladder without falling. She considered that coal was too generous for Martin's stocking.

Matt and Lizzie were eager to help with the ornaments and had already torn into one of the boxes, sending glass balls rolling across the floor. Bettye packed them off to play while she handled the lights but discovered a missing key element: extension cords.

There was only one place to find them—the mass of male disarray known as Martin's work area, a corner of the garage filled with dusty boxes and bins of hand tools, electrical tools, nails screws, clamps, spray paint, tarps, and miscellaneous junk. Multiple shoe boxes lined a shelf, none of them marked. This took another twenty minutes. She thought of things entirely inappropriate for the day before Christmas.

With all the accessories now at hand, she took to lighting the tree, which went surprisingly fast. The co-conspirators were recalled to hang decorations and add tinsel. After setting a star atop the tree, the time arrived to turn on the lights and admire their handiwork.

It looked glorious.

Martin arrived home an hour later to find his decorating regency usurped. Instead of his tree of light, there stood a tangible, thoroughly decorated, fully real fir.

"The tree?" he asked, partly from bewilderment and part in search of an explanation.

"The tree," she answered simply. She stepped up behind him and wrapped her arms around his waist, giving him a warm holiday hug. He stood there with the dawning realization of the holiday subversion while he was away.

"It's a pretty tree," he finally said with a nod of acceptance.

And it was.

Later that night, he found the deposed Holographic unit in the middle of his study, projecting a tree nearly as wide as the room itself, and the Elf mode turned to maximum. More notable were the ornaments on the tree and the subsequent mystery they presented.

It was evident that someone had spent considerable time customizing and uploading the images to the unit; they were too personalized to be anything else and therefore required someone with a moderate amount of computer know-how.

That pretty much ruled out Bettye, who had trouble working a TV remote. The kids had neither the age nor technical savvy to pull it off. So it was a conundrum never solved, despite Martin's constant prodding for Bettye to come clean. She said not a word, never confessed, and never indicated how the tree came to look the way it did.

But whenever Martin became too full of himself, she reminded him of his tree and the ornaments, all of which displayed the rear end of a donkey with three words scrawled in bright holiday red across both cheeks. Words of meaning and sentiment for the season that read "Merry Christmas, Marty."

Thus ended the struggle for evergreen dominance, and every December after, Martin made the trek to the tree lot without question or argument. He suffered the occasional scratches and all the tree droppings, and the subject of artificiality was never broached again. After all, what's the point?

As for the virtual tree, Martin sold it the following year to his neighbor, Harry, who got it for a real bargain. Harry was thrilled; he could hardly wait to surprise his wife with it.

AN INTRODUCTION

NOT SO WONDERFUL

This story found its roots in the #metoo movement and the allegations against way too many in society. There comes a time when all the chickens come to roost and those must atone. With this came a story, not one of tinsel and mistletoe but one of the times. It's not a feel-good story—but some deserve to be told regardless.

NOT SO WONDERFUL

THE BARTENDER PAUSED, then slid the whiskey shot across the bar. "You may want to slow down a bit. Let me get you a glass of water."

"I don't need no fuggin' water. Just keep 'em coming." Tony held the glass up to the light, studying the reflection in the amber liquid. "Charge it to my room." He took a sizable gulp, relishing the scorch that ran down his throat. Medicine for the traumatized.

The bartender stood at attention, mouth open, ready to offer a response—most likely about limits. Then, apparently thinking better of it, put a zipper on it.

"Doesn't matter anyway. I'm not driving anywhere, so you can get off your professional responsibility high horse." Tony cast a glance around the near-empty hotel bar. Only a couple seated in an isolated corner chatted quietly. At the far end of the bar to his left, two women sat talking about God knew what. His eyes met one and he raised his glass in salute. "Ladies," he greeted. She turned her head. He returned his attention to the bartender. "What's your name, son?"

"Bernie."

"Well... Bernie..." he tapped his glass, "this is one thing that never disappoints."

"Staying long?" The bartender's tone suggested he hoped not.

A snort filled with as much sarcasm as alcohol slipped out. "I've no fuggin' idea. This is my home now. Lost my own... and everything else."

Bernie nodded. "From the flood?" A common story, people displaced from too much rain at one time in a region prone to storms. The Gulf Coast offered infinite varieties of flooding opportunities.

"Nah. That woulda been too easy." Tony grinned, flashing five decades of coffee stains across his teeth. "I earned my expulsion, but it was one hell of a good ride, every last one. Now, I got no home, my wife's gone, friends, business deals, kids, they don't want to talk to me." He took another slurp.

Bernie's eyes darted past his customer as if looking for a quick exit. No use.

"You know the word *pariah*?" Tony asked. The bartender shook his head in response. Tony pulled out his phone and tapped the screen, bringing up an app. "So here's the definition: An outcast. A person despised. That is *moi*, my friend, the ultimate deplorable. And everything I spent a lifetime building ain't worth a steaming pile of shit."

He cast another glance at the end of the bar. The two women stared at him while whispering between themselves. Well, let them talk. Everyone else had. "So here's to a career down the tubes along with everything else." He downed the rest of the whiskey in a single gulp.

He stared at the counter, rapping his knuckles against the surface. "So how about you, Bernie? You got a happy life? Wife and kids? Girlfriend? Boyfriend? You don't strike me as the cheatin' kind."

"Happy enough."

"I figured. Good, upstanding character, probably never screwed anyone over, faithful to a T. That's the kind of morality that gets you a good job behind a bar, listening to a drunken ass who's just hit rock bottom. Keep up the good work." He tapped the glass on the counter as an exclamation point. He'd be winning no marks for friendship here, not that he cared.

A voice came from behind. "Excuse me?"

He turned to face the two women from the end of the bar, now standing before him. He looked them over from head to foot, admiring the curves, the lush lips, the silken hair, the whole package times two. Given another time, he might have made a move. Even tried for a *ménage à trios*. Not now.

The taller one with medium-brown hair hanging past her shoulders stared at him with an unreadable expression. She still held her glass of red wine in hand. "Excuse me, but aren't you Tony Whitman?"

He studied her for a long moment before answering. "Guilty as charged, my dear."

Her hand snapped up in an instant. The contents of her glass crossed the distance, exploding against his face, deep red staining his white shirt. He jerked back. Without a missing a beat, she set her glass alongside him on the bar. "You're a pig. I hope you rot in jail." She turned and marched toward the exit.

Her friend, shorter, blonder, remained long enough to add, "Me too." Then she stomped out the door.

Tony watched her leave. A drop of wine fell from his nose. He reached for the nearby napkin dispenser, pulled a clump out, and dabbed at his face and shirt. No way would the stain come out, not with that amount. "See what I mean?" he mumbled, then pushed his glass toward Bernie. "How 'bout another one. I need it."

The bartender shook his head. "Sorry, sir, but there's no more."

"Course not. I expected that. The perfect kicker to the perfect day."

"You should go to bed, sir. You'll feel better in the morning."

Tony eased himself from the stool onto unsteady feet. "I doubt that very much." With a wobbly turn, he exited the bar.

Across the hotel lobby. Past the front desk with a lovely receptionist, brunette. Past the nearby unattended concierge desk. Past the massive Christmas tree with its twinkly lights and promise of peace and goodwill toward men. Finally, to the bank of elevators with floor-to-ceiling glass walls that looked out on the atrium decked in festive decor.

He pressed the button and waited, allowing the moments to tick by, feeling the cold dampness of the wine-soaked shirt against his chest. Feeling the anger build. *How dare the bitch?* She didn't even know him, only hearsay—but that's the downside of fame.

The doors opened and he stepped inside, pressing the button for thirty-two. As the elevator ascended, he stared through the glass at the changing perspective of the lobby, growing ever smaller. The upward motion slowed. With a soft ding, the doors opened onto his floor.

How had it all come to this, living out of a suitcase, and a brilliant career now apparently over? Hotels were nothing new. He'd stayed in the best across the globe, more often than not, with a changing roster of sexy bedmates. Some he managed to turn into stars. Most he forgot soon after, but that was a perk of the job. He made certain of that—before his life imploded.

He stepped from the elevator, but after a few yards, he paused and drew himself closer to the ledge looking over the atrium. Visually, the architecture conveyed a stunning design, especially from the height. Angles and curved railings shrunk in the distance, reaching the marble floor thirty-two levels below. A wave of vertigo swept over him. He clutched the railing tightly until it passed.

How long did it take for him to ride from there to here, forty-five seconds, a minute? How long would the return trip take on a direct route? He lost himself in the calculations, a matter of feet per second applied to the distance, aware that in the grand scheme of things, it served as a simple solution. Quick and easy for one not ready to pay the piper.

He didn't notice the man beside him until the fellow spoke. "It's quite a view."

Tony said nothing, only acknowledged the other's presence with a grunt.

"A lot of floors, a lot of people," the man added, then allowed silence to fill the gap. He wore his perfect posture as a fashion statement, one hand placed over the other against his solid white suit.

Who the hell wears all white anymore? Tony thought. In an earlier time, the man could be selling ice cream and burgers at a soda fountain. He decided not to encourage the stranger with conversation.

It made no difference. "Funny thing, hotels," the man said, "sort of like a way station for the masses. Lives pass by, sometimes intersecting, sometimes not. But even the slightest chance encounter can have ramifications to change a life. And here it is playing out before us. Is this mere happenstance, or is there a higher order to things? Fate, perhaps?"

Tony stared at the man. "Do I know you?"

"No, I don't think so." The man grinned, full of warmth mixed with a mystery. "But I, on the other hand, know you quite well."

"You and everyone else. Not my preference."

"But you're practically a household name. Anthony Joel Whitman. Famous director of the Broadway stage, acclaimed writer, numerous awards including five Tonys, which must be a thrill to pretend an award's named after you. Rich beyond measure. Wife... well, wives. Kids." The man raised his brow, like a wink in reverse. "And then, of course, there are all the other women and their... allegations. But you called them out as liars, didn't you?"

Tony felt the irritation building. "Who the hell are you?"

"Why, haven't you guessed?" The man cocked his head. "I'm your guardian angel."

"So you're a lawyer. Seizing on a prime opportunity? I

already got one, a damned good one." If a reply could sneer, Tony's stole the show.

The man brushed off the attitude. "Seriously. I am your personal guardian angel. I've been with you your entire life."

"Sure. So where are your fuggin' wings?"

"Wouldn't do well for me to parade through the hotel with them flapping about, would it?"

Tony shook his head, trying to figure a way out of the conversation. "Of course not."

"We have a lot to talk about, Tony. Your past. Present. Future. And you have plenty of free time now. So how will you spend it?"

"What's it to you, buddy?" He paused, then sighed through clenched teeth. "That's right. You're my wingless guardian angel." Caustic laughter spilled, enhanced by the alcohol. "So this is like *It's a Wonderful Life*? You going to tell me how my life was so great, how it changed all the people around me?"

The man's expression turned somber. "No. Not so wonderful. The sad truth is that many people would have been better off without you in their lives. You caused some serious damage over the years. And now you have to figure out what to do about it."

The words did little to quell the incoming storm. Tony stared at the man for several seconds. With everything he had to deal with, the last thing he needed was some self-righteous prick selling him a morality clause.

"That's bull. You don't have a clue about my life. And for the record, I've brought joy to a lot of people. I've built careers. Made investors wealthy. Donated to charities. Lots of charity. I can go down the list."

"I don't discount any of that. But you are avoiding the point."

"Which is?"

"You're not a nice person. You hurt the people around you, business associates, friends, strangers... family. Everything you've done is motivated by self-interest. I can go down a list, as well, if you want specifics."

Tony clenched his fist, restraining an urge to throw the man against the wall. He took a breath, then another. "You got a name?"

"Why don't you call me Jamie. It's a good unisex name. I don't want to play favorites."

"That's not funny."

"What's wrong?" After a moment, the man's eyes widened. "Of course. The same name as the plaintiff in your..."

"Enough!" Tony erupted. "You've had your little joke. Now get to the point or get lost."

With a knowing smile, the man leaned against the railing, arms crossed. "You'd like that, wouldn't you? For me to just walk away as if everything is hunky-dory. But it's not that simple. Why, just a few minutes ago, you were looking over this ledge, considering something very drastic. Very permanent. That's why I'm here—because sometimes you have to take that leap of faith to make things better. *Capisce?*"

Tony rubbed his fingers against his brow as if it might wipe away his troubles. "I'm not in the best of moods, ya know. And kinda drunk."

Jamie put on a comforting face. "I understand. Especially with Ellie walking out on you today after, what, nineteen years?"

"Twenty. She reminded me it was our emerald anniversary."

"And for what it's worth, she was faithful all that time, even though she had numerous opportunities to stray. Remember that producer you worked with some years back? Robert Ellstree, I believe?"

"Eldrich," Tony corrected.

"Right. You nearly lost her that time. He was nuts over her and would have treated her like a queen. Meanwhile, you've managed to seduce almost every girl that caught your eye, whether they wanted to or not. Mostly not. And the ones who said no? Well, their careers always seemed to suffer setbacks after, didn't they? Either way, some took it rather hard. Which is why they're all coming out of the woodwork now—together. They smell blood."

"I didn't want Ellie to go." Tony closed his eyes, a fresh stab from recent events shooting through him.

"Not enough... otherwise, you might have acted differently." Jamie paused, letting the words sink in. "There's someone I want you to meet."

Tony opened his eyes to find a young woman standing alongside them, so quiet, he hadn't heard her approach. She might as easily have appeared from nowhere. Youngish, perhaps mid-twenties, with long dark hair hanging to ample breasts. Shapely hips. Full lips. Dark, rich eyes, but set to a pale face, and an expression void of cheer. Something about her seemed vaguely familiar. Out of habit, he immediately undressed her in his mind, liking what he saw.

"Let me reacquaint you." Jamie gestured to the girl. "This is Melanie."

Tony extended his hand. She did not reciprocate, only stared at him. He shifted uncomfortably. "What do you mean *reacquaint*? I've never met her before."

The girl shot a look at Jamie. "I told you he wouldn't remember."

Jamie kept a pleasant demeanor. "Memory's a funny thing. Sometimes it requires a trigger, especially when there's been so many. Let's go eight years back, give or take a few months. Revival production of *The Pajama Game*, a suitable title if there ever was one. Melanie was a young hopeful, vying for a role. After the audition, you invited her up to your apartment. When she arrived, you were still in your robe after a shower. Yes, I know you've pulled that stunt many times. Usually, it worked. You made advances. She declined. You had her anyway."

Her eyes turned three shades darker. "Then nothing. No call the next morning. No flowers. No role."

"Sorry," Tony muttered.

"And that's all I get now. A half-assed apology. By the way, you're a lousy fuck."

Tony found an ounce of his former bravado. "Whatever. And if you didn't get the role, that means you weren't good enough."

Dark eyes turned red. "Just good enough to rape, is that it? I'm better in bed than on the stage?" She turned to Jamie. "Although we never made it to the bed. He attacked me right there on the floor."

Tony ignored the accusation, scratching at his ear. "Well, I did hope for the best for you. Actors are resilient. How have you gotten along since then?"

She gave another look to Jamie and he nodded. She held her hands up, palms facing Tony. Clearly visible on both wrists were the tracks of red, still oozing where they once gushed. He felt a shudder at the growing comprehension.

"I should have explained," said Jamie. "Melanie's dead. Has been for going on... five years?"

"And four months," she added.

"It's so hard keeping up with time. Such a human concept. Anyway, Melanie had one bad experience after another. The night with you left a lasting wound. Finally, she decided to check out—rather like what you were considering."

Melanie managed a grim smile. "And my last thought was joyful—that I'd never have to see or think of you again. Imagine my surprise." She elbowed Jamie. "Like I said before, he's the scorpion, not the frog."

Tony wished for another drink if only to try to wash the experience away. "You lost me. What scorpion?"

After a comforting tap on Melanie's shoulder, Jamie replied. "Surely you know the fable. The scorpion asks a frog to carry him across the river, but the frog refuses, knowing he'll be stung. The scorpion argues that if he did so, they would both drown. The frog agrees. Halfway across, he stings the frog, and as they drown, the frog asks why. The scorpion answers, 'It's in my nature.' So here's the question: in your life with its many rivers and many frogs, what will you do now to make amends?"

The inner fire erupted. Tony had never been one to back down from a fight, never retreat. "I don't need to make amends. I plan to fight every charge, deny any wrongdoing." He turned his attention to the girl. "And I refuse to accept any guilt in what you did to yourself—assuming that's what actually happened. All this means is that you're weak and can't handle the real world."

Melanie rolled her eyes as if not surprised at his outburst. "Can I go now?" she asked Jamie.

"Yes, I'll take it from here. Thanks."

In an instant, she disappeared, the vanishing as surreal as her appearance. Tony looked around him. "How did... where?"

Jamie appeared unfazed. "Humility's a virtue. You might try it."

"I've never needed it before. I got where I am today by determination, and to hell with anyone in my way."

"And where exactly are you now on the success ladder? It doesn't look like the top—rather the opposite."

For once, the snappy retorts Tony excelled in failed to come. Jamie tugged on his shirt, straightening a wrinkle. "Melanie had a rough life well before you showed up. She didn't have to die the way she chose. Some alternatives required courage, but she decided not to take a leap of faith. Only after did she see the big picture, but by then, it was too late. We all reach these crossroads sooner or later. Now, it looks as if you have hit yours." He took a step closer. "Things are about to get really nasty for you, between the lawsuits and lawyer fees, divorce, expulsion. What do you do now?"

"They didn't mean anything," he muttered, more to convince himself.

"Perhaps not to you. For others, it was a big deal. Do you have any idea how many women you've slept with over the years, not counting Ellie or your previous two wives? How many random grabs, fondles, insinuations, and inappropriate remarks?

Do you have any understanding of the effect it's had? You've left some sizable scars. Do you remember Jeri, the underage girl in New York, eleven years ago?"

"I've never—"

"Yes, you did, but probably didn't realize she was only sixteen at the time, not that it would have mattered. You were pretty wasted that night."

Tony looked to the floor and noticed how his shirt, still red from the wine, had dried to a clammy dampness. Amid this intervention, he'd forgotten about it. The stain reinforced his awareness of current problems. "I take it you have a way to make things right?"

"Not really." Jamie laughed. "This is one time where you can't slip a wad of bills on the sly and make your problems go away." He paused, allowing the moment to sink in. "You've dug yourself a hell of a deep ditch, and I don't think any amount of clawing will pull you out completely. However, hope springs eternal when it comes to redemption. Anything might help."

"Like what? Donate more money? Do charity work at a women's shelter? Apologize?"

"At this point, *sorry* only goes so far. It didn't fare well with Melanie. And I don't think a shelter would want you right now."

"That girl saw me as an insect."

"An arachnid, to be precise, but she's got a point. So ask yourself 'What am I?'" Jamie held up his arm, checking his wristwatch. "Well, Tony, I must be going. I still have other people to see—but I've enjoyed our little chat."

"What? You drop this crap on me, then bail? You said you're my guardian angel."

"I am. But even angels can only do so much. After that, it's up to the individual. This is all your doing, not mine."

At once, Tony felt lightheaded, his legs ready to give, and he reached for the nearby railing, needing support. "I need to sit." A glance around him confirmed the absence of chairs.

Jamie gestured to the carpet with its decorative motif of maroon swirls. "Make yourself comfortable."

Tony lowered himself to the floor and grounded himself, arms cradled around his legs as a security blanket. "I've no one left to talk to except my lawyer—who loves me based on dollars per hour."

Jamie joined him on the floor. "You should choose your friends wisely, and hold them dear, the same as your family. Good ones are hard to come by, and you've run through the lot."

"So what you're saying is I'm screwed? Is that it?"

Jamie looked to the heavens, considering. "Pretty much. Sorry not to have better news but you reap what you sow. What you do from here is your decision."

"Got any more surprises?" Sarcasm dripped from the question.

"Life is full of surprises, especially for one as busy as you. For example..." With a wave of his hands, much like a master magician, Jamie conjured a wall of fog in front of them, roughly six feet in shape. It hovered midair like a portal to another realm. In the mist, a figure appeared, manifesting into a female form. "Another one of your transgressions. The girl before you is Sarah. She's nineteen years old and lives in Oklahoma City."

Tony shook his head. "Don't try to pin that on me. I've never been to Oklahoma."

"True. You two have never met, but there is a connection. Sarah is your daughter."

"I don't have a daughter," Tony growled.

"On the contrary. Her mother's name is Constance. You knew her as Connie but probably paid no attention to her name. She was one of your one-night hotel conquests, this time in New York. Sarah arrived nine months later."

Qualities in the girl's features— the jaw structure, the shape of the eyes—caused Tony to pause. He saw the similarities, passed down a generation, and needed no further convincing. "Does she... know about me?"

"Nope. By the time she was born, Connie found a husband. Best to bring a child into the world with a proper family. Unfortunately, he was not good father material." Jamie got to his feet. "Sarah suffered abuse whenever mom wasn't around. Lost her virginity at twelve. Funny how the wheel keeps rolling, isn't it? But I wouldn't worry about her too much. She's grown into a strong, determined young woman. You might even be proud. As to the dad, well, his time is coming."

Words came with difficulty. "I... didn't know."

"Of course, you didn't. Constance was simply a quickie to pass the time. She had plans for her life, but those got scrapped with the child."

"I could have... I guess... helped somehow if I'd known."

"You could have." Jamie looked at the girl in the fog. "But would you? More likely, you would have passed Connie off as an opportunist."

"You don't know that."

"Don't I?" Jamie smiled. "What would a scorpion have done? Consider the whole of your life until now." With a snap of his fingers, the image within the fog shifted, and Tony stared at what first appeared to be an explicit porn film. Then he recognized himself, clawing at Melanie on the floor while she repeatedly told him to stop. He paid no mind and thrust himself in.

The image changed to Tony, much younger, perhaps high school, bullying a younger boy. He pushed and laughed as the kid fell to the ground. The mist shifted to another scene, Tony shouting at an actress when she failed to deliver to his expectations—a norm for him when directing. Flecks of spit hit her face. She moved to wipe it. "Pay attention to me!" he yelled. Before the image changed, Tony saw the tears streaming down her face.

The foggy screen became a slide show of his past, each image held just long enough for Tony to recognize the events. College. The frat party and the girl who passed out after too much alcohol. An easy lay. The two simultaneous girlfriends who didn't know about the other. He had that going for a while. Childhood, rummaging through his father's issues of girly magazines. Whacking off behind locked doors. Copping a feel behind the curtains at an awards ceremony. Getting his face slapped. Good. That meant the babe had spunk. Promises of roles for extra attention and rehearsals under the sheets. Crass remarks, regardless of gender or race. Special disgust leveled at queers. More women. Sex in hotel rooms. Sex in the shower. Blow jobs in the limo.

Somewhere in the midst were his wives. Patsy. Helen. Ellie. Moments of affection, and ones filled with hate. Ellie. That hurt the most. Then back to yet another nameless girl, more of them than he ever realized. The pictures flashed by so fast, he could no longer recognize one from the rest. He thought he saw Connie, or someone like her—he'd always had a thing for blondes.

Then, abruptly, the roller coaster ended. Tony had no words, only stared into the murky depths before him. After a long moment, he looked up for some explanation.

Jamie sighed. "Show's over, but you get the general idea. You've got a lot to think about."

Tony shook his head. "You're not being fair."

"What's fair? And for whom?"

"Me. Where's your compassion?"

In response, Jamie knelt, locking eyes. "This..." He rested his hand on Tony's shoulder. "This is compassion. More than that—an opportunity. You know all about opportunities, right? You've had a lifetime of them."

At once, Tony felt his conscience collide with the assured exterior he'd spent a lifetime honing. This played out like a master script, exactly as he might have staged it, culminating in a perfect moment of the emotional arc. The sudden revelation. The transition for the final act. Except he had written himself into the storyline with no clear ending—the ultimate writer's block.

Jamie stood and glanced again at his watch. Shook his wrist as if checking to see that the timepiece worked. Held it to his ear. "I must be going now. Sorry to rush, but that's the life of an angel." With a gesture of his hand, the fog diminished into nothing.

Tony pointed to the watch. "I thought you didn't pay attention to time?"

"It's one of my little indulgences. Helps to remind me of what I once was." Jamie extended his hand and gave Tony's a shake. Solid. Firm. Comforting. "Good luck, Tony. Treat people better. Do good things. I'll be watching you."

With that, Jamie simply wasn't there. Tony stared at a void in space where moments earlier a person, a — something — stood. All at once, he felt more alone than ever before.

He remained sitting, clutching his legs close to his chest, rocking from one side to the other. As much as he desired to discount the last hour, this had been no hallucination. Even if it had, the substance of the encounter was real. He knew his past, had lived it, and remembered far more than he ever let on. He denied his doings to the press, the public, and the world at large. Putting up a good front came easy. But denial failed when looking inward.

With a sigh, he rose and stepped to the railing. He gazed across the atrium to the other side, floors of rooms set above another. Inside those rooms, lives played out. He watched a couple, the same man and woman he saw earlier in the bar, strolling along the corridor two floors below his. They walked hand in hand, deep in a conversation no one else could hear. She slipped her hand around his waist. He returned the gesture. They opened the door to a room and walked through together. Consensually.

Down below, occasional ant-sized figures moved across the lobby floor. Who could say from this height if any of them might have a lasting impact on another? The sounds from the atrium wafted upward, echoing against hard surfaces into a muffled combination, further proof of life in flux. What was he other than one more voice in a greater mix? Somewhere above him, the elevator made a stop. A bell dinged.

Jamie spoke of faith, choices, and how they might make a difference. Tony had a lifetime to unravel with its many intrusions and abuses. Okay, perhaps he had crossed the line on occasion—but surely there were some good deeds too? His life could not be that wrong. He'd been a good husband and provider, father to his children. Excellent at his craft. Tyrannical at times, yes, but it reaped rewards for all involved. The lucky ones made names for themselves, launched careers. So what if he took liberties? He deserved it all.

Still...

He thought of the girl's accusation, and that damned fable. She might as well have held up a mirror for him to see. He knew himself better than anyone else, his strengths and shortcomings, and where his future might lead. He'd directed his life based on his particular preferences, giving only when he felt inclined. It had been a wonderful life until now.

Even if no more allegations were leveled against him, his career was over. The media recognized a good, juicy story, and struck gold in parading the sordid details of his life for all the world to see. The rest fell like dominoes. In the court of public opinion, he'd already been sentenced. Stick a fork in. He was done.

Too bad, really. He knew the ins and outs of the theater better than anyone, paid his dues early on, and knew his importance. Even a month earlier, when he spoke, the industry stopped to listen. Now it had turned its back on him. How was that for gratitude?

So, too, his marriage. "I can't pretend any longer," Ellie said before she walked. "God knows I've tried. But I'm not one of your productions where everything's resolved in the final act." Once, love radiated from her face. Now she wore bitterness from too many experiences.

Tony saw what lay ahead. Despite the bravado, he also knew his inner yellow streak, the one he never shared. Always in control, always—and as any good director knows, it's best to let the curtain fall at the right time.

He took off his shoes, one after the other, feeling the softness of the carpet through his socks. He set the shoes against the wall, perfectly aligned ninety degrees. He'd always had an eye for detail. Then, without further thought, he climbed over the railing ledge, fully aware of his nature, and committed to making a leap of faith.

AN INTRODUCTION

PEACE ON EARTH, GOODWILL TOWARD ZOMBIES

Confession time—I love horror movies. This may not be the proper thing to admit in the middle of a holiday anthology, but there it is. I grew up on a steady diet of Universal and Hammer scary movies. My shelves were lined with models of Dracula, the Mummy, and the Phantom of the Opera. *Famous Monsters of Filmland* was my magazine of choice. Then Stephen King arrived on the scene and there was no turning back.

For me, a good scare fits in just as well during the Christmas season as Halloween especially since both are a decorator's dream holiday. Pull down the skeletons and ghosts and put up the wreaths and mistletoe while using the same hanger. It's seamless.

If chills are not your thing, so be it. This story takes a noticeably ominous turn, not full-on *Chainsaw Massacre*, but more like *Toy Story* meets Chucky. So to paraphrase with glee from Edward Van Sloan in *Frankenstein*, "This may thrill you, shock you, even horrify you. If you prefer not to strain your nerves, now is your opportunity to... well, you have been warned."

PEACE ON EARTH, GOODWILL TOWARD ZOMBIES

JANET PICKED UP THE SEASONAL DOLL with resignation, aware that its time had come and gone, at least until next October. All the other vestiges of Halloween had long since been either stored or chucked, the plastic skeletons, the orange and purple string lights, the fake cobwebs and spiders, and Cassie's fairy princess costume.

Okay, the latter hung inside the child's closet and likely would resurrect itself whenever Cassie got the urge to play Cinderella, Elsa, or Anna. As to the trick-or-treat candy, that all vanished by November third. Janet had not eaten a single piece, narrowing the culprit to one.

With the decorations now packed away, this left only the doll before her, an eighteen-inch skeletal figure with blue-green rotting skin and bright orange hair that stuck out in all directions as if jolted with electricity. The plush creature figure resembled a cross between Frankenstein and Beetlejuice with a hint of South Park.

Hank—Cassie's father and Janet's ex—bought it for Cass when she was a toddler, one of his many poor parenting choices. Ironically, the girl fell in love with it and insisted "Zoombie" be given a place of prominence at Halloween every year.

"He'll guard over you when you have bad dreams," Hank told his daughter at the time. Janet felt otherwise, figuring Zoombie to be the stuff of nightmares. Cassie won out with the doll on exhibit each year.

This time, it managed to stick around through Thanksgiving amid the other dolls in the girl's room. Next stop, Christmas, only a week away.

She set Zoombie aside as the front door opened and Cassie burst in, followed by Hank, this being his weekend of custody. Per the settlement, he had Cassie for two weekends a month, an arrangement he seemed fine with. That gave him ninety percent of the time to work, drink, watch football, and generally screw off. That's the way of things, leaving the female to parent. Fine with her as well.

"Look, Mommy," Cassie shouted while holding a mass of red and white up for her to see. It took a moment to register. The girl clung to a ragged Santa doll, similar in size to Zoombie but fatter and worse for the wear. The plastic face hid behind a mangy beard that at one time might have been white. Overly large eyes meant to twinkle with glee were cracked, paint chipped in places. Its red and white suit bore stains and weathered patches as if used as a dog's play toy. As Santas go, this one had been on one too many sleigh rides.

"Where the…" She caught herself mid-sentence, editing out the expletive. "Where did you find this?"

"Daddy and I stopped at a garage sale. They had lots of Christmas ornaments. I got this. It's Santa's helper."

Janet shot her ex a disdainful glance. "And why did you go to a garage sale?"

"We did that all morning. Miss Vicky joined us. Said she does it all the time because it's like a treasure hunt. You never know what you'll find."

Janet's temperature rose a few degrees. She'd already argued with Hank about the presence of another woman during his time with Cassie. It set a bad example and might be confusing. Hank countered that children were smarter and more accepting than she gave them credit for. A year into the divorce, he had no trouble finding another woman to shack up with, while she… well, the idea of dating left her queasy. Work and Cassie kept her busy enough.

Janet took the Santa doll. "He's a bit worn." Instinctively, she wanted to wash her hands and throw the thing away. No telling where it might have been. She kept her feelings in check and handed the doll back.

"I thought so, too. But Vicky said it means that he's well loved."

"I bet she did." A good thing the child didn't yet grasp the subtleties of sarcasm.

"I'm going to my room." Cassie grabbed Zoombie and ran up the stairs with both dolls.

"Really? Garage sales?" Janet shook her head at her ex.

"Cassie had fun. It was an adventure for her and a great way to spend the morning." Hank wore the perpetual half-smile that at one time had charmed her into marriage.

"And we've talked before about Vicky."

"It's not a big deal, not to Cassie. I tell her that Vicky is just a friend."

"Yeah. One that you fuck."

His smile disappeared. "Who, when, and where I fuck is no longer your concern. I'm a model parent when Cassie stays over. Perhaps if you got a good fucking, you'd be less judgmental."

A half-dozen hostile replies came to her mind. Instead, she gestured to the door. "We're done. You can leave now."

Hank opened the door, paused, and looked back. "We need to talk about New Year's. Any way you can take Cassie that weekend? Something's come up."

"As in?"

His voice diminished in volume. "Vicky wants to go to Napa. I said… you'd be okay with it."

How typical. "Later, Hank."

He nodded and closed the door behind him. Happy holidays. Good riddance.

Santa joined them for dinner that night. He sat on a stack of books in a chair next to Cassie. Janet spooned out the chicken broccoli casserole onto their plates, a staple recipe due to its ease and multiple days of leftovers. Did she grow tired of it time and again? You bet, but as no one else agreed to do their cooking, she opted for the path of least culinary resistance.

Cassie plopped a morsel onto a saucer and slid it in front of the doll. Janet smiled at the gesture. "I don't think Santa's hungry."

"But you're always supposed to give him milk and cookies or something when he visits," Cassie replied with a pout.

"I'm sure he appreciates it." She now noticed a detail previously overlooked. Below the scraggly beard, he smiled, teeth crooked and dingy yellow. That, along with the deformed eyes, gave Saint Nick a less than saintly appearance. A shiver ran down her back.

They spent the evening watching holiday cartoons, the classic with *Rudolph and the Bumble*, as well as *Frosty, the Snowman*. Cassie kept her new doll close by. Bedtime arrived, with Santa snuggled in bed with Cassie as Janet read a final story followed by a good-night kiss. As she left the room, she noticed Zoombie tossed unceremoniously in a corner, looking like—appropriately enough—a lifeless corpse. Favoritism is a fickle thing, lost as easily as gained.

With the rest of the evening to herself, she cleaned the kitchen and paid several bills online before going to bed. A cold front had blown through, the wind tossing tree limbs to and fro. Even in that short time, the interior temperature dropped several degrees. With the weather alternating between the typical Texas warm and cold, she'd resorted to changing the A/C switch on an almost daily basis.

Dressed in a cotton nightgown, she slid below the covers, goose bumps rising on her legs from the chilly mattress. For times such as this, she missed the warmth of companionship in bed, along with the other delights. Instead of sex, she had only a book to look forward to, a best-seller about life in the swamplands and singing crawdads. Now on chapter three, she flipped the page as her skin warmed the covers. She looked up, noticing an object outside her half-open door partially illuminated by the hallway night-light.

The Santa doll faced her with its back resting against the wall. Staring.

Cassie must have dropped it before going to bed. Except she recalled it nearby as they read together. Of course, the girl could have gone to the bathroom and left it behind. Still, it creeped Janet out. She rose, took Santa to her daughter's room, and put him on the chair.

Back in bed, she read a few more pages before her eyes grew heavy. She placed the book on the side table and let sleep take her away. When she woke the next morning, she found Santa back in the hallway in the same position as before as if guarding her. Or stalking.

"Cassie, did you leave your Santa in the hall last night?"

"No, Mommy. He was in my room." Cassie answered the question between bites of her Sugar Pops.

"Did you get up during the night? Go potty?"

"No."

"Hmm."

Of course, the girl might have gotten up, half asleep, walked to the bathroom with her doll, and dropped him along the way. It seemed the only logical explanation. Objects didn't move on their own. She looked at Santa, once more placed on the kitchen chair as a guest. The thing grinned back at her, teeth more visible than before.

Janet sighed, feeling as if an unwanted pet had been brought home, this one with a red and white coat. The thought crossed her mind that Hank planned this as a covert way to annoy her. Just as quickly, she dismissed the thought. That gave her ex way too much credit.

"You ready to work on the Christmas tree today?" The artificial tree sat in its box in the corner of the living room. She should have started on it weeks ago. In the past, she had a husband to drag it from the attic and set it up for her. She considered herself a trooper for finding it in the first place. Still missing were the boxes of lights and ornaments, her upcoming task for the day.

"Yay!" Cassie cheered while shoveling another spoonful of cereal into her mouth.

It took well over an hour, but Janet finally found the elusive ornament box buried under a painting tarp in the garage. But no lights.

By early afternoon, she'd made a run to several stores in search of multi-colored lights, Cassie's request, only to find them sold out with only the white remaining. Eventually, she discovered a single twenty-five-bulb strand of colored lights in a torn box, stuck way in the back of the lowest shelf in a pharmacy. Figuring one was better than none, she opted to mix them with the soft white.

The day became a game of spot the Santa, who never stayed long in a single place. Why the girl moved him so often became a mystery since Janet never saw her do so.

"Have you seen Santy?" Cassie asked at one point, having wandered around the house looking for it. They finally discovered the doll perched on the kitchen counter between the microwave and the knife block, one arm draped over the butcher knife handle.

The final straw came in the evening after Cassie's bedtime story. With the daughter now asleep, Janet poured herself a glass of wine, ready to chill for the evening. She strolled into her bedroom. There on her bed—on the pillow where she rested her head—sat the Santa doll, legs wide open as if displaying his junk. He grinned wider than ever.

She stared at the horrid thing, took a good swig of her wine, and set the glass on the dresser. No way would she have that thing on her bed. She approached the doll, prepared to take him back to Cassie's room, then paused, noticing the damp spot on her pillow. Between his legs. As if he…

No. With a growl, she took it by the neck and threw it out of her bedroom. It skittered down the hall, hitting the wall before coming to a stop near Cassie's room. She pulled the door to and took another gulp of wine, now for medicinal purposes. She turned and felt that warm wine glow turn cold. The doll sat on her pillow once more, dead eyes glaring at her. A scream lodged in her throat.

She backed to the door, tempted to look down the hall and see if it was still there—but no. What's the point? For long minutes, the staring contest continued as she weighed her options. No way would that thing remain in the house. Had she a fireplace, she would have let it burn. After all, Santa and chimneys were best buds, right?

With a determined stride, she marched across the room, ready to escort him from the premises. Now only feet away, she paused, no longer willing to touch him. The pillow still bore the wet spot, and she knew,

knew, knew, she'd never use it again. The mere idea of resting her cheek against the… piss, cum, doll jizz, whatever, disgusted her.

She took the ends of the pillow, using it as a large mitt, and scooped the doll up. Then she ran to the garage and stuffed it all in the trash can, then slammed the lid with a sound of finality. For good measure, she lifted a nearby box of old dishes and set it on top of the can, the weight solid to keep the lid closed.

"Try getting out of that, fucker," she muttered before leaving the garage. She closed the door, locked it, then rechecked it. Twice.

Only as she reentered the bedroom did she pause, looking nervously at the bed. All appeared exactly as it should, the bed normal minus the pillow. After a quick check of the room, feeling less nervous, she picked up the wine glass and finished it off in several good gulps.

Out came her cell phone. Speed dial. Hank answered.

"You're calling late."

"Hank, where did Cassie get that horrible Santa doll?"

"At a garage sale, Janet. You know that already." His exhausted tone suggested he'd fought this battle one too many times. That summed up the last year of their marriage.

"Yes, but where? Whose was it?"

"I dunno. Some lady with a sign in her front yard. We saw it and stopped." He paused. "Why? You want a matching pair?"

"No, I don't want a pair," she snapped. Damn, he could be so annoying. "Do you remember where her house was?"

"No, just some street in the Montrose area. Old ranch-style house. Lots of clothes for sale, lamps, and decorations. Your usual crap. So, what's the big deal."

"Nothing. You're no help."

Hank snorted at the slap. "Funny thing, though. The lady seemed real happy to get rid of the doll. Practically gave it to us. Offered to throw in some other decorations as well, but Cassie just wanted the toy."

"Did she say anything about it? Where it came from?"

"Janet, you're asking some weird-ass questions," Hank laughed. "You been drinking tonight?"

She didn't dignify the question with an answer. "Good night, Hank." End of conversation. She tossed the phone on the bed.

There'd be little sleep for her tonight, her mind whirling with thoughts that defied reality. It must be stress, an active imagination, superstition, even though she'd never been one to throw salt over her shoulder. After turning the lights off, she slid into bed and closed her eyes.

Within minutes, the door to her bedroom opened. Cassie stood in silhouette, the night-light from the hallway casting a yellow glow about her.

"Mommy, can I sleep with you tonight? I'm scared."

Janet tossed the sheets back as an invitation. "Sure, honey. What's bothering you?"

Cassie snuggled next to her, pulling the covers close. "I'm hearing noises. You told me there's no such thing as monsters, right?"

"That's right," Janet answered while having doubts.

"I feel safe with you."

Janet tucked the sheets around her daughter and held her close. "Everything is fine. You just go to sleep."

So she did. Janet followed her example soon after, allowing the events of the day to fade from her mind. Cassie always had that effect, the near-ness of her, and the body memory of two who were once one. They kept one another warm as the hours moved through the night.

Janet roused herself at some point, aware of the child shifting her position. In that dreamy half-sleep, she felt a light weight at her feet, moving across the sheets and blanket as if a cat had leaped upon the bed and made its way across the covers. Her dreaming synced up to the sen-sation with a tabby come to snuggle. Only as it reached her waist did she wake with sudden clarity. She had no cat. Nor dog. Nor any pet to speak of. Yet the weight remained.

Her eyes shot open. In the dim light, she saw a diminutive figure straddling her and Cassie, its arms raised. Even in partial shadows, she recognized the worn red outfit, the straggly beard with rotten teeth below, and the cracked eyes. Santa stood before them holding a kitchen knife, ready to strike. How he managed to hold such an object seemed preposterous, but in the cold, quiet dead of night, it made no difference.

She yelped while shifting her body, waking Cassie as the doll brought the blade down. Metal dug into flesh. What had been intended as a strike for Janet's chest grazed the side of her rib cage, not mortally but enough to draw blood. Cassie let out a piercing shriek as she recoiled from the figure. Their combined movement should have toppled Santa from his perch. Somehow, he rode the wave and raised the knife for another strike.

Janet could have sworn she heard him laugh.

The blade came down once more, this time striking Janet's arm. She felt the sharp cut work against muscle. She screamed again. By now, the doll had repositioned itself, wielding the knife to deliver a death blow.

Then a second silhouette appeared and latched onto the first.

"Mommy!" cried Cassie as she scrambled backward.

It took a moment for recognition. Blue-green fabric skin. Sullen face. Even in the dim light, Janet knew it to be Zoombie. She pushed herself back on the bed while watching the impossible. Two dolls struggled for control of the knife, an absurd puppet show turned on its head.

Santa gained the upper hand pushing the other against the sheets. A moment later, Zoombie struck back. Somehow, he managed to wrangle the knife away and with a quick movement, skewered jolly old Saint Nick through his stomach.

The red man froze momentarily, then flopped about as if in an epileptic seizure. Zoombie pulled the knife, raised it, and brought it home once more, slicing through Santa's abdomen. Cassie and Janet watched in horror as one doll reduced the other to a pile of fabric, the white stuffing pulled apart like disemboweled intestines. Casting the knife aside, Zoombie took hold of Santa's head and ripped it open, then fed upon the cotton fiber brains. After all, that's what zombies do.

Once sated, the doll paused and examined his work. Satisfied, he glanced at the mother and daughter. He nodded—then collapsed on the bed, as lifeless as before.

Cassie wrapped her arms around her mom, crying. Janet stared at the bloody discoloration on the sheets that formed a terrible Rorschach pattern. In response, her arm and torso wounds began to throb. She'd need to look after herself.

But not yet.

She rose and gathered what remained of the Santa doll. "Wait here for me," she said to her daughter.

"Don't leave me," Cassie whimpered.

Janet nodded. Of course, the child did not want to be alone. Together, they walked to the garage, placed the doll in a metal bucket, and carried it outside. She took a lighter normally used for lighting candles and set the contents ablaze. For the next few minutes, they watched the fire consume the red and white fabric, leaving ashes behind. Without a word, they left the bucket and returned to the bedroom.

"I don't want to go back to my room." Cassie's eyes expressed the fear within.

"Then stay here with me." Janet examined her arm, the cut deeper than she expected. "I need to find a few bandages first." She wondered if she had any large enough. Even in the dim lighting, she winced at the bed spotted with blood and small remnants of stuffing. "And I need to change the sheets."

"What about Zoombie?" asked Cassie, staring at the doll.

Janet thought for a minute, aware that this was a time of magic and good deeds done, a kind, forgiving, charitable, pleasant time as described by Dickens. "I think… it's good to have someone watch over us as we sleep. Like a guardian angel."

"Is that what he is? I don't see any wings."

"That's the thing about angels. They can look just like you or me, and you'd never know they're angels. They keep it secret."

Cassie picked up Zoombie and examined his back for telltale signs. She frowned. He appeared as he always had, green, still, and very dead. "I don't understand."

Janet smiled and wrapped her arms around her daughter. "That's okay. I don't either. But you see, sometimes zombies wear their wings on the inside."

AN INTRODUCTION

DISASTER BECOMES HER

While the "meet cute" has always been a key element to romantic stories, it entered the larger public consciousness with the 2006 romantic comedy, *The Holiday*, with Kate Winslet, Cameron Diaz, Jude Law, and Jack Black.

The term refers to the initial meeting of a couple in an amusing or memorable way. Indeed, the movie features multiple occurrences, most notably the one with an elderly screenwriter (Eli Wallach) who later explains its importance.

Of course, a meet cute doesn't necessarily need to be cute. It can be awful. Movies are full of unpleasant first impressions which can make for an even better situation. So with this story, I wanted to put the boy through all sorts of hell. Let him suffer. Break some bones. Does he deserve it? Nope. But it raises the stakes and creates some equally uncomfortable situations for the girl. I like where it leads. So give him hell, Maggie.

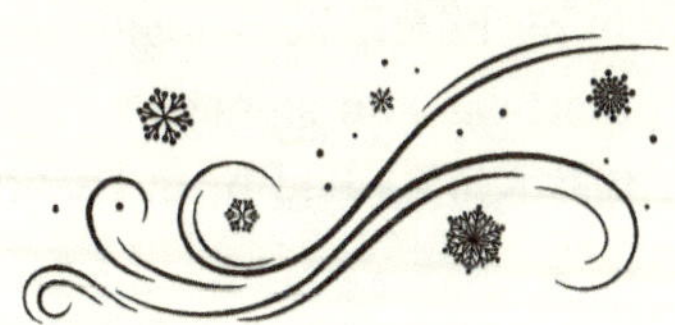

DISASTER BECOMES HER

"I'M AN ELEPHANT," Carson grumbled as he arranged the bags on the table. "I'm actually working for peanuts." He maneuvered within close quarters, the six-by-six-foot booth at the Nutcracker Market allowing enough room for a table, chair, and the stacked plastic storage bins. Next year, he'd get a bigger space—if there was a next year.

He had his doubts. Mom Prescott's candied peanuts had been a seasonal delight since he was a child. His mother concocted multiple nut recipes including a spiced rum variation. He eagerly anticipated the aroma of sugar and spice that filled the kitchen every year. She'd died two years prior, leaving Carson and his older brother with a mortgage, multiple unpaid bills, a house full of worn furniture… and her recipes.

Dealing with her estate left additional collateral damage by way of a failed relationship. His ex-girlfriend had her fill of him spending more time dealing with legalities than her. In retrospect, it was for the best. Since then, he'd avoided the dating scene.

Missing Mom's holiday snacks, Carson set himself to recreating her formula last year. Cinnamon. Ginger. Brown sugar. Most importantly, the secret ingredient, or so she always told him: love. As a child, he bought the line. Later, after outgrowing his naïveté, he figured it to be bullshit.

His recreations never quite matched up to her level so perhaps there was truth to her special addition. Still, he made a few batches, primarily for himself, but also shared with friends. Upon encouragement to take the nuts to an entrepreneur level, he did just that with visions of mass sales and easy money. Yeah, right.

Thus arrived the current holiday season. He'd spent the entire last week cooking and packaging in prep for this, his first real attempt at a pop-up. Now standing in his booth, he recognized the depth of his folly. He had no marketing materials, no signage or business cards, and the stick-on labels on the plastic bags had been hastily made on his home printer.

A glance at the other booths on the market floor depressed him further. All were glitzed out with polished, branded displays. His reeked of being a first-time amateur. In an attempt to add some sparkle, he'd bought several strands of white twinkle lights to hang along the top of the booth divider, connecting them with zip ties.

Only when he ran the cord down did he realize the logistical problem. The male plug hung a foot away from the outlet. He'd need the extension cord he packed in his car. Good thing he'd worked up a checklist of possible necessities beforehand.

He briefly considered tossing a sheet over his table, then nixed the effort, figuring he'd be gone only a few minutes. With this being vendor setup day, his booth seemed safe enough. He made his way through the building and out the door toward his car, not a short walk.

In retrospect, he should have arrived earlier. All the close spots were already taken, forcing him to park at the far end of the lot. As he exited the building, he pulled his coat close. The cold December wind struck his face and tossed his dark brown hair about. Northerners would consider him a wimp, grimacing at the mid-forties temperature, but hey, Texas boy.

He walked across the lot mostly filled with SUVs and other variations, the popular car for the region. As was his. The extra room in the rear had come in handy more times than he could count, this trip being no exception.

Along the back row, he spied his car, a white Toyota RAV4 sandwiched between several other similar vehicles. The sunlight gleamed off the surface, making it appear cleaner than normal. He'd let it go unwashed for far too long, laziness on his part, but damned if it didn't look freshly washed now, an apparent trick of the sunlight.

With the fob in hand, he tapped the unlock button moments before tugging on the driver's door handle. No movement—peculiar since it should have opened by proximity alone. He jiggled the handle again, expecting it to connect and open. Still nothing.

Only then did he look through the window and see a woman staring back at him. Cute, youngish, probably in her twenties, medium blonde hair hanging to her shoulders. Wide, blue eyes—extremely wide as if in shock. So, what the hell was she doing in his car?

She let out what must have been a yelp, muffled through the closed door. He cocked his head and tapped on the glass, expecting some explanation.

"Excuse me, but you're in my car," he shouted.

She looked down and fumbled with something in her lap as he stood looking at her. The rest occurred within seconds. Behind her on the passenger seat, he noticed a box of tissue papers, not something he had in his vehicle. Nor the bottle of water in the cup holder. Dawning raised its sleepy head as he noticed the ever-so-slight differences between his vehicle's interior. She rolled her window partway down and raised her hand. In the moment before she pressed the nozzle, he saw the can of pepper spray.

A split second later, he collapsed on the ground, his face a mass of unimaginable pain. It accompanied twin screams, his and the woman's for entirely different reasons. They formed a two-part harmony as if in prep to sing a verse of "Jingle Bells."

He still clutched his face five minutes later as the police arrived.

Only by the grace of the angels did Carson not spend the night in jail. It soon became obvious that this was a clear case of mistaken car identity with his White RAV4 parked alongside hers.

"What are the odds?" he asked his brother over the phone later that night. "Same make and color, same year-ish, even had an Astros sticker on the back window."

"You shoulda bought a Jeep and made a statement." Perry's laugh indicated he enjoyed the story, probably too much. Sibling rivalry never fully fades, only becomes more civil.

"So, I never finished setting up. That gives me an hour in the morning before the doors open."

"You'll manage, bro."

Carson tilted his head back and squeezed a drop of saline solution left in his cabinet from a previous infection into his eyes. Even after several hours, his eyes still ached from the spray.

"I could use some help this weekend. Just saying."

"You're on your own, Carson. I got work and family. Y'know, responsibilities."

"What the hell? You were the one who talked me into this. Said it would keep Mom's memory alive, spread the love, and all that."

"Yeah, but I didn't think you'd take me seriously. We talk shit all the time."

"And now I've put a load of money into this. I could use some support, especially from family."

His brother laughed again. "You never learn. You should know better than to listen to me. Gotta go. Merry Christmas."

The line went dead. Carson sighed, expecting all the worst the season might bring. Ho, ho, ho, indeed.

Carson reached his booth at sixteen after nine. He'd planned to be there an hour earlier. Setting the alarm to wake up would have helped, and while his hotel was near the market center, unexpected traffic due to an accident compounded his delay. Already, an eager crowd packed the auditorium, many dressed in bright shades of red and green. Some already had bags in their hands from purchases made within the first few minutes.

Had he closed the booth properly the previous night, he would have covered the table with a sheet. Instead, his display appeared as he left it with several conspicuous holes from missing product. Someone had already helped themselves to a free morning snack at his expense. With an extension cord now in hand, he plugged in the strand of lights, making his booth appear budget-festive. After restocking his display from the storage bin, he stood in wait for customers.

The booth to his right had been bustling since his arrival, a corner space filled with stylish clothing mostly for women. He noted it as he passed by only due to having to navigate around the crowd. Whoever ran the booth obviously did something right. Perhaps he should chunk the peanuts in favor of clothing, even though he knew Jack Frost about fashion. A sign at the rear said it all: Apparel in a Pear Tree. Yeah, he got the joke, twelve days and all.

Hour one proved to be a bust. People walked by, casting a half-interested look at his booth before moving on. A few paused for additional seconds, enough to give him some hope. He'd smile, say hello, attempt light conversation, all with the same result. At fifty-one minutes in, he sank into his chair, tired of standing guard over his array of holiday snacks.

By the second hour, his spirit sunk to Scrooge-like levels. Who was he kidding? He'd bombed at every business attempt before. Why would this be any different? Jesus, peanuts, really? If his mother wasn't so caring, she'd be looking down at him and laughing.

The curtain separating his space from the next suddenly gave way as something large and heavy fell against it, knocking his stacked bins to the floor, domino-style, bags of nuts scattering like marbles and hitting his lukewarm Grande Starbucks. Coffee spilled across the floor and on his white Nikes, rendering them less than white.

The object—a metal clothes rack—slid through the separation in the curtains, snagging the white holiday lights and pulling the non-zip-tied sections loose from the railing. Several cans of cold soda hit the floor and rolled across from the adjacent booth.

A commotion arose from the other side along with a female voice shouting, "Sorry. Sorry." Carson attempted to push the rack back into place but met resistance. Its owner struggled with it from the other side, inadvertently pushing it farther into his space. After a few moments, he gave up. Let them deal with it. As he leaned closer, a face appeared between the drapes, only a foot away from his. Blonde. Wide blue eyes. The only thing missing was the pepper spray.

"You." It came out as an accusation. Déjà vu swept over him and he involuntarily winced at painful memories from yesterday. He prayed she wasn't armed.

She blinked several times, slow to recognize him. "I know you," she said, an understatement of the day.

"Unfortunately."

"Ohhhhh." Now she made the connection: the car, the spray, the stranger at her window. "Wow. What are the odds?"

"Not high enough."

She studied his face and smiled. "Sorry about last night. How is your face?"

"It's been better."

"No, really. I'm so sorry. You surprised me yesterday and, well, a girl can't be too careful, especially alone in a parking lot."

At least she seemed apologetic. He looked back at the mess across the floor and his brown-stained sneakers. This qualified as strike two.

She noticed it as well. "Ohmygod," she gasped. "Did I cause that?"

He attempted to be diplomatic. "The clothing rack did."

"It's top-heavy. I need to fix that." Together, they maneuvered the rack back to her side. Then he started to pick up the strewn bags of nuts. "Let me help you," she said, attempting to squeeze past the rack and curtains. Instead, she tripped, stumbling into his booth—and him—as he bent over. He fell to the floor with the bags scattering once more.

"Sorry! Sorry!" she repeated.

"I got this," he snapped. "Just go back to your side."

Her face took on an expression similar to a sad-eyed-orphan painting, the kind usually found in garage sales. He picked up the cans of soda that rolled over, handing them back to her.

"No, you take one," she said as she accepted the other. "An appeasement?"

He looked at her and experienced a flashback from the previous day—of first seeing her and thinking, *Yeah. Cute.* Her current attire included a fuzzy pink sweatshirt with the word GRINCH emblazoned in bright green across the front. Surely, she meant it as humor since she hardly seemed the grinch sort. If anything, she was more of a Max.

She gave a meek smile as she popped the top of her soda and raised it as a gesture. Let bygones be bygones.

He nodded and pulled the tab on his can.

Pressurized soda spewed up, across his shirt and into his face. He dropped the can as his eyes burned once more, this time from the carbonation.

"Sorry!" she cried, the phrase becoming a standard for her.

As he did a little dance, she frantically looked around the booth for a cloth for him to wipe his face with. At last, she grabbed the base of the booth curtains and handed it to him. He pulled it to his face, hitting resistance, and bent forward. Then tugged again. This time, the upper support bar for the curtains gave way. A portion of the fabric came loose.

Carson lost his balance, falling backward with the now loose curtain, and slamming into one of his bins of product. It, in turn, spilled over, additional bags of peanuts scattering across the floor willy-nilly. He landed on his side amid a sea of candied nuts.

Through stinging eyes, he looked at the devastation around him. All the hours of work getting the booth set up had been laid waste. Half of the curtains on one side hung loosely from the disconnected wall rod, along with a portion of his Christmas lights. Bags covered the floor, sandwiched between upended storage bins. A now-leaking can of soda dribbled on the floor.

Carson looked from the can to the woman standing above him wearing an expression of pure mortification.

"I'm so, so…" she began.

He lifted his finger for attention. "Stop. Not another word. Please go."

"But I…"

"In the spirit of Christmas and goodwill for all, please. Go."

If she had possessed a tail, it would have been tucked between her legs. She dejectedly exited his booth, leaving behind the carnage.

"Peace on Earth, my ass," he mumbled to himself. Perhaps Scrooge was right.

After gazing at the mess, he began the cleanup. Several shoppers who'd watched the catastrophe occur took pity on him and bought a few bags. Well, it was something. Perhaps, he should put on a show every hour on the hour and charge admission, "The Great Market Booth War." Concessions available. Get your peanuts here!

He paused, actually considering it. Oh, how pathetic. Now, he'd lost all dignity.

He spent the next hour cleaning his booth, putting bags of product back in their bins, repairing the curtain rod and divider, restringing the lights, and doing his best to wipe the floor. It now felt sticky from the soda. His brown-stained tennis shoes made a sucking noise with every step. At last, he finished his setup and plopped into his chair, exhausted. With expectations low, he watched as the patrons continued to walk past his booth.

By mid-afternoon, his already poor disposition had grown in acidity. Excited shoppers filled the pavilion, walking past with bags in hand, buying from everyone except him. In particular, he'd noticed the constant chatter from the booth next to his. Finally curious, he opened a crack between the curtains to see.

Whoever this girl was, she rocked the business. The booth—filled with all sorts of dresses, shirts, jackets, hats, and other apparel—had nary a free inch of space available from the customers milling about. Whatever she did to attract business worked. He spied her near the other side, chatting with a customer. Their eyes met. She gave a nervous wave with her fingers. He quickly shut the curtains, looking back at his empty space.

The afternoon proceeded at a snail's pace. Shortly after four, she appeared at his booth, approaching cautiously. "Hi."

Even with a front table separating them, he instinctively took a step back. Once bitten, twice shy. "Yes?"

"I wanted to stop by for a moment. Again, I wanted to apologize."

"No need." He figured the sooner she left, the better. This woman was an accident waiting to happen.

Somehow, the universe heard him. She stepped toward the table, bumping into it. Several packages of nuts fell to the ground. Served him right for stacking them so high. She froze for a moment, perhaps reliving their morning all over again. With a sigh, he crossed to the aisle to pick them up. As he bent down, so did she. Their heads butted, sending a bout of pain across his forehead.

"Sorry," she said. It flowed out as if it were a mantra.

With the packages in hand, he stared at her. "So you've said."

She offered a weak smile. "I don't know how I lost my balance."

"Things happen."

She cleared her throat. "Look, I feel like I need to make amends of some sort. I've caused you a lot of problems, so…" She held out a scarf for him. "It's the least I can do."

"That's not necessary." He shook his head, immediately feeling bad for his less-than-charitable thoughts about her.

"Please. I insist. I think the color would look good on you."

The scarf was quite nice, a weave of browns and blues that fit his color preference. Had he been in the market for a scarf, he might have picked it out himself. Still, he hesitated.

Not taking no for an answer, she stepped forward and wrapped it around his neck.

"Really," she commented as she examined it on him. "It suits you." She smiled and—oh, damn, she was rather cute. Not in a glamorous way, almost as if she tried her best not to attract attention. She wore only a bit of makeup, just enough to accent the eyes. Her hair hung limply about her face, but somehow it brought out her features.

She gave the scarf a small toss across his shoulder, pleased with the way it looked. At that moment, they both heard a commotion behind him. A loud series of barks erupted to the jingling of tiny bells, followed by a woman shouting, "Toby! No! Come here!"

They turned to see a small Terrier puppy wearing a red elf collar adorned with jingle bells. It barreled for them with unbridled glee. *Scarf! Play toy! Yes!*

Before he could react, the dog leaped for him, breaking a world record for puppy jumps. Paws struck his chest, sending him backward as the dog sunk its teeth into the scarf. Packages of nuts sailed through the air. He landed on the ground, breaking his fall with his arm as a jolt of pain shot up his wrist. Toby remained on top claiming his prize. A moment later, the woman appeared, pulling the feisty puppy back with his leash.

"Mercy me," she exclaimed. "Somehow, he got away. Are you okay?"

He shot a perturbed glance at all three, first the dog, the woman, and finally Scarf Girl.

"I'm fine," he answered as he rose, knowing he wasn't. With the fall, he heard something crack. Now his lower arm ached something fierce. Already, it had changed color.

The woman hurriedly walked away with her pooch in tow, no doubt wanting to avoid any repercussions.

"Your arm," the girl said, noticing how it had started to swell. "That's not good."

"No," he answered. "It's not." Just what he needed. With the day already a bust, he realized he'd have to close early and search for a nearby minor emergency clinic. So much for business.

"Can I help you?" the girl asked.

"I think you've helped enough."

Without another word, he retreated behind the table to find a sheet. He'd cover the products and close down for the day, then leave in search of a doctor.

He arrived at his hotel, his arm now in a cast. It had taken the full afternoon to find a nearby clinic, deal with paperwork, and see a doctor. Conclusion: definitely broken. He and his cast would be best buds for the next six weeks. He tried not to think about how he'd manage the next few days, let alone tear-down with one functioning arm.

He scolded himself for getting a hotel room. At the time, it seemed the logical move, avoiding an hour-plus drive each way. If today indicated the rest of his time, he'd be lucky to make back the cost of the booth space.

As of now, he had one mission in mind: a good stiff drink at the bar. He deserved it and more. At the stool, he removed his coat while leaving the infamous scarf on. No sooner had he sat at the counter and ordered a drink did he hear a familiar voice behind him.

"Oh, no. Did you really break your arm?"

Oh, c'mon. What are the odds? He recognized the voice without even turning.

"Yes, I really did break my arm." *Thanks to you, the scarf, and a pip-squeak dog.*

She came into view at his side. "It's not been a good day for you, has it?"

"I've had better."

"I'm so…" She paused before adding, "I keep saying that, don't I?"

"You should have a shirt with those words on it."

That brought on a quiet, awkward moment. It might have been the elephant in the room, larger than either of them and just as silent.

"Can I join you?" she asked at last. She still wore her pink sweater and matching bright fuchsia tights and tennis shoes.

He considered scooting to the next chair, putting more distance between them. Disaster seemed to follow her like an obedient pet while pulling him along for the ride. He wasn't sure if he wanted any more. Still, she seemed apologetic. Reluctantly, he gestured to the next chair.

His beer arrived, a well-deserved IPA, extra hoppy to fit his mood. "You hardly seem the grinch-type," he commented, nodding at her shirt.

She giggled, a light, airy sound that might disarm the harshest enemy. "We all have a bit of grinchiness in all of us. Some more than others. I can be a real sourpuss when I want." She plucked at her sweater. "I sell these. They're quite popular."

"I bet they are."

She turned to the bartender. "I'll have a Pinot." He nodded and left.

Carson managed to smile. "I would have pegged you for a rosé girl."

"Actually, I considered a mimosa, but reds rule today. It has a happy flavor, if there is such a thing. Cabs are way too intense." She extended her hand. "I'm Maggie."

He started to reach, then paused with his right arm in the cast. Instead, he switched to his left. "Carson. You seemed to do okay at the market today."

She beamed. "I did. Lots of people shopping clothes for gifts—mostly for themselves." Her smile faded. "I guess you didn't do well. It's partially my fault. First the clothes rack and then the scarf."

He gave a shrug. "The booth was dying even without your help. Candied nuts aren't the hot thing this year."

"That's too bad." She tilted her head, studying him. "The scarf looks good on you—just the right color. After all that's happened, I'm surprised you're still wearing it."

"It's warm." He caught himself, aware that politeness was in order. "And it was very generous of you. Thanks."

"No biggie. I'm not sure what happened earlier. Usually, I'm reasonably coordinated."

The bartender returned with a filled wine glass. She reached for it as he set it on the counter. Somehow—her hand went left as his went right or vice versa—they connected with the stem in between. The glass tipped over, splashing its contents across the counter and soaking Carson's cast.

Maggie's eyes grew double the size as Carson pulled back. The bartender grabbed a nearby towel, offering his apologies while attempting to sop up the mess. "I'll get you another wine and the drinks are comp," he said, now flustered. Carson inspected his cast, now in shades of pink and red as if it were a watercolor painting.

"Will it wash off?" she asked. "I didn't think they stain so easily."

"Apparently so." He stared at her for a long moment before scooting his chair a foot away. Her expression dropped. "You're a dangerous woman," he added before taking a gulp of his beer.

"I'm—"

"Sorry? Yeah. I know."

"Really. I'll put it in writing." Her voice took on a defiant tone.

"Sure, you will," he scoffed.

"You don't believe me?" She looked over the bar, finally seeing a marker a few feet away near the register. She hopped from her chair and grabbed the pen. "Give me your arm."

Before he had a chance to refuse, she started to write on his cast. He watched, now amused as she signed her name and set the pen down.

"Good enough for you?"

He read the words on the cast.

This is my fault. Maggie

"You know, this is admissible in a court of law."

"So sue me. I'll blame it on the dog."

The bartender returned with a fresh glass filled to the brim. She reached for it.

"Whoa," Carson demanded. "Not so fast."

She froze.

"Now slowly, be careful," he said with an even voice. "Take the glass by the stem. Gently. Now lift it with a steady hand," he coached. "That's it. Nice and even."

She paused, shooting him a look equally amused and perturbed. "Now you're just being mean."

"I'm simply looking out for your best interests… and mine."

She laughed. Again, disarming. No, he'd hold off on suing for now.

Carson arrived at the market the next morning right before opening, enough time to restock and rearrange his table and plug in the lights. Maggie had already prepped her space, ready for business. Her booth jammed with a holiday playlist, currently the classic Mariah Carey tune.

"Good morning, Carson," she chirped. Okay, good enough. Under normal conditions, he always needed a couple of hours and a dose of coffee to get his pleasant face on. How someone could wake up all merry and light baffled him. With one arm in a cast, he'd need to work extra hard to get in the holiday spirit.

"Good morning, Maggie," he answered.

The front doors opened for business. The crowd flooded in, all ready for seasonal festivities and shopping. In an instant, Maggie's booth flooded with people, pulling apparel from the racks and holding them up to a mirror. How did she do it? Was there a trick to having the right merchandise? Meanwhile, he hosted crickets.

Suddenly, she appeared at his table with a plastic bowl. "You need this. Pour some nuts in it as samples." Just as quickly, she vanished. Duh. Why had he not thought of that before? It seemed so obvious. He did as told. It seemed to help. Over the morning, he managed to sell a few bags—not enough to cover his booth cost, but at this stage, he'd take what he could.

His arm itched. He looked around for something to ram into his cast for relief. Nothing in sight.

Noon rolled around. His stomach grumbled. There was a sandwich booth at the front. He could either shut down the booth to go on a food run or pacify his appetite with candied nuts.

Maggie appeared again at his table during a lull, this time with a serving tray in hand. "I have an idea. You like baseball?"

"What red-blooded male doesn't?"

"So, you know the guy who walks up and down the steps hawking popcorn and beer?"

"Yeahhh?" He wasn't sure where this was going.

She held up a red and white striped apron along with the tray. "Time to hawk. If the customers don't come to you, then you go to them."

"And who watches my booth?"

"I do. We move the curtain back so I can see both. I got you covered."

He stared at her, dumbfounded. "Why are you doing this?"

"I still owe you for yesterday… and the day before."

He rose from his chair, still dubious. "So how does this work?"

She handed the tray and apron to him. "Simple. Walk the floor. Give out samples. Have a few bags with you and direct customers back to me. I've got your back." She paused then added, "Trust me."

Then came her secret weapon. The giggle. Carson was doomed.

A minute later, he found himself carrying the tray laden with his specialty nut mixes balanced on his cast. He took to the floor, offering free samples, and selling an occasional bag. He found his spirits lifting.

That ended shortly as he heard a cry behind him along with the jingling of bells.

"Toby! Come back!"

He turned to see the familiar pooch bolting for him, no doubt aware of the treats he carried on his tray. Toby took flight, knocking him back to the floor. He broke his fall with his good arm as bags and loose nuts scattered across the aisle. As he looked at the mess, he noticed how his arm throbbed.

"I can't believe it," said Maggie as she and Carson sat at the hotel bar. "What are the odds?"

"Not in my favor," he replied as he nursed his beer—now difficult to handle with his other arm in a sling. At least it was only fractured, not broken. "Who brings a puppy to a holiday market?"

"The market manager does. Apparently, she's the top dog here and Toby is the unofficial mascot." She sighed as she looked him over, a pathetic sight with both arms now bound. "Carson, I am so—"

"I know, I know. This time, it wasn't your fault."

"Yeah, but I gave you the tray and sent you out. If it hadn't been for that…"

He tried to shrug it off. "Then you watched my booth for the rest of the day while I was at the emergency clinic. I appreciate that." He paused before adding, "I still think you're an accident waiting to happen."

Her lips tightened as if aware he spoke the truth. "You haven't asked if you got any sales."

"I'm not sure if I want to know. So far, it's been a bust. And I haven't figured out how I'm going to handle tear-down and packing when it's over."

She slid a white envelope across the counter with a figure written on top.

"What's this?" he asked.

"Your day's sales."

He looked at the number. "There's some mistake. It says $847."

"No mistake. I didn't bother with the cents though. I hope that's okay."

He looked at her with an expression of bewilderment, the kind reserved for Powerball winners.

"How? Did you hold them at gunpoint?"

She beamed at what she considered a compliment. "A package deal. If a customer bought your product and mine together, they got a certificate for twenty percent off their next purchase with me."

"But that means you'd be losing money on a sale."

She shook her head. "Nope. It means I lure them back for another sale. Less

profit is still better than no profit." She followed it with a giggle. Yes, *the giggle.*

"I'm… I'm impressed." He maneuvered his glass to his mouth for a sip of beer. "How did you get involved in selling clothes?"

Her face stiffened. "My dad. You?"

"My mom. These were all her recipes. I'm simply bringing them to the masses."

"She's probably proud of you for that."

"I'd like to think so. But she passed a few years back. That's why the brand has her name. I'm keeping the legacy alive."

"I'm sorry for your loss."

"It's okay. So, your dad got you in the biz?"

She sipped at her wine before speaking as if looking for the right words. "Indirectly. He told me I'd never amount to anything. Just get married and be done with it. I decided to prove him wrong." She set the glass down less delicately than before.

"Damn. That's harsh."

"He lacked some basic skills when dealing with the opposite sex. But you can't choose which family you're born into, right?"

"I guess so."

She reached for the glass again, her finger striking the stem. It teetered to one side, about to fall over and spill. She quickly grabbed the glass with the other hand.

"Good catch," he said.

"I'm getting better." Her eyes rolled upward for a second. "Honestly, I'm making this all up as I go along. The booth looks slick but only because I watched a lot of YouTube videos and copied them. I'm no marketing genius. But it seems to work so far."

They chatted for another hour as people came and went, and holiday music softly filled the background. Through it all, Carson studied her face, her mannerisms, her way of speaking, and wondered if she was a classic example of desiring the thing that was worst for you.

Did she fall in the same category as refined sugar, alcohol, red meat, and smoking? So far, she'd been either directly or indirectly responsible for way too many mishaps at his expense. So here he was, contemplating how much fire a moth might stand.

At last, they rose, ready to go back to their respective rooms. As he moved behind her, she slipped while sliding off the chair, stumbled, and fell into his arms, such as they currently were. She looked up, their faces only inches apart. She blushed and regained her footing. "Sorry. I lost my balance. Are your arms okay?"

"I'm fine," he answered while feeling anything but. This only magnified his train of thought. No, best not to get involved if he wanted to live a long, fruitful life. They said their adieus in the elevator with her exiting on Floor Four and him on Six. She stepped out, giving a final glance at him over her shoulder. The doors slid shut.

He rode the remainder with the soft hum of the elevator to keep him company. Only later did he replay the scenes. Her fall from the stool, the subsequent catch, and that last look from her. The thought occurred to him: Was that accidental or deliberate?

Maggie's chirp broke the silence. "Good morning."

She stood in front of Carson's booth exuding more bubbles than a glass of champagne. Again, he marveled with some disgust how she managed to put on such a cheery face at such an early hour.

"How are you?" she added.

"Decent, all things considered." The morning had been a trial. Activities normally taken for granted became difficult with two injured arms, certainly getting dressed. He ended up on the floor attempting to get his shoes on. Driving to the market also proved to be a challenge, but he managed without wrapping his car around a tree.

"Would you be up for doing a repeat of yesterday?" she asked.

"What part? The falling, the injury, and the costly second doctor visit?"

She bit her lip, apparently reconsidering the question. "No, not that. I still feel really bad. But I think we were on to something. If you walk the floor again, you can sell your nuts and promote both of us. I can cover the home base, the same as before. We work as a team."

On the surface, it seemed like a good strategy. "You're forgetting one thing. Toby, the demon dog from Hell."

"Not to worry. The manager promised to keep him on a tight leash."

He thought back to the cash-filled envelope from the previous night—not something he would have accomplished on his own. She gave a hopeful smile, further eroding his resistance. "Sure. What else can happen that already hasn't?"

Shortly after, he hit the aisles with his nuts in hand. Clever girl, she'd tied ribbon from the tray handles to hang around his neck, making it easier to carry the products. He spent the morning making the rounds and finding customers to be receptive, especially with the bowl of free samples on his tray.

All went well.

Then it didn't.

He'd returned to Maggie's well-populated booth. She gave him an exuberant wave.

"How goes it?" he asked.

"Really good. You even got a couple of repeat customers. Your mom must have been a wiz in the kitchen."

As she stepped out to greet him, her foot snagged against a string of the plastic garland she'd wrapped along the clothing rack. It trailed behind, unraveling into a long strand.

"How're your arms?" she asked as she circled him.

"Aching but fine."

The garland pulled taut, one side fastened to the rack. Maggie felt the tug and looked down. "Oh!" She moved, only pulling the strand tighter as it now had wrapped around both of their legs. Her action caused Carson to move back, only to find resistance. They attempted to move in opposite directions, wobbling as they did so.

For a brief moment, they hopped together as if participating in a three-legged race. Then, as with Humpty Dumpty, there came the big fall, them tied together. Carson landed first with her on top. He cringed on impact, not using his hands to soften the blow. The bags of candied nuts flew in all directions.

Once more, their faces were only inches apart. Again, a nice face, he thought. A troubling face. For that matter, she was all trouble, probably more than he needed. Still, at this distance, he momentarily lost resolve.

She rose first, her face flush, with the now familiar repeat of "Sorry. Sorry." She bent to unravel the garland from their feet as he sat up.

"Should I get a restraining order?" he asked.

"Let me get this off." She tossed the strand to the side and helped him to his feet. As he put weight on his left leg, a bolt of pain shot through his ankle. No, not okay. He stared in disbelief before attempting to walk. Another stab followed.

No, not again, he thought.

"What is it?" she asked.

He replied by pointing at his foot.

Her face fell, going white. "Oh, no."

"I'd better sit. Help me to my booth." He paused, looking at her as multiple thoughts ran through his mind. "On second thought, I'll manage on my own." He handed her the tray before hobbling back to the chair behind his table.

Carson returned to the pavilion after the four o'clock closing time, the market officially over. He now sported a black orthopedic walking boot, a suitable match to his arms. Maggie looked up from his booth with a familiar expression of horror. "Broken?" she squeaked.

"Fractured."

"Oh, Carson, I'm so…"

"I think you need a new word. That one's losing its value."

She pouted, another expression that seemed to get under his skin. "I'm sad. Regretful. Heartbroken. Guilt-ridden. What else can I say?"

He noticed that his booth had been nearly disassembled. Bags of product had been stored in their bins, the holiday lights removed from the curtains, and the table set to the side. "I figured you might need help with this," she explained.

She had a point. It would have been difficult to tear down in his condition. Still, she didn't need to do so, considering she still had her own booth to contend with.

"Thank you." He gestured to her space. "But what about you?"

"Mine's easy. All the racks are on wheels. I just roll them out to the SUV." She moved closer. He took a step back. She paused. "Do you have far to go? I never asked where you live."

"About an hour away. Spring area."

"That's not far from me. Nice area."

"Yeah," he answered, not sure what to say next. "Um, I guess you should start on your booth. I can get mine from here."

"Are you sure? I mean, I can…"

He shook his head. "I'm parked right next to the dock door. With a dolly, I'll probably be done before you."

"If you say so." She reluctantly moved to her space. In silence, he set to work, getting a nearby cart and moving his wares. Occasionally he'd glance at Maggie. Once, their eyes met. She quickly looked away. As it turned out, they both finished at the same time.

She approached him with an expression of one who's accidentally run over the neighbor's cat. "Look, I know this has been an ordeal for you, but I…"

"Yes, I know. You're sorry."

"That's not what I was going to say. Despite all the injuries I may have caused, I enjoyed talking with you. I wish it could have been under better circumstances."

He offered a smile. "I enjoyed it as well. Well, not everything. I could have done without this." He raised an arm. "Or this. Or this." He gestured to the other arm and foot. "Or my face on the first day."

"Ohmygod. I forgot about that." She winced. "Not a good meet cute, was it?"

"I should have run for the hills after that."

She took a deep breath while reaching into her pocket and pulling out a pen. Then she approached him.

"You probably never want to see me again. I wouldn't blame you. But… like the song, jackpot question in advance, and all that. If you ever want to talk…"

She took his cast in hand and wrote her phone number under her name. "Here's how to find me."

With a final smile, she walked away, leaving him with cracked bones and a car full of candied nuts.

"So, thanks for no help whatsoever," Carson told Perry over the phone a few days later. "Some family you are."

"Think of it as a learning experience," his brother responded. "Actually, I wish I'd been there. I always relish another's misfortune, especially yours."

"You're so thoughtful."

"Listen, bro. I gotta run. Family's calling."

They said their goodbyes and hung up. Carson leaned back on his sofa, replaying the events of the weekend. Thinking back, it reminded him of the journalists navigating a war zone, doing their job while trying to avoid the line of fire. He'd be wearing mementos of the experience for the next six weeks. His arm itched. He ran a ruler inside of the cast to scratch.

To one side of his front room sat the multiple bins of leftover candied nuts. He'd not yet decided what to do with the remainders. Of course, he could always hand them out as Christmas presents—but they did become a popular item at the market. He couldn't have done it alone. If not for Maggie, his business venture would have been a bust.

Maggie.

She'd been in his mind as well. For every misadventure through the weekend, every fall and injury, her voice followed. Always the same words. He recognized bad news, an error in judgment when one should know better. A wise man would stay far, far away. Run like hell. Hide in the deepest cave until the coast was clear.

Too bad he never seemed to take his own advice.

He looked at his cast, stained pink from the wine, and the words written on one side:

This is my fault. Maggie

"You're damned right it is," he said to himself, still hearing the giggle impossible to resist.

He picked up the phone and dialed her number.

AN INTRODUCTION

CAN I TAKE 'EM ALL AT ONCE?

This is the longest story in the collection. Charles Dickens' *A Christmas Carol* has served as a great inspiration to me on multiple occasions, beginning with a novel wholly influenced by his work. I returned to it in 2010 intending to turn the storyline on its head. Inversion is a delight, especially for a storyline used so frequently.

In this case, I weaved Dickens in with Edgar Allen Poe, Dr. Seuss, *Jane Eyre*, and the immortal bard's *Hamlet*, all combined into an absurdist retelling of the *Carol*. Within this, I found some serious moments. Having come back to it a decade later, it may be one of my favorites.

The moments between Poe and Amelia serve as the emotional core of the story, and this might have worked as a stand-alone story. Somehow, it takes on greater significance when sandwiched between the circus pieces. Poe never met Amelia in real life. Perhaps he should have; it might have changed his path.

CAN I TAKE 'EM ALL AT ONCE?

CASK ONE

Poe was dead: to begin with. There was no doubt whatever about that. He had been wholly dead since 1849 under mysterious circumstances worthy of his own tales. His burial had been presided by a few relatives in weather dark and gloomy—again way worthy. Burial registers had been signed, and the clergyman, clerk, undertaker, and the handful of mourners all played their parts. Yes, Poe gave a doornail a run for its money.

And still, he proved to be as unrepentantly depressed and annoying as ever.

"And so I ponder, weak and weary. Nevermore," he mumbled for the millionth time just to prove the point.

"Oh, shut the hell up," Hamlet replied, another ghost but of the literary sort.

"With sorrow for my lost Lenore," Poe continued, ignoring the Dane.

Fists clenched, Hamlet took a step forward but was gently restrained by Lenore and Ophelia.

"It will do no good, my lord," Lenore said apologetically. "I have thrown myself at him time and time again, enticing him with my radiant and nubile maidenly charms, but he will have none of it. Truth be said, I'm used to it. That's his way."

Ophelia gave her a comforting pat on the sleeve.

"Then have him put a cork in it, and have him go anon," retorted Hamlet.

"And on and on," added Hamlet's father, resplendent in his ghostly armor with a sleeping beaver atop his head. "The lad will not be quiet."

But Poe, a master wordsmith of poetry, articles, tales, and academic diatribes, continued with his pontifications much to the ire of everyone around him.

"A blood-red thing that writes from out the scenic solitude," Poe exclaimed. "It writhes, it writhes with mortal pangs. The mines become its food, and seraphs sob at vermin fangs in human gore imbued."

"Okay, now that's just gross," Ophelia said in disgust.

"I've heard worse," added Lenore.

"How do you deal with it? All day long, he laments your passing, yet here you stand, if not in the flesh, then at least in ethereal body."

Lenore looked herself over. "Yes, and what a body. Would that I looked this ravishing when I was alive. More's the pity. He doesn't realize what he is missing."

"Agreed. My lord Hamlet and I have long since come to terms on that account. He abandoned that silly nunnery nonsense."

"She's quite the little vixen," added Hamlet.

Ophelia giggled. "He especially likes it when I pretend to go mental. It drives him wild."

"Madness!" cried Poe with arms outstretched. "Is not madness the sublimity of the intelligence?" And knowing the optimum time for a dramatic exit, he took a bow. After fumbling about for a book in his coat, he wandered off into the nothingness, head buried within the pages.

"It's not as if we can simply ignore him and he will go away because he returns time and again. A solution is what we need," Hamlet replied. "There has been too much ado to this end without a quiet resolve. I have spoken to him repeatedly, tried to cheer him up, and told him bawdy jokes, to no avail."

"Does he know 'The Man from Nantucket'?" asked his father.

"All and more. Still, he speaks endlessly about things most miserable—I am open to suggestions."

"Dearest Hamlet, I know how this must weigh heavily on your soul," said Ophelia with a comforting arm caressing his shoulder. "Is there anything I might do to lighten your load?"

This was followed by a series of furtive glances by both parties. "Later, when we are alone, we can... discuss," he replied, causing her to stifle a giggle.

Lenore sighed. "I must admit, I, too, grow weary of this. Is there not someone, anyone, who might be able to help? A person of advice who could talk sense into him, or at least give him a touch of humor?"

"What about his contemporaries?" asked Ophelia. "Colleagues and fellow writers? Surely, there was someone among them that he admired?"

They all looked at one another in hopes that the other would answer. "Anyone?"

"Rufus Griswold?" Lenore offered weakly.

Hamlet cleared his throat. "Well, I guess that clears up our first option."

Ophelia shook her head in dismay. "I don't get it. Here we are with an eternity to enjoy all the riches of peace and contentment, right? Yet we are saddled with a person who brings forth the opposite. Where's the joy in that?"

Hamlet smiled at the thought. "Is that not plain? For our dreary friend, the very despondency that wears us down brings him the utmost satisfaction. Our problem is that it is a cycle to be repeated *in aeternum*."

"Rather like a bad song that we can't get out of our heads," noted Lenore.

Ophelia grimaced. "Oh, I hate that. Like the ballad 'Tie a Yellow Ribbon Around Yonder Old Oaken Tree.' You know the one."

Not being musically inclined, Hamlet's father shook his head.

"Here is the point," said Hamlet. "See, there, those two portly gentlemen, pleasant to behold in their overcoats, scarves, and top hats. See how they make their way to our depressive friend over there. Watch what transpires."

Without as much as a raised curtain, Ophelia, Lenore, Hamlet, and his father turned their attention to the drama about to unfold. Poe stood in the distance, deeply engrossed in a book by H.P. Lovecraft. As everyone understood, this was always a favorable omen; the result of his reading meant that he'd not be talking, thereby, not driving those near him batshit crazy. In this instance, he did not see the two gentlemen until they were right upon him.

"Have I the pleasure of addressing Mr. Poe?" asked the first, thus beginning the assault. Poe frowned and closed his book. "At this festive, er, place," continued the gentleman, "it is more than usually desirable that we should make some slight provisions for the poor and destitute who suffer greatly at the present time. Many thousands are in want of common comforts, sir."

"Are they not, in fact, dead, as we all are, and beyond the pale of such needs?"

"They are," returned the gentleman. "I wish I could say they were not."

"And being dead is not all it's cracked up to be," chimed in the other. "I do so miss the telly."

"And the Union workhouses?" asked Poe. "Plenty of prisons? The Treadmill and Poor Law still in full vigor?"

"Well, yes, but not up here. For that, you have to go, um..." he said in a softer tone while pointing downward, indicating a heated locale way below his feet.

"And since you and I are quite deceased—as are all those unfortunates of whom you speak—is it not a massive waste of my time for you to be rattling on about such concerns?"

The gentleman shuffled his feet. "Yes, well, old habits die hard, and I was quite good at this when I was still..."

"Breathing," said the other.

"But since you are here, you can give me an audience as I read aloud one of my favorite poems," exclaimed Poe with relish. The two gentlemen exchanged worried glances as he cleared his throat.

"Hear the loud alarum bells-

Brazen bells!

What a tale of terror, now, their turbulency tells!

In the startled ear of night

How they scream out their affright!

Too much horrified to speak,

They can only shriek, shriek,

Out of tune,

In a clamorous appealing to the mercy of the fire

In a mad expostulation with the deaf and frantic fire..."

"Pardon me," said the first gentleman, "but don't you have anything a bit more upbeat? Something like 'Tie a Yellow Ribbon Round the Ole Oak Tree?'"

"Oh, yes," replied the other. "That's a good one. Or 'Muskrat Love.'"

At this, they put their arms around each other and began to sing about Muskrat Suzie and Muskrat Sam doing a jitterbug in muskrat land. Poe eyed them carefully before raising a hand and bringing them to silence. They stopped, and after he was sure that he had their undivided attention, he continued.

"Oh, the bells, bells, bells!

What a tale their terror tells

Of Despair!

How they clang, and clash, and roar!

What a horror they outpour

On the bosom of the palpitating air!

Yet the ear it fully knows,

By the twanging,

And the clanging,

How the danger ebbs and flows."

As he continued his recitation, the two gentlemen looked at each other, shrugged in unison, and walked away.

"Ohhh, that's new," said Hamlet. "Good comeback."

"How's that?" Ophelia asked. "You've seen this before?"

"Indeed. Part of our joy here is in the doing of what we liked doing best in life. Those two yonder gentlemen get their jollies from helping the impoverished even though there is no such thing here. Time and again, they have accosted our poetic associate, full in the knowledge that it is a losing proposition. Mostly, it plays out the same way, but every now and again, there's a new twist."

"Then I'll put my money on the poet," said Rochester, joining the group with Jane Eyre at his side. "I know a sure thing when I see it."

"Would it not be fair to say that dear Edgar is doing what he likes best?" suggested Lenore.

"What?" countered Hamlet's father. "Driving us looney."

"Well, the aim of any good artist is to incite a response," noted Jane, "be it standing in a courtyard in the rain, burning a madwoman in her own home, or reading depressing poetry aloud. It's all the same."

Hamlet snorted. "Yes, I'd like to incite a response on his—"

Lenore waged her finger at him. "Now, now, now, we don't talk like that here." He started to reply, then thought better of it and held his tongue.

"So call him what you will," continued Jane. "He has the soul of a true artist."

Hamlet shook his head. "Artist. Shmartist. His level of pleasure is counter to ours. None of us find it pleasant. It is truly a rotten state to be chained to such an individual."

Hamlet's father let out a short gasp, eyes widening as a smile spread across his face. "Chains? Of course, why did I not think of it before? Yes, I may have the answer." He began pacing with an agitation that woke his sleeping beaver, but he gave it no consideration. "Mind you, 'tis a long shot on any account. He may not succeed, but then again, it worked before. He could do so again."

"What are you talking about?" asked the younger Dane.

"I pray, thee, wait but a while. I must go in search of someone who may be of help. Wait. Stay. He! He!"

Hamlet, Lenore, Ophelia, Jane, and Rochester looked at one another with quizzical expressions as the elder ran off, laughing loudly with cries of "Chains! Padlocks!" and the beaver holding onto his head for dear life.

All in all, it had been a very good day.

Poe managed to give several lengthy oratories, reciting from his favorite, most morose poems and prose to whosoever would listen (regardless of whether they were interested or not—Mostly, they weren't, but that did not hold him back). He found time to edit his massive tome, *The Fraudulent, Plagiarized Poetry of Henry Wadsworth Longfellow*, and even squeezed in a drink or two. Now he returned to a home of his own making.

Of course, those structures were unnecessary in a place such as this, but he enjoyed the creature comforts of solitude. Despite the constant need to inflict his creative whims upon others, he had come to enjoy the quiet and took to oyster-like seclusion for his respite. It was a gloomy, isolated house, set at odds with the surrounding, the perfect statement to his style.

The first indication that things were amiss was when he arrived at his doorstep and his doorknocker called his name. True, it might have been his imagination, but he could have sworn the knocker cried out, "Poe!"

This, in and of itself, was absurd, the idea of a talking doorknocker. Anyway, he might have misheard with it exclaiming "Pow!" or "Poo." Of the two, *pow* made more sense as the knocker made similar noises whenever rapped, usually a hard "Thump!" or similar onomatopoeia. As to the other word, well... who ever heard of a doorknocker shouting a bodily function?

While startled, he chose to ignore the knocker, entered, and slammed the door shut. The sound resounded through the house like thunder, although he could have sworn that he also heard an additional noise from without as if the same doorknocker had shouted, "Ouch!"

Poe fastened the door, walked across the hall, and up the stairs to the far reaches of the darkened house. Poe liked that. Darkness was cheap, even in an afterlife where currency had no real use; more importantly, it was the perfect atmospheric element to create a dismal mood, and Poe liked that even better. Any color as long as it was black, any mood as long as it was somber.

As if to relish the home's depressing quality, he strolled from one room to the next, seeing that all was proper. Sitting room, bedroom, lumber room, library, all as they should be. No corpses under the bed, no black birds perched outside the window, no cats entombed behind the brick walls.

Quite satisfied, he closed the door and locked himself in his chambers, then double- and triple-locked it as was his custom, thus securing himself against any unwanted visitors. Once done, he sat at his writing desk and prepared to tap into his muse.

But wait as he might, the creative spark did not come rapping on his chamber door. The mortal enemy of any writer, the artist's block, set itself upon his shoulder and tightened its grip. So Poe sat there, pen in hand, pondering weak and weary and staring at the sheet of white paper, finding it more terrifying than anything else he had ever created.

Inspiration never came, but something else did.

At first, the sound was almost undetectable, a light jingling noise from below as if a person dragged cheap jewelry over the casks of Amontillado in the wine merchant's cellar. The cellar door flew open with a booming sound, and then the jingling grew louder on the lower floors, up the stairs, and straight toward his door. Without a pause, the cacophony passed through the heavy barrier and into the room.

Jacob Marley stood before Poe, dressed as he always had in his pigtail, waistcoat, tights, and boots. What had changed was the chain he bore. Once made of cashboxes, keys, padlocks, ledgers, deeds, and heavy purses wrought in steel, now, he wore a set of stylish gold necklaces adorned with small, golden good-luck trinkets in the shape of tiny padlocks and cashboxes. These hung around his neck and were clearly visible from the halfway unbuttoned shirt. All in all, he looked very fashionable in a seventies kind of way, very disco.

"You know me, Poe?" he asked in his best ghostly voice.

"I do," answered Edgar. "You are a well-used plot device created by Charles Dickens to set off a series of events in a Christmas fable, and one that has been blatantly stolen by every hack writer since."

At this, Marley grimaced, lips apart, showing a set of clenched teeth. But he said nothing.

Poe continued. "Yes, I know you. You're the undigested potato, the undigested bit of beef, the crumb of cheese, the…" At this, he stopped, but the words hung there, waiting to be spoken. Both of them knew it.

"Go on," said Marley.

"There's more of gravy than of grave about you."

Marley sighed. "God, I hate that line," he said to himself. "Well, let's get on with it."

With that, he raised his arms and let out a frightful cry, accented by a full reverb, and a round of thunder and lightning to enhance the effect. Alas, the lengths of chain he once possessed had been so reduced that it merely jingled to the melee. Still, the overall effect did the job, commanding Poe's undivided attention. To add a final touch, the phantom took off the bandage around his head, allowing his lower jaw to drop down upon his breast.

"Mercy," cried Poe. "You live up to your reputation. Dreadful apparition, why do you trouble me?"

"Are you listening now?" replied the ghost.

"Yes! Yes! Er, will you sit at least?"

At this, Marley smiled. "Thought you'd never ask." He retied his bandage around his head and plopped in the weathered chair opposite Poe. "You wouldn't happen to have a nice bourbon by any chance, would you?"

Poe shook his head. "Sorry, I have trouble keeping liquor around."

"I understand. No matter then."

Then followed an awkward silence for Poe, not knowing what to say. Marley simply sat there, looking around the room, quite content to say nothing else. Finally, Poe broke the lull by picking up a nearby toothpick.

"I have a toothpick," he said feebly.

"So I see."

"It's a very nice toothpick."

"It is."

"If I were to swallow it, I could be forevermore persecuted by a legion of goblins, all of my own creation."

"Yes," replied Marley. "I've heard that line before."

Poe fumbled with the toothpick and set it on the table. "Yes, well..." He picked up a nearby bowl of candy. "I also have some jelly beans."

"Ah, most excellent," cried Marley. "I've not had jelly beans in what seems to be a century. Cherry, by any chance?"

Poe passed the bowl over, and Marley rummaged through the candy, finally finding a red one in the mix. "Aha!" he cried and popped it in his mouth. "God, I love cherry."

Poe took back the dish, found a tasty licorice for himself, and returned the bowl to the table.

"So why do you trouble me?" Poe asked at length.

"Ah, yes, that is the core of the matter, isn't it?" answered Marley. "It is required of every man that the spirit within him walk among his fellow man, travel far and wide, and if that spirit does not go forth in life, it is condemned to do so after death, blah, blah, blah, etcetera, etcetera, etcetera.

"The point now is that you are quite dead, have been so for a very long time, and there is another lesser-known requirement that comes into play once a person croaks. Simply put, once you're dead, the spirit within him needs some happy time. Lord knows there is enough pain and suffering when you're alive, so who needs it here? That requires a bit of cooperation between all here to make things work. One bad apple, and so forth, if you get my meaning."

Poe shook his head, not quite seeing the big picture.

"See here, Poe, you need to get with the program. This is a pleasant place. No strife. No worries. No past due payments, money lenders, no murderous uncle marrying his sister-in-law, and no bad poetry."

"Ah, but it is all a mask, a charade," countered Poe. "To think that after such a sordid life, and embracing the conqueror worm, this is all that remains, much of madness, more of sin."

"The point of the matter," continued Marley, "is that there is no reason not to enjoy the merriment of ourselves and others. Come then. What right have you to be dismal? What reason have you to be morose? You're dead enough."

"What reason have you to be merry?" snapped Poe. "You're lifeless enough."

"Dead is as dead does," smiled Marley. "Personally, I have come to enjoy eternity."

"Leave me be. You have no business in my affairs."

"On the contrary, my somber friend, your common welfare is my business. Charity, mercy, forbearance, benevolence, and advice, whether asked for or not, are all drops of water in the comprehensive ocean of my business. Too long have I heard in disdainful tones asides about your gloomy demeanor. I feel the time has come to set things right, so I am here to aid in your reformation."

An uneasy feeling grew in the pit of Poe's stomach. He had his suspicions on where the conversation was heading and he didn't like it one bit.

"Let me guess," he said. "I will be haunted by three spirits. I can expect the first one when the bells strike one, the second the next night, and the third the next night at the last stroke of twelve. Am I right?"

Marley's lips curled into a knowing smile. "You know of my methods?"

Poe smirked. "I do read, you know. Give me some credit."

"Well, then you would be right, but you would also be wrong. There will be visitations—a set of three, to be precise, on three consecutive nights. But I do hate repeating myself. For you, I have something very special planned."

"You're a good friend to me," grumbled Poe sarcastically. "Thank'ee."

"You, Edgar Allan Poe, shall do the visiting. Indeed, you shall leave this place and pay a visit to three mortals who have not yet become one with the spirit world. You will give them your attention, and you will learn from them, for only through this interaction may there be some hope for your welfare."

"What welfare? I'm already dead. You don't get farther from welfare than that." Marley started to speak, but Poe cut him off. "And don't give me the reclamation line either. Save that for the Scrooges of the world."

Marley smiled at this, but it was perfunctory, without amusement. "Fair enough. It changes nothing. You will go a calling, beginning when the bell strikes one. The second will follow on the next night, and the third the next night at the last stroke of twelve."

"And I don't suppose that I can take them all at once and get the damned thing over with?"

Marley shook his head. "It doesn't work that way. Anyhow, we could use some peace and quiet around here, even if it's only for three days."

"Moron, time doesn't exist here. You know that as well as I."

"No matter. My time with you is done, praises be. Get thee hence, and do try to come back a little wiser than you are now."

Marley raised his hand and snapped his fingers. With that, he disappeared with a low pop, leaving Poe alone once more.

"Welfare, indeed," he grumbled. Like hell, he was going anywhere. One of the comforts of being non-corporeal was that the rules of the living no longer applied, including doing things just because you were told to. He planned to stay put in the home of his own making, and no bell was going to say otherwise. Anyway, there was not a single timepiece in his home, neither pocket watch nor grandfather clock. No clock, no bell—so how about that, Marley?

A soft noise seemed to emanate from the window, and Poe approached it for a better look. To his consternation, the normal view he would have had was now obscured by a thick blanket of swirling snow, and the sound he had heard was that of the gusts of wind outside.

He opened the window to see better. Immediately, the myriad of snowflakes took the opening as an invitation, blowing past him and into the room. But there was something else to all this, and Poe stared intently into the shifting powder for some explanation. The swirls grew dense, quickly obscuring the room around him, and he soon found himself surrounded by the spiraling flakes, seeing nothing else.

Then the room vanished. There was only the blizzard and him within it, and as it whipped around him, causing a degree of lightheadedness, he thought he heard the tolling of a bell, once, twice, three times, and on until it pealed a full dozen.

And as everything went white, he mumbled to himself, "Marley, you're a real shit."

CASK TWO

Poe found himself on all fours entrenched in several inches of snow. What immediately struck him was the intense cold, something he had not felt in ages. Come to think of it, he'd not felt much of anything since he died.

"Interesting," he said to himself while drawing his hand across the snow, feeling its texture as might a newborn. His knees tingled from the dampness running the lower length of his trousers, but he made no effort to change position. Instead, his attention was drawn to the surroundings.

The wintery maelstrom surrounding him now dissipated, and he saw he knelt on a city street or in an alleyway. Visibility was still reduced to a short distance, but he could make out the weathered brick pavement that peeked out from the mounds of snow. Not far was the wall to a building also fashioned from brick. But what commanded his attention was the shape not three feet away, marked on top with red.

As the snowfall lessened, he discerned that of a person huddled in the corner against the wall as if to find meager shelter from the elements. Clothes were worn and sparse, offering little protection from the cold, but it was apparent that at one time, the garments had been well-kempt.

The red was that of hair, long and tangled, a radiant auburn color, and it moved with the wind as if it had a life of its own. Judging from the size and shape, this was a young girl, most likely an orphan.

Without any forethought, he instinctively reached out to touch the hair to see if it, too, had substance. Fingers came into contact with strands. He ran them through the hair in a state of fascination.

With that, the figure jerked as if woken from a deep sleep, pulling herself back against the wall and looking directly into his eyes. Likewise, he pulled his hand back from her head, somehow snagging a few errant strands in the process, which remained tangled between his fingers. For him, now returned to a world governed by seconds, minutes, and hours—time suddenly came to a stop.

This was no child. The eyes that stared back into his were that of a young woman, perhaps in her twenties, but one who had clearly seen far more than her years. She took in a deep breath, shuddered, and pulled her shawl closer around her, but still kept her eyes locked on his.

"I'm sorry," he managed to say. "I thought you were... might have been..." The rest of the sentence trailed off as he realized he was not sure what he had expected.

She licked her parched lips, pausing as if considering his words and how to answer. "Are you... he?"

"I beg your pardon?" Poe responded, not entirely sure of her question.

"Are you the spirit whose coming was foretold to me?"

"I am," he answered. "Possibly. I think I might be."

She cocked her head slightly. "Don't you know?"

It was a good question. Logic suggested that if he was meant to come courting people in the mortal world, then they might have been given some advance warning. As to what was disclosed, and who did the disclosing, that was another matter. For all he knew, she might have been told far more about him than he of her. Then again, she could know absolutely nothing.

Her eyes remained trained on him, and he now noticed their intensity as well as their color—the softest of blues, clear as water but flecked with a fiery intensity that made the hue all the stronger. Or perhaps it was simply the way she looked at him. Her eyes contrasted the hair, blue against red, water to fire. He found himself quite nervous under the circumstances.

"Sorry. I'm new at this, so forgive my lack of certainty."

"Oh," she said more like a whisper to herself. Cautiously, she drew a hand from underneath the shawl and reached out to him, stopping an inch from his face. Then, ever so cautiously, she closed the distance and flesh met substance. There was an almost inaudible gasp, and with that, the hand withdrew.

"I can touch you as if you are real, yet..." she hesitated, and for the first time, her eyes shifted, taking in his whole figure. "I can see through you, so you must be a spirit."

Indeed, he was as transparent as any phantom. The brick wall was visible through his body. He could see that for himself when he held his hand in front of him—and yet he could feel the ground below him and the cold of the snow.

What was more, the girl before him could see him and touch him as well. Indeed, the rules of ghostly existence included solidity. Still, there were all the tales of spirits passing through solid objects. Thinking that by all rights, he should be able to pass through the wall, he pressed his hand against the brick surface. Immediately, his hand disappeared up to his wrist.

He retracted his hand from the surface while pondering how it could be. *Must be some sort of power of will. A manifestation based on intention,* he thought. Obviously, he had a lot to learn about being a ghost in the real world. He repeated the action, this time faster, and then a third time. In each instance, his hand vanished behind the brick façade.

What if he were able to choose what was tangible and what was not? Would the wall then be as substantive as the snow around him? *The wall is solid,* he thought to himself. *I can touch and feel it.* Again he reached out, but this time, his fingers met resistance. They trailed along the mortar lines between the bricks, feeling every bump and crevice. He concluded there were rules and strategies to this form of existence.

He paused, aware of being watched. At once self-conscious, he brought his attention back to the girl who stared at him with a curious expression. His actions must have appeared ridiculous to her.

"Amusing yourself?" she asked.

"Not exactly."

"So you punch the bricks for no particular reason?"

"Yes. Particularly."

Again, those eyes shone with an intensity that caused him to flinch. He took a moment to compose himself, all the while realizing that he had not felt uncomfortable, not like this, since...

"I hope I did not startle you."

"What's to startle? I see ghosts all the time," she answered, and he looked at her credulously for some sort of elaboration. It did not come. Only when a smile crept across her face did he grasp that she was having him on. One thing was certain, she hardly seemed frightened by his apparition.

"Anyway, I have more pressing concerns than seeing spirits," she continued, all the while, pulling the thin shawl tighter around her.

At once, Poe felt profoundly stupid for not making the connection. What was a young girl doing outside in weather such as this, dressed in the barest of shabby clothes? It was not a fit night for any purpose other than to get from one warm location to another, yet here she sat, huddled against the wall and making no effort to find shelter.

"My dear lady, you should not be out on such an intolerable night. You should be somewhere warm."

"To do so, a person must have a place to go, and I am—shall we say, between positions."

"But you can't just sit here. You will catch your death."

"As I said, a pressing concern, one among several."

She added no more to this, leaving Poe more curious than ever to know what her circumstances were. How did she come to this place, and why was she not trying to find a haven from the elements?

The girl broke the silence. "So you are here to tell me something, I suppose? Show me the error of my ways or some similar matter?"

Poe was taken aback and laughed before he could stifle the urge. "Me? I think it somewhat backward. Are you not to instruct me for the betterment of my welfare?"

"What welfare? You're dead!" She bit her lip after saying these words, realizing that it might not be prudent to remind ghosts of their own ghostliness. "You are dead, aren't you?" she asked nervously.

"Fully and wholly," he answered.

"So let me make sure I understand this. I was told to expect a visitation by a spirit and that his purpose would soon become clear to me. You are here and you are by all evidence a spirit unless this is my imagination due to exposure and lack of sleep and food, in which case you are absolutely nothing at all. Assuming that you are genuine, you do not have a clue as to your purpose, but here you are anyway. Is this correct?"

"I think you put it rather well."

"And am I your first?"

Poe smiled. "The way you put it sounds rather personal, but yes. You are my first."

"As you are mine. Then perhaps we might start with introductions?"

"Of course," he answered but somehow felt it better not to give his full name, possibly residue from his mortal life when his name brought immediate recognition. In this case, anonymity might be the better approach. "My name is Edgar."

"A nice name. Very strong." She examined his face. "Somehow it doesn't fit you. It is too harsh."

"Some people have said that I *was* harsh."

"Does not anyone call you Eddy? It suits you better."

"Some do," he answered, immediately thinking of those in his life who called him by that name.

Family.

Friends.

Virginia.

"Then may I call you Eddy?"

"It would give me no greater pleasure."

"My name is Amelia. Amelia Beille."

"It is indeed a pleasure, Miss Beille. Or is it missus?"

"You may call me Amelia. I think we are beyond proper formalities, you being dead and all."

"Very well then," he answered, extending his hand to her while hoping that it would remain solid. "Pleased to meet you, Amelia."

She took his hand and it was indeed solid. Her fingers were cold, no doubt from the weather, reminding him that they must find sanctuary for her sake. He did not immediately release his grip. It felt good, the sensation of her hand in his, and somehow energizing as if some sort of force was shared between them.

"Likewise, Eddy."

Reluctantly, he released his grip.

There came a sound of footsteps, soft at first, but growing quickly in volume. Poe turned just in time to see a man well dressed in full suit and hat, upon them as if in a great hurry. There was scarcely any time for Poe to move. The man walked through him as if he were nothing, which he was, paying him no mind. As he passed, the man shouted, "Move, woman. Out of the street."

"Hey!" Poe yelled after him. "Blaggard! Who the hell do you think you are?"

No response came as the man disappeared once more into the darkness.

"Such rudeness," Poe said. "Then he ignored me."

Amelia laughed. "I don't think he heard you—or saw you. You're a ghost, remember? I may be the only one who can see you."

"Still, that is no reason for such treatment."

She looked down, immediately sad, "Yes, that's the way of the world, isn't it? Compassion, forbearance, goodwill to fellow human beings, love for one another. It all sounds nice, but little of it actually exists."

"That's a harsh thing to say."

She nodded. "It is. I would like to think otherwise, but I've been shown the error of those ideas." She followed this with another shiver from the temperature.

Poe was struck with a thought. If he was able to choose what was tangible, then might his garments do the same?

"Come. We must find you shelter. In the meantime, let's see if you can wear this for warmth. Stand up."

"Might you give me assistance? It has become more difficult recently, but I shall try."

With his help, she rose to her feet, and several things happened in quick succession. As she leaned on him, he felt the warmth of her body against his, a sensation at once alien and comforting. He immediately wanted to hold her all the closer. Her hand slipped and a small object fell from her grasp—a book which landed in the snow at their feet.

Instinctively, he bent to pick it up, but his hand swept through the pages. Concentrating on being solid, he tried again, this time picking up the book and brushing off the dampness from its cover. Only then did he notice, as he rose and was at eye level with her abdomen, her proportions which had been camouflaged when she was sitting against the wall.

Not only was she pregnant, but judging from her size, she was very nearly due.

"Dear heavens, child, I had no idea."

She laughed at the comment. "Hardly a child, sir, I assure you. It takes adult behavior to acquire this situation."

He removed his coat and placed it around her shoulders. It remained there as solid as the ground at their feet. Immediately, she pulled it closer around her.

"You are very kind."

"Not at all, but I must get you somewhere warm, for both of your sakes. Come."

He led her down the street, looking both ways for a reprieve from the cold. *It must be late*, he thought, judging from the lack of people on the streets. There was something startlingly familiar to his surroundings, so much so, that he was at first unable to figure out why.

To the left and right, structures loomed, adding an omnipresent atmosphere to the snow-filled night. Poe looked around him, noting the street signs as they walked. Hamburg Street. Past William and Johnson, a public square, and then past Covington, then finding themselves at a wide expanse of water on both sides. In the distance was the neighboring shore, also lined with streets and buildings, and to the left, the inlet curved before coming to an end.

"I know this place," Poe said, looking at the basin. "The Patapsco River. This is Baltimore, is it not?"

The answer came somewhat muffled, her head buried inside his coat. "Yes. You could have asked me that before."

He turned, accessing his surroundings and the best destination. It came quickly.

"We must go back. I know of a place, but it is a ways off. Can you make it?" Her head turned up to his and nodded.

They backtracked along Hamburg to where they first started, and then a little farther to South Charles Street, taking a right and moving north. After a half dozen blocks, the river, having curved in their direction, came into view. It reached an end as they crossed the tracks to the Philadelphia, Wilmington & Baltimore Railroad. Onward, they passed West Baltimore, Fayette, and Lexington, finally arriving at East Saratoga Street and Parish of St. Paul's. The entire trip had been made in silence.

"We can find shelter here for the night," he told her, trying the door to the church. It was locked. He frowned, considered the barrier for a minute, and then took his arm from her shoulder. "Wait but a minute. I shall be right back."

Poe stepped into the door, vanishing as he passed through. Amelia heard a fumbling on the other side, and the click of a latch, and then Poe was back with her, opening the door as if it had never been barred.

The silence was profound. Even during the light of day, the church commanded serene respect. In the deep of the night with no one else around, it was even more so. She knelt and crossed herself before moving farther in. It felt good to be out of the wind and the snow, but she made no effort to remove the coat. Instead, she walked to a pew halfway in and sat to rest. Poe closed the door and relocked it for good measure before returning to her.

"Better?" he asked.

"Much." Her eyes were closed, head leaning on the back of the seat. She needed the rest and Poe was content to let her do so, but there had been a question nagging at him since he first saw the river.

"Amelia, what year is it?"

"Don't they have a newspaper where you come from?" Even though exhausted, she retained a sense of wit.

"I'm afraid not."

"It is December 1849."

She said no more, leaving Poe to his somber thoughts. In this city, he had spent so much time, a city he died in only two months before now. Elsewhere in this city, at the Westminster Hall burying ground, his earthly remains were lying at rest, still somewhat fresh in the earth.

"The curtain, a funeral pall, comes down with the rush of a storm," he recited softly to himself. He knew the words well and had tossed them out with way too much dramatics in the non-corporeal realm.

True, he had done it partially to antagonize the heavens, but the words had ceased to be anything more than mere words. Now, all those poems he had written during his life came back to him with a meaning most profound. "And the angels, all pallid and worn, uprising, unveiling, affirm that the play is the tragedy 'Man,' and its hero…"

"Are you talking to me?" Amelia asked, half asleep.

"No, child. Just talking to myself."

"I like the sound of your voice."

"You should rest now."

And so she did, and he sat there as guardian, taking in the solemn stillness of the church, increasingly lost in all that was once his life.

"Have I slept long?"

Poe was unsure of when she woke, but she now stared at him, one eye partially covered by the red hair that had fallen during the night. He brushed the strands back, noting how soft her skin was.

"Some time. How do you feel?"

"Better." She stretched, arms extended to touch the sky while turning her head from one side to the other. "As well as to be expected, considering my condition. But I have no comfortable position to sleep anymore."

"Pews are hardly the most relaxing to sleep on," he replied with a smile.

"Ghosts do not need to sleep?"

"No."

"And you have been here the entire time?"

He nodded.

"It's still dark outside," she said, noting the windows.

He nodded again but said nothing. They sat in silence, Amelia lost in her thoughts just as he had during their stay. At length, she placed her hand on his arm.

"You have been very kind. Thank you."

"I'm still not sure of my purpose here."

She smiled. "Perchance to lead a lost woman to shelter and warmth?"

"Anyone might have done that."

"Yes, but no one did. None but you."

Poe turned to her, watching her closely in the pale church light. By now, he knew well the contours of her face as he had studied her closely as she slept. But the face had been passive and unconscious to the depths of slumber. All her secrets were held deep within, with only hints suggested by an occasional shift of the face, a twitch of the mouth, or the slight fluttering of closed eyes.

If he had been uncertain of his purpose when he first appeared in the snow, he now found the situation more confounding with no sense of understanding of their circumstances. What he was sure of was that during the time she had rested, he had somehow fallen utterly in love with this abandoned girl—or as much as a spirit could love a person on the other side.

"How did you come to this?" he asked. "Is there no one to take you in?"

She smiled, the expression mixed equally with amusement and sadness. "Is this the time for telling tales? I don't know that mine would be much different from others. The only variation is in the end."

"I would like to know," Poe replied. It may have been the empathic tone in his voice that gave her pause.

"Then here it is, in simple terms. I grew up believing the world to be a good and honorable place with care and compassion as common virtues. Then I met a man who swore his love to me with promises to honor, obey, and protect as long as we both should live. I left my world, my family, and traveled far to be with him. He had his way with me under the pretense of marriage. Only after I found myself with child—his child—did I find that the marriage was false, as was he. You see, he was already married. Then he abandoned me, leaving me with nothing save the clothes I wear."

"Can you not go back home?"

"I have nothing to go back to—and those that I thought were my friends were his alone, and they have likewise turned their backs. The one thing that gives me strength to endure is the life that grows within— and the hope that he or she will fare better in this world than I."

For once, Poe, who had always been so good with words, had none to give. If a ghost could shudder at a mere thought, now was his time to do so. Hers was a horrible situation—probably not that uncommon—but inexcusable for any human being to treat another as this without compassion.

No, it was insidious, far more than anything he had ever written in any of his stories. Torture chambers, encasement behind brick walls or within coffins, madness—all this was mere child's play to the simple cruelty dealt this woman beside him. There were no words he could offer that would set things right, so he offered his hand instead upon hers.

Then her tears came. Tears that may have been held back for far too long, longing for release. For her, it was a purging, appropriately set in this house where so many people seek refuge to unload the trials of their lives. After the tears ran their course, Poe helped to wipe them from her face. She shifted in the pew, and in doing so, her book fell once more to the floor.

"You seem to keep dropping your Bible," he noted.

"Not a bible. However, it has traveled far with me, and is one of my few remaining possessions."

"It must be dear to you then," he said, picking it up and handing it back to her.

"More so than you can imagine," she replied and held it out for him to see.

"Shakespeare's sonnets," Poe observed. "Fine works indeed."

"Yes," she said softly.

"If it is not too forward to ask, why is the book so precious? Is there some sentiment attached?"

She leafed through the pages. "When I think of love—pure adoration from the heart, I think of this. Shakespeare was able to put into words what is meant to be left to the senses. It is what I always believed love to be, and is what I thought I had found. Alas, I had the misfortune of choosing unwisely. But I still believe in the power of devotion. So in even my darkest days, I have this to remind me of all that is best in this world."

"Words can be quite powerful."

"Indeed. I have read much of Shakespeare, but I find the majority of it quite tragic. It is too easy to see parallels. I would prefer the stories to take a different course. Such is Hamlet; he should have not been so cruel to Ophelia. It was clear that they loved one another. They were meant to be together."

Poe smiled at this, knowing the outcome. Once leaving the mortal world, Hamlet and Ophelia made up for lost time, usually in a horizontal position—or as the Dane had once described, Ophelia's dexterity at riding the pony.

"I believe the essence of Hamlet was that he could not make up his mind," Poe commented, deciding to avoid the topic of lust in the afterlife.

"And where did it get him in the end? No, Shakespeare's tragedies are too close to real life. So I shall stay with my beloved sonnets."

"Rough winds do shake the darling buds of May, and summer's lease hath all too short a date," he replied, the line coming to him instantly.

"You know the eighteenth," she said, obviously impressed.

"I am a man of words, having written much in my own time. I also have paid attention to others."

She looked at him with a level of curiosity. "Should I know you?"

The time for anonymity had come to an end. With some hesitancy, he replied, "My last name is Poe."

Dawning came slowly to her, but it came, nevertheless. "Yes, I know of you. Oh, you passed away only a few months back. I am so sorry for you."

He smiled and patted her hand. "Don't be."

She smiled and looked into his eyes as if seeking some deeper meaning to who he was. "You should have written happier stories."

"It was not in my nature."

"Yes, it was, Eddy. Some of your poetry was quite beautiful. Full of love and longing." She stopped and the smile disappeared. "Sorrow too. Great sadness."

"Words come from emotion."

"Were you not happy?"

"Only sometimes."

"And the rest?"

"Not so much."

"You deserved more then. Love. Joy. You should have spent more time outdoors on a summer day. Taking in nature. Enjoying the company of friends."

"I appreciate your recommendations, Amelia," he said. "Some days are naturally gloomy."

She smiled at his informality. "And now. Are you happy now?"

"I'm dead, for one thing. Happiness—it should be reserved for the living. What I have are regrets."

Amelia moved closer to him. "But that time has passed. You should let them go. You should be happy."

In a flash, he saw all of the errors of a lifetime—wrong choices, missed opportunities, rash behavior—and without even thinking, he responded bitterly, "Easy to say. I shall remember that on the next summer day."

Immediately, he wanted to retract the words. It came out too harsh, a bit mean-spirited, and she deserved anything but callousness. "Sorry. I know you mean well, and I appreciate your kind thoughts. It is hard to undo either a lifetime or its residue."

"Then for me, will you try to be happy?"

This time, Poe smiled and it came with ease. "I will try." At that, he concluded that Shakespeare may have been on target in his verse about the summer day, for at that moment, she was indeed lovelier and more temperate, dimming the gold complexion of Heaven's eye.

"Right, then. Tell me of happiness," he asked of her.

And so she did. In the dim light of the church, she told of growing up; of childhood dreams and what she would do when she came of age; wishes made upon the moon when it was full and bright and days spent as if there were no tomorrow; the books she had read and the ones yet to read; her likes and dislikes; what made her heart melt and what chilled it to the bone. Not all was pleasant: There was her father's passing when she was young and the struggles afterward. And the man who proved to be false.

She asked Poe of his life, and he told her tales in return. It became a game of sorts, one speaking and then the other, and as time passed, they let each other into that private inner sanctum that was usually so guarded. The walls fell so effortlessly that Poe questioned his openness, wondering if it had anything to do with Amelia having no one else to turn to.

Or might it be that there was the vast divide of life and death between them, a chasm so vast that they both felt comfortable opening to the other since there was no possibility of a future beyond the brief time they had together? It was a thought he quickly pushed away, not wanting to know the answer.

They talked until the interior grew light from the morning sun, and still more—and as they talked, they found even more to say. The interruption came only when her stomach grumbled, and she confessed that she was quite hungry.

"Not to worry," she said as she knew of a place where she might obtain food. She gathered her few possessions before attempting to rise. Immediately, Poe rose to his feet, helping her to the door. Together, they left the sanctuary of the church to a morning that was clear and bright, the world around them covered with white from the snow that had fallen the night before.

There was something else to the surroundings which he did not immediately pick up on. It was only after they had passed a dapper gentleman on the street, who bowed and wished Amelia a Merry Christmas, did Poe focus on the seasonal décor hung about on all of the buildings. Wreaths and holly stood in stark contrast to the cold brick facades and snow.

Amelia led the way from Saratoga to Frederick Street and down to Fayette, but the travel was slow. He might have been able to walk at a quick pace, but she was in no condition to do so.

Abruptly, she came to a stop and there was another softer sound. "Oh Lord," she whispered and looked down to see the wetness spreading across her skirt, while at her feet, steam rose from the fresh liquid that had fallen onto the snow. She looked at Poe with an expression of fear. "It's starting. What shall I do?" At that moment, he saw in her eyes all the uncertainties of a frightened girl at a point where there was no going back. With a sudden burst of clarity, he took her hand.

"Come. I know where we can go. It is a distance but we must hurry."

They began the journey eastbound on Fayette Street, but all too soon came to a stop when the first contraction came. She gasped, clenched her teeth, and waited for the sensation to subside.

"Is this what it's like?" she asked.

"Only in the beginning. It gets worse." He hated to be so honest but felt she needed to prepare herself. "But you will be fine. People have been doing it since the dawn of time."

"Men don't," she answered. "Why don't you take my place?"

"That may be difficult," he countered lightly. They began the walk again, passing by High Street. There were people about now, passing by the two of them, although from all outward signs, there was only a single woman walking alone. Occasionally, a passerby stared at Amelia for talking to no one in particular, but she gave it no mind.

Instead, she focused on the waves that arrived at regular intervals. In more than one instance, a pedestrian walked straight through Poe, only to stop and shiver as their whole body had been given a sudden chill. With only a few blocks left, Amelia doubled over from a particularly intense contraction and remained on her feet only because he helped to steady her.

"Hold on, Amelia. Almost there," he said, and once the pain leveled off, they continued along the street.

At last, they turned a corner and the Washington College Hospital came into view. Poe felt a shiver of his own, having known the building intimately in his own way. He had been brought there only a few months earlier, and it was there that he breathed his last. Little time had passed since then, and yet it seemed like an eternity.

"Come," he said, leading her to the building, and as they entered, another contraction hit, this time sending her to the floor. The staff in attendance came to her immediately and took charge.

"Don't leave me," she implored of Poe.

He took her hand. "I'm not going anywhere."

The attendants took her to an open room lined with cots and set her in a corner bed with Poe at her side. As the labor ran its long and strenuous course, he spoke encouragements, wiped her head, and held her hand. She panted and screamed as the day went on until the newborn emerged into the world.

For Poe, who had never before experienced such an event, it was a revelation as mesmerizing as the woman who brought the child forth.

It was a boy. With eyes still wet from tears, Amelia stared into the face of her child. "I want to name him William," she said to the nurse, who noticed that she then looked to her side and smiled before saying, "William Edgar."

As the nurse carried the infant away to be cleaned, Poe took Amelia's hand in his.

"He is a remarkable child. You should feel proud," he said.

"I am," she whispered. "If only it was easier for me to breathe. I did not know I would feel so weak."

"Relax. Your hardest work is done."

"I was so frightened."

"I know."

She shook her head. "No, not that. Of course, I was terrified at the birthing, but I was more afraid of how I would feel about the child—that I would hate him because of who his father is and how I was abandoned. I know that the baby is an innocent with no control over who his parents might be, but I was terrified of what my feelings might be once he was born. But then I looked at his face and knew I could never feel anything but love for him."

"I doubt that it could have been any other way," Poe said softly. "You are too good to think otherwise. And you are far too good for the animal who wronged you so cruelly. You deserve far better—and in time, you will find someone who cherishes you for who you are."

She tightened her grip on his hand as she looked at him, and her eyes grew moist again. "If only..." she said, and it was clear that a world of impossibilities passed through her mind. "If only."

The words lapsed into silence. Poe remained at her side as she rested. He watched the nurses and doctors come and go, unsuspecting that they were being observed, or that the woman who had just delivered a child still had company.

He listened to the sounds around him, that of the hospital with its echoing halls and distant rooms, as well as those that came from beyond the walls. If he listened closely, he could hear the heartbeats of the multitude far down the streets and all throughout Baltimore.

Yes, the city was a living, breathing thing, a macrocosm built from many individual lives. Indeed, he found himself privy to the life pulse of the entire world, but in all this, he could still feel the rhythm of the girl's life beside him with the intake of air into her lungs and the slow exhalation followed by another breath.

And by degrees, he became aware of an irregularity to that breathing. Poe leaned closer, placing one hand on top of hers, and the other on her forehead. Her eyes opened at his touch, and she gave up a weak smile.

"It's you," she said softly and reached over to pull the sheets closer around her. "I'm cold." In the last few minutes, her face had grown pale, her lips parched. She ran her tongue across them in an effort to moisten them, but her mouth was dry as well. "And thirsty."

Poe rose to her request, but her eyes grew wide. "No. Please don't leave me."

"As long as you want me here," he replied, all the while caressing her hand.

"Tell me a poem, one of yours, but not a sad one."

"Whatever you desire," he answered and thought of one he had written in his youth. The words came back effortlessly.

"Fair river. In thy bright, clear flow of crystal, wandering water, thou art an emblem of the glow." He spoke the words softly, but with an inner fire, and as he continued, he found a new meaning, very different from what he had intended when the words were first penned. When he finished, she squeezed his hand in appreciation.

"Beautiful," she managed to say. "I'm so very cold. Are you cold?"

He shook his head but was unable to answer with words. There was so much he wanted to say, but syllables seemed to be held captive in his throat.

Something in Amelia's eyes changed, an understanding of things, and she looked intently at Poe. "Eddy," she said. "I want you to be happy. It is important. Will you do that for me?"

"I will," he managed to say.

"No more sour poems?"

He managed to laugh. "A tough request, but very well. No more sour poems."

"Be happy."

"Yes." And at that moment, with all its finality, he was happy. She smiled and closed her eyes.

"I love you," he whispered, but she did not hear.

She was gone.

In the distance, a bell tolled. Poe held her hand close to his chest even as the world around him began to fade, becoming more transparent with each chime. With the twelfth and final ring, he too vanished.

The nurse in the room glanced at the corner bed and her patient. She saw only a girl who had so recently given birth to a healthy baby boy. The girl lay motionless except for her arm, extended as if clasping something invisible—then falling limp to the bedside.

CASK THREE

The blurring of the world around him came to an end at the same moment as the last tolling of the bell. Poe found himself once more on all fours, this time on a cushy surface, and his face mere inches from another man. They could have rubbed noses if they desired—not that he would want to.

"Whoa, dude," the man said, hitting Poe with stale breath that reeked of hours-old pizza and beer. Poe retreated as quickly as possible from both the man and aroma while taking in the situation. He nearly fell from the edge.

He was on a bed, apparently a single, judging from its size. The man opposite him was dressed in a black T-shirt and boxers, but still clinging to his bedsheets. Judging from this and the tufts of curly hair that stood up at odd angles, he'd just been woken.

"It's true," the man said in slack-jawed wonderment. "You're really him. The other dude said you would visit me, but I thought it was a con." He threw himself back against his pillow, laughing hysterically. "I can't believe I am sitting in bed with Edgar Allan Friggin' Poe."

Poe stepped away from the bed and straightened his clothes, all the while looking at the somewhat unbalanced individual before him. "And you are?"

"Me? Dude, I'm your number-one fan. I mean, I really dig your stuff. Oh man, this is so totally awesome!"

The man climbed from the bed and pulled on a pair of well-worn jeans. They had been lying in a crumpled heap on the side of the bed and looked as if they had not been washed in ages. After some searching, he also located a pair of flip-flops from underneath the bed and slipped them on. All the while, he never stopped talking.

"This is so fricking amazing, you being a real ghost and all, but here you are, all semi-transparent and everything. It's kinda like that Christmas Carol story, except there's only one of you, and there are no chains and padlocks. I guess there's no Tiny Tim either? So what's the deal? Are you supposed to get all mystical and woo-woo, and show me my checkered past? Anyway... yeah... wow. So you really are the dude, right?"

"Pardon me," Poe interrupted, "but would you mind telling me who you are?"

"Oh, yeah. Right. I'm Nat Crandall and I'm your biggest fan."

A sinking feeling settled in the pit of Poe's non-stomach as he took in his surroundings as well as the individual before him. Nat might have been in his thirties, but it was hard to gauge. Judging from his weight, he probably spent most of his time in a sedentary position rather than active, and the less said about personal hygiene, the better.

He wore a black T-shirt depicting a raven swimming underwater in a swimming pool. Below was the word, NEVERMIND, which had been scratched out and replaced with the word, NEVERMORE.

Likewise, the unkempt apartment was filled with books, papers, half-filled cups, and a miscellany of other items strewn across the floor and covering practically every horizontal surface. What bothered Poe the most was that everywhere he looked, he saw himself.

Little wall space was visible since most of it was covered with posters and framed pictures, all of which were images of Poe and things related to his life. Numerous portraits, paintings, movie posters and lobby cards from Poe-based films, and illustrations by Wilfried Satty were scattered throughout.

On one side were pictures of places from his past: his dorm room, Fordham cottage, Washington College Hospital, and others. In the midst hung a portrait of Virginia. A small desktop shrine with a velvet scarf included a variety of framed portraits, a single, plastic, black rose in a vase, and a small engraved card in front that read *To One in Paradise*.

One wall was taken up by a large poster of Vincent Price from *The Masque of the Red Death*. Looking closer, Price's face was made up of dozens of squirming semi-naked bodies. Standing on shelves and tables throughout were busts of Poe, as well as ravens, including one, appropriately enough, positioned next to the window.

Obsessive much.

On the other side of the room stood a bookcase crammed tightly with books, and the whole accented by several Poe busts, as well as a miniature cat statue—naturally, it was black. Looking closer at the shelf, all of the books were either by him or about him. Multiple editions, hardback, softbound, paperback, children's books, and pop-up books all lined the shelves. At the bottom was a collection of volumes centered wholly on the unpleasant details of his death.

"Check it out, dude. I collect editions. Impressive, huh?" Poe realized that Nat had been talking nonstop since he had arrived, and showed no indication of slowing down. "I've even thought about writing one myself," he continued. "My pitch is to draw parallels between your work and the stories of Beatrix Potter. No one has done that yet, so I figure now is my time. Holy, shit, this is so friggin' cool."

Poe held up his hand, hoping that this might shut Nat up for a moment. "Why do you have all of these... things?"

"Like I said, I am so into you. You speak to me, really get to me right here." He thumped his chest in rhythm to a heartbeat. "Hey, check this out."

Nat pulled a picture frame from a table and held it out for Poe to see. The image was of Nat standing next to Poe's grave, with both hands in a thumbs-up position and a goofy grin on his face. "See, it's the two of us together. Pretty cool, eh?"

Poe was at a loss for words on this one, so Nat rattled on.

"So listen, I have several thousand questions I would like to ask you. You don't mind, do you? Nah, course not. So tell me about Virginia. Was she really a hottie? Must have been, the way you carried on about her. You seemed to be kind of hard on Longfellow. Do you still feel that way? What about Griswold? Why the hell would you leave it all to him? He was a seriously screwed-up dude? Surely you knew that. And what's with the whole laudanum thing? Is that really the best way to off yourself? It doesn't seem that romantic. I mean, for a normal guy, yeah, but it doesn't have that poetic edge."

Poe sat in a moth-eaten chair, and for the next thirty minutes, he listened to Nat ramble on about this and that, all centering on his total Poe compulsion, a fact Poe determined early on. Nat threw him a question only to interrupt the answer almost immediately as a new thought superseded the old one.

At present, Nat asked about the symbolic meaning behind the gorilla in "Murders in the Rue Morgue," and if he had an affinity for circus animals when he came to a stop mid-sentence. Mouth halfway open, he gawked at the ghost with new wonderment. Apparently, he had been struck with a particularly brilliant revelation.

"Whoaaaa," he exclaimed. "The Society needs to know about this. Your visitation is way too epic to go unnoticed. I mean, I'm honored that you're here and all, E.A. I mean, why me? I'm totally into your stuff, but I'm just a guy, right? But you need to make this official and talk to the right people. I'm talking the Edgar Allan Poe Society. I'm really tight with them, ya know, and that's where you need to be."

Poe shook his head. "I don't think it works that way."

But Nat wasn't listening. "Yeah, we can arrange this. Yeah. Yeah," he said, more to himself than Poe as he paced back and forth. Then he changed direction and picked up the phone, dialing a number so fast, he obviously knew it by heart.

"I'm calling Phil Howard," said Nat with one hand cupped over the mouthpiece. "He heads up the society. Smart guy. He'll know what to do."

"This may not be a good idea," Poe countered, but again, his words went unheard.

Nat paced with nervous excitement as the phone rang and continued to ring for a good thirty seconds before it was picked up on the other end.

"Hello?" The voice sounded low and groggy.

"Phil, it's Nat. Nat Crandall."

There was silence on the other end.

"I have something really epic to tell you. Are you listening?"

More silence. Finally, a reply came. "Do you know what time it is?"

Nat looked at a nearby clock, an old Victorian-style timepiece with a plastic blackbird taped on top. "Yeah, it's two twenty-five. Were you asleep?"

"What the hell do you think?" replied the voice, obviously irritable at being woken in the middle of the night.

"Sorry about that, but this is way important."

"Nat, I have told you to stop calling me at home. You want to say something, wait for a meeting or something. I have no control over that. I still don't know how you got my new number after I changed it."

"Yeah. Yeah. Yeah. Listen, buddy..."

"I'm not your buddy," came a quick reply.

"Okay, okay, but I have something to tell you that is drop-dead a-maze-ing. This can't wait. Are you sitting down?"

"I'm in bed. What the hell do you think?"

"Just as good. You will never guess who is here in my apartment with me..."

Nat waited a few seconds for a response that did not come and then barreled ahead. "You ready? I am standing here talking with the ghost of Edgar Allan Poe!"

Silence.

Even the crickets that had been chirping outside were now quiet— probably dumbfounded by the statement or curious to hear the response. Poe merely shook his head.

"I'm not kidding, dude. He really is here, sitting in my chair. I'll prove it. Ask me a question for him, and I'll get him to answer."

Nat waited for a question from the other end. None came. Instead, there was a soft click as the line disconnected.

Nat looked at the phone in shock. "He hung up. I don't think he believed me."

"Did you expect him to?" Poe asked.

"Well, yeah. Why would I lie about something like this?"

Poe sighed. "You might give him some credit. Anyway, you woke him in the dead of night."

Nat stood up straight, shaking himself as if ridding his body of some bad residue. "No. This is too important to let it slide. He needs to know about this."

"Even if you call him back, I doubt he will answer," Poe commented. For good reason, he could not blame Phil. He had experienced his share of admirers in his time, including those that were a few drops short of a pint.

Now he found himself stuck to one, at least until the clock bells rang again. He might as well settle in for the rest of the evening and hope it passed quickly. Afterward, he'd move on to the next and final mortal. As to Nat, well, there was little for him to learn here.

Nat busied himself around the room, picking up a set of keys, change, and other scraps of paper and shoving them into his pocket. He gave Poe a purposeful look as he pulled on his coat. "Come on, E.A. Our audience awaits."

Poe looked at him with a sinking feeling. "Where are we going?"

"If Rome won't come to us, we shall go to Rome. We're going to Phil's house."

This was too much. Poe crossed his arms in defiance and made no effort to rise from the chair. No way would he participate in such lunacy. If Nat wanted to go on his little journey, he was more than welcome to do so, but he would do so alone. Poe planned to stay right where he was.

Unfortunately, this was not to be.

Nat threw open the door and marched out. As he did so, Poe felt himself pulled forward as if some sort of vise had taken hold of his stomach and dragged him from the chair.

"Uhhhph," he grunted as he was hauled involuntarily after Nat. All too soon, he found himself in the passenger side of Nat's little Toyota Celica, an old and ill-kempt model in much the same state as his apartment. Without time for Poe to brush away the pile of papers in the front seat, he shifted uncomfortably on top of the stack. Already, Nat started the car and backed out onto the street. This did not bode well.

Enough was enough, Poe thought. "Nat, the time has come to talk..."

"Yeah, of many things, shoes, ships, sealing wax, cabbages, and kings. So you like Lewis Carroll? He's a bit of a lightweight for me."

"What are you talking about?" asked Poe, clearly confused, but Nat had already started on another rant.

"All you have to do is stand next to me so Phil can see you."

"That's not possible."

"Sure it is, E.A. You're here with me."

"Will you please stop calling me that?"

"Sure, E.A. No prob. So you ready for your big unveiling?"

"No, I'm not, and neither are you. You can see and hear me, but no one else can. This is purely a one-on-one relationship."

Nat paused. "You think so?"

"I think so."

Nat thought this over. "But you're not sure?"

"Well, no, but in my experience..."

"Good enough for me," he replied, clearly not taking Poe's advice seriously. Instead, he began questioning the ghost about his alcoholic benders. Poe felt it best to simply keep quiet.

A short time later, after running several red lights and nearly taking out a stray cat, they pulled up at their destination.

The house was large, very upscale, set in a posh area of Baltimore. It stood in the center of a well-manicured lawn elegantly lit with decorative lights that illuminated the surrounding trees and the beds awash in color from perennials. By Poe's estimation—the car clock no longer worked—the time was probably well past three in the morning.

Nat wasted no time in getting out of the car, and Poe immediately felt himself being dragged behind him, across the driver's side and through the steering column, then up the sidewalk to the front door. There Nat stood, ringing the doorbell, over and over.

Poe idly shifted his weight from one foot to the other, all the while expressing how this was—to use Nat's adverbs against him—really, really not a wise plan.

At length, a light came on inside the house, and then another as its occupant made his way to the front door. Then the porch light lit them both, and Poe noticed a face looking through the curtain in the small side window alongside the door.

"Phil. It's me, Nat! Open up. I gotta talk to you."

The figure stood there, obviously considering his options, before making a decision. The curtain fell back into place and the face disappeared from view. A moment later the porch light went off. Soon after that, the other lights went out as well.

Nat was slack-jawed. "I don't understand. Why did he walk away?"

"Hate to say I told you, but—"

"No. No. No. This is too important." Nat began beating on the front door and then rang the bell repeatedly. When this elicited no response from inside, he walked to the front of the house and started yelling.

"Phil! Hey, dude, I know it's late but ya gotta check this out. I got Edgar Allan Poe right here with me! Come on out. And, hey, he looks much better in person than he did in those old photographs. Annie Richmond was right. It doesn't do him justice."

When the police arrived fifteen minutes later, Nat was still shouting at the darkened house, occasionally grabbing a downed branch or pebble and throwing it at the windows. They tried to calm him down—might have let him go home with only a warning had he not been so belligerent. It's never wise to call a law enforcement official "an illiterate jock." All too soon, Nat found himself handcuffed in the back of the patrol car with Poe at his side.

"Bright move, Nat," Poe said softly.

"Phil could have at least come outside and explained to the cops that he knew me."

"I think you're missing the point."

"Which is?" Nat hissed.

"Who do you think called them in the first place?"

"All I wanted to do is share this experience." Nat pursed his lips in defiance. "Well, then, so be it. I have you all to myself. His loss." Then Nat beamed at him. "So what shall we talk about, E.A.?"

"I've asked you to stop calling me that—and perhaps you might want to keep the dialogue to a minimum," Poe said, motioning toward the front of the car. Both policemen had been casting glances in the rearview mirror at what appeared to be a lone person carrying on a conversation with thin air.

"Oh," Nat replied and stopped talking.

His vow of silence was only temporary. By the time he'd been booked, photographed, and fingerprinted, he had resumed his nonstop conversation. The police took this all in stride. They dealt with all sorts from homicidal maniacs to the harmless fruitcakes that populated the city. One more oddball with a penchant for chatter was hardly anything new.

They escorted Nat to the holding cell, already full of that night's arrests, unaware of Poe at his side, passing through the bars as Nat was locked tight.

All things considered, it was just as well that the officers never saw him. Jail cells were meant for containment, not particularly useful on a ghost.

Poe saw how the cold reality of the situation bore down on Nat, who nervously surveyed the other occupants of the cell. The lad surely realized now that he'd been a bit too hasty in his actions. Certainly so with Phil, first on the phone, and then the second act at Phil's front door.

Likewise, he could have been more passive with the police. Any deviation at any of those points might have kept him from landing here. He looked over the lot in the cell, clearly aware they were checking him out as well—and knew this was not a good place to be.

"This is definitely not my night," he said, casting a sideways glance at Poe.

"For your own welfare, you might want to keep quiet," Poe whispered, not that it made a difference. No one else heard him speak.

"Better than your welfare. You're already dead," he replied sarcastically.

Poe nodded. "So I've been reminded."

They found a less populated corner and sat on the floor. Nat bore the uneasy sensation of being watched and wanted more than ever to be invisible—like his companion. He kept his eyes averted to avoid any confrontation with the other people in the cell.

This was a rough bunch. Some had been tossed in for the usual reasons: disorderly content, DWIs, and the like. Others had all the makings of a street gang. They held tight as a group and were given a wide berth by the rest in the cell—and they were the ones that stared at him.

It was going to be a long night, what was left of it.

Nat kept quiet for the first hour, and Poe actually felt some sort of sympathy for him. True, he was incredibly obnoxious—Poe could not wait to be far away from him once their time had passed—however, this was a terrible place, and he was not entirely sure that Nat's actions deserved a stay in the city jail.

"Sorry," Nat said at length.

"No need to apologize to me. You're the one who has to live with this."

"Sometimes, I..." Nat said, pausing as he made some inner evaluation. From the expression on his face, it was not a pleasant assessment. "Sometimes, I get carried away."

An understatement if there ever was one. Poe nodded but said nothing. There was no sense in adding salt to the wound.

"I guess calling the policemen names was not one of my better moments. Or driving over to Phil's. Or..." He lapsed back into silence. "So why *are* you here?" he asked after a time.

"That may be the first sensible question you have asked all night," Poe replied. "Unfortunately, I don't know that I can give you an answer."

"I have to figure that out for myself?"

"Something like that."

Nat considered it for a minute. "Kind of like the Dickens story?"

Poe smiled. "You have no idea."

"So is the afterlife all it's cracked up to be?"

"Oh, it has its merits."

Nat shifted uncomfortably on the hard floor. "But you wrote so much about death. You must have given it great consideration. Is it what you expected?"

Poe shook his head. "Nothing is ever what you expect. That is a universal constant. I guess that is what makes life worth living, and..." he smiled at where the conversation was going. "Let's just say that if ever you get bored with things, you only have yourself to blame."

Poe was the first to notice the shadow, that of the four inmates who had been watching them earlier—but were now standing in front of them, and only looking at Nat, he being the visible one. Nat was in mid-sentence when he looked up. The remainder of the sentence died in his throat.

Most big cities had their share of gang activity. This one was no different. If anything, gang rivalry had been growing more blatant and dangerous in recent years, leading to a zero-tolerance approach by the police. Members were herded whenever spotted, but even with the crackdown, activity remained high. Its members were dangerous and not to be messed with.

But the downside to getting gang members off of the street was that they had to go somewhere. Putting them behind bars could be an altogether unpleasant experience for anyone else sharing the cell.

The four now faced Nat, all with the same expression that a starving wolf possessed when cornering a defenseless sheep. They were all young, mid- to late-teens or early twenties—one did not even appear to be shaving yet—but street-smart existence had added its own set of years to them.

The one in the center, not the tallest, but certainly the most intimidating spoke first.

"Who you talkin' to?"

Nat shook his head and averted his eyes, having noticed the tattoos the three of them had on their faces—a small teardrop near one eye. If he remained quiet and small, perhaps they might walk away.

The leader asked again. "I'm talking to you. Who you talkin' to?"

Again, Nat shook his head but said nothing.

"I asked you a question, and I don't like being ignored. You talkin' to yourself?"

Nat looked to Poe for some help. "What do I do?" he whispered, but Poe shook his head and motioned for him to be quiet.

"Please," Nat continued. "Help me."

This quick interaction did not go unnoticed. "Oh, so you are talking to someone," the hoodlum said, looking from Nat to the empty space at his side. "You got a friend there?" A grim smile swept across his face, and he nudged the youth beside him. "We got a live one here. Whatcha think about that, Rudo."

The youth, Rudo, stepped forward and bent down until eye level with Nat. "What's the story? You can talk, right?" He looked from Nat to the space where Poe sat, looked straight at him but only saw blank space. "You can talk to me. I'm right here."

One of the other hoodlums laughed. It was not a jovial tone.

"If you know what's good for you—know what I mean? Who are you talking to? You got a friend there?" He glanced back at his cohorts with a smile before continuing. "It's okay. Your friend's right there, right?"

Poe shook his head, "Nat. No," he whispered, not from fear of being heard—no one but Nat could hear him—but not to cause Nat any more distress than he already felt. Unfortunately, Nat was already nodding for the most irrational of reasons: fear.

Rudo leaned in closer. "So you do got someone here. Will you introduce us to your little friend? A he or a she? Is this your pussy squeeze? Or do you like men better?"

"No. A friend," Nat managed to say.

"Well, I think we should be properly introduced." He looked back at the others. "Right, Alejandro?" the leader nodded and Rudo turned back to Nat. "C'mon, man. What's his name?"

"You don't want to do this," Poe said, this time louder, but Nat was beyond listening.

"Edgar Allan Poe," he said.

The four looked at him in dead silence. Once the name had fully registered, there was an outbreak of laughter from the three of them.

"Who's that?" said the remaining one, not a literary type.

"Don't jack with us, dickwad," snapped Rudo. "Not if you like breathing." With that, the four launched into a verbal assault.

"Don't say any more," Poe urged. "It will only make things worse."

His words went unheeded. Something clicked in Nat's brain, and he decided that the best approach was full, honest disclosure. Raw fear certainly played a part, but there was another factor—ego-driven validation. His attempts to convince Phil had failed and landed him behind bars… but now he had an audience.

With a suddenness that startled Rudo, he reached out and grabbed the youth's shoulders.

"Yeah. My friend is Edgar Allan Poe. He is sitting right here beside me. I can see him as clearly as I can see you. You've got to believe me."

"Hey! Get off me," Rudo shouted, stepping back while brushing Nat's hands away. This led to a shouting match between the two of them even as Poe shook his head in dismay.

"Stand down, Blood," said Alejandro, now stepping forward to assess the situation. Rudo did as he was told, moving back several paces.

"Someone here with you? How come we can't see him?"

"Dunno," whispered Nat.

"Right. Your friend's the writer man?" asked Alejandro. "Wrote them scary-ass stories? Got them black cats, and killers, and the dude with the bad eye?"

Nat nodded in response.

"He's dead, ain't he? Croaked a long time ago?"

Again, Nat nodded.

Alejandro leaned in close until his face was a foot away from Nat's, and the details of the tear tattoo visible. His face was hard and cold, and Nat could see what was behind those eyes. It was cold and soulless without a shred of humanity. All of the villains in Poe's stories, those that Nat had read so often, were nothing more than playful pups when set next to this man.

And Nat knew that he was in deep shit.

"You're makin' fun of us," Alejandro said. "Think we don't know nothin'. I don't take kindly to that, nor do my players. I know all about this Poe and his stories. You want us to think that you got someone here? Let's see what he thinks of this." He looked back at the others and gave a jerk of his head. It was an order. They obeyed.

Multiple sets of hands grabbed Nat and dragged him to the center of the cell. The few other inmates, those not part of the gang, stayed as far to the sides and corners as possible, not willing to be a part of the action.

"No!" Poe called out and tried to help Nat, but his hands kept passing through all that he tried to touch. To become solid with his surroundings required concentration, something he did not possess at this moment. Nat was on his own.

"Hold him down," Alejandro instructed. "Arms and legs out." He reached into his jeans and fumbled around for a minute before pulling out something small and opening it. He held up the Swiss army knife for all to see.

How he smuggled it into the jail went unanswered. Standard procedures should have prevented it from happening, but somehow, he had managed the feat, possibly through concealment in a body cavity.

"Yeah, I know a Poe story," he said, staring down at Nat while brandishing the blade. "About a man tied down, can't move, and there's this pendulum that swings back and forth over him. It has a real sharp edge like a knife. It goes like this."

He stood over Nat and swung his arm from one side to the other, the knife pointed directly over Nat's chest. With each swing, he lowered his arm a little, so that by inches, the razor edge closed the distance.

Laughter came from the gang members. Sobs of fear came from Nat. And there was the pacing around them all, that of Poe, frantic to come up with a means to help.

The blade swung low, this time snagging on Nat's shirt. It rose, and then came back, this time catching again and tearing the fabric. Another time and the blade made contact with the skin. Nat cried out, this time louder. The blade returned, making a deeper cut and drawing blood.

"Now, let's see what you're made of," said Alejandro, and he brought his arm back down for another pass.

Poe thought back to the events with Amelia earlier in the evening—or was it yesterday evening—and how he had been able to do simple things by force of will. It took a level of concentration, but when focused, he could unlock doors or keep someone warm with his coat. If only he could rally his attention this time, it might make a difference. He knelt at Nat's side and held his arms out as a baseball catcher might do for an incoming ball. He set his intention and prayed.

Alejandro's arm swing back down, now dropping another inch, and positioned to make a sizable cut. His teeth were clenched in an expression of malicious joy. The blade fell quickly for its destination, coming within a mere inch to make contact...

And it stopped. For all in the room, it looked as if Alejandro brought his arm to a complete halt. Nat saw differently. Poe had stopped the blade in his hand, right before it would have drawn considerable blood.

"Wha?" Alejandro's reaction was one of shock. Not only had his hand stopped from moving, it now felt as if someone held it firm. It remained there motionless, the blade a mere inch from Nat's chest.

Everyone in the room now watched as Alejandro took one hand in the other, flexing his muscles as if he was struggling with something unseen, something that caused his arm to involuntarily rise until it pointed at the cell door.

He clenched his teeth, not from amusement as he had moments earlier, his eyes wide with fear. For some reason that defied all the norms, he no longer controlled his own body. Then he screamed as he moved swiftly toward the bars of the cell. It was the most extraordinary sight. For all who watched, it appeared as if he was being dragged across the floor, arms extended, and with a loud thud, the arm holding the blade went through the opening in the bars and his shoulder hit hard metal.

He remained in that position a minute later when the policeman marched in to investigate all the screaming. Whatever Alejandro had done to land himself in jail was now compounded by an additional weapons charge.

For the remainder of the night, the other inmates gave Nat a wide berth, but not without occasional curious stares.

"Thank you," Nat said to Poe when no one was watching.

"You're welcome. You might want to watch what you say and who you say it to. That sort of thing can get you into trouble."

"Like talking to ghosts?"

Poe patted Nat on the shoulder. Curious, he thought, for a person as loud and obnoxious as Nat, he found himself growing fond of the fellow. Nat's actions weren't malicious, simply unskilled in social disciplines, and maybe lacking a bit of standard common sense.

But there was something else as well, and at first, Poe was not ready to accept this, but he could see some of Nat in his own actions. True, he'd made his share of enemies in his lifetime. Sometimes that was on purpose, but at other times, it was from him acting on impulse.

Soon enough, daylight arrived, and a policeman appeared at the cell door to let Nat out. His one phone call had been to his parents who made the proper arrangements for bail. Nat was free to go. As they walked from the cell, Poe heard a distant bell sounding.

"Nat," Poe said, "my time with you has come to an end."

"Yeah, I figured as much," Nat replied. "Funny, I had all these questions I wanted to ask. So much about you I wanted to know, and I never was able to do so."

"Oh, the answers were there. You never took the time to listen. You might have enough time for one final question though."

Nat nodded. "Okay..." He thought on this for a moment before asking quite simply, "What's your favorite color?"

"Black," Poe responded. Even Nat could see the humor.

Nat giggled. "Very funny, E.A."

The laughter continued through the final tolling of the bell and as Edgar Allan Poe faded out of view and out of Nat's life.

CASK FOUR

At least this time, not a bed.

Poe found solid flooring beneath his feet, but everything else remained a literal fog. Only by increments did the mist clear, just enough for him to see the tombstones that surrounded him on several sides. The softest of blue light shone overhead, most likely that of the moon. He felt no breeze. Instead, the fog hung in the air about him with no sense of purpose.

The silence of his surroundings ceased with a footstep, followed by another, each growing closer, but ever so softly as a bare foot might make on a hard surface. Then the fog parted and Poe saw a human shape coming into view before him, a shadowy figure usually reserved for nightmares.

It stood quite tall, dressed in flowing black robes and a hood that completely covered its face. Only the hands were visible, light as snow, with fingers long and spindly. The figure came to a stop before him, and Poe waited for what was to come next.

Nothing happened. It stood there, occasionally twitching its fingers as if waiting for Poe to make the first move. Then something else came to his attention, a truly unreal quality of his surroundings. The fog still billowed around them, but now Poe could see the fog machine in the distance that pumped out the mist.

The tombstones around him were imitations made from cardboard and Styrofoam and painted in shades of gray to appear old and weathered. Above him, the bluish light turned out to be a spotlight, one of many that hung overhead.

As Poe watched the fog flow to one side, he noticed how it dropped off mere yards away, beyond which he saw row upon row of seats in a darkened auditorium.

While still unsure of why he was here or who he was supposed to meet, his surroundings were now confirmed. This was the stage of a theatre or opera house, wholly empty of an audience and no other person in sight, except for the hooded figure before him.

As if on cue, the figure raised one hand in a beckoning motion. Right, he might as well get it over with. Poe approached, but the figure then pointed at the grouping of mock gravestones. Poe drew closer to examine the markers, expecting to find his name on them. Instead, he read the names of those who were equally familiar: William Wilson, Julius Rodman, Arthur Gordon Pym, Napoleon Buonaparte Froissart.

Yes, he knew these people quite well. They were the results of his creation, people from his stories he had given life. Roderick Usher and poor cataleptic Madeline; M. Valdemar; the arrogant and ultimately reddened Prince Prospero; William Legrand; Fortunato and Montresor who'd had their differences over a cask of wine; Dr. Tarr and Professor Fether; Lady Ligeia and Lady Rowena; and the brilliant criminologist, C. Auguste Dupin. Yes, they were all here. Even little deformed Hop-Frog had his own resting place.

If Poe was fully familiar with these individuals, he was equally clueless as to their symbolic meaning. Poe turned to the hooded figure for an explanation.

"And your point is?" he asked.

The figure tilted its head in an exaggerated manner as if to say, "Don't you get it?" It scratched its head in grand pantomime before extending its hand to the graves once more, Poe shook his head in exasperation as the figure went through a series of incomprehensible hand gestures, most of which were lost due to the bulky nature of the robes it wore.

"Look, I don't have a clue what you want," said Poe. "Can you try to be a little more clear?"

The figure paused, thinking for a moment, and then raised a finger as if struck with a clever idea. At once, Poe felt an uncontrollable shiver run through him as the entity fumbled with its hood. He was not sure he wanted to know what was underneath it.

The hood was pulled back to reveal a face void of color, completely white, with eyes surrounded by black as were the darkened lips. But this was not the face of some reaper or deathly entity. Instead, it was something that Poe found far more frightening.

It was a mime.

The clown sported the traditional whiteface makeup with black lines accenting the eyes, eyebrows, and mouth, and topped with a small French beret, also black. It gave Poe a giant smile and waved to him. Then the mime examined its robes, shook its head out of disgust, and let the robes fall. With a flair of bravado, it threw out its arms, showing off its wardrobe of tight-fitting black spandex. If it could have shouted "Ta-dah!" it would have.

Poe immediately wondered if he might have been better off with Nat. "Let me guess," he said to the clownish figure, "my welfare, right."

In response, the mime wagged its finger, and then cocked its head to one side, tongue protruding out while positioning one hand above as if holding a noose.

Poe got the message. "Right. I'm dead. Thank you for clarifying that."

The mime brushed off its shirt and then went into the classic "walking against the wind" routine before pulling up a chair (invisible, naturally) and sitting, gesturing for Poe to do likewise.

"I believe I will stand," Poe answered, all the while growing more impatient at its antics.

The mime appeared to be in no hurry. It pretended to pour itself a cup of tea, offered one to Poe, and then casually took a few sips.

"Is there a point to all of this?" Poe asked with increasing irritation.

The mime nodded with glee as might a small child unable to hold a secret—pointing first at the gravestones, and then at its face which took on all the characteristics of a tragedy mask. It shook its hands, suggesting that all those stories that Poe had written were way too downbeat. Then it pushed the edges of its mouth into a silly grin. Again, the outstretched arms, having successfully changed tragedy into comedy.

Poe got the message. "You have a problem with my stories?"

The mime eagerly nodded while pointing to its toothy smile.

"So... you think I should tell happy stories. Perhaps something with flowers and bunnies, extra-fluffy clouds, and soft, cuddly kittens?"

The mime patted its chest, suggesting that it not be forgotten.

"And you?"

This brought about a thumbs-up from the mime. Poe shook his head.

"Sorry. It's called artistic license. I am proud of my work, and I wouldn't consider changing it."

This brought about a dejected expression from the mime, who pointed its finger at Poe, and then went through the motions of reading a book while laughing at its passages.

Poe shook his head at this. "I appreciate your opinion, but humor is not my style."

At this, the mime jumped up and down enthusiastically. Then it ran over to the tombstones, tapping on one after another. As he did so, spectral figures sprang up from behind, entities that were neither mortal nor from the afterlife. There, standing aside the marker for Roderick Usher was Usher himself, a physical manifestation of the literary character with his wild, silken hair and somber attire.

What appeared distinctly different was the face of Usher. Instead of a gloomy expression, he wore the same wide grin and white makeup as the mime.

At each tombstone stood Poe's familiar characters all in the same mime makeup. These were the creatures of the imagination, Poe's imagination, but now distorted into some sort of humorous masquerade.

The mime gestured for Usher to come forward. Usher responded with a stately bow before stepping up to the front of his grave. He cleared his throat—actually, he went through the motions of doing so, but like the mime, did so without a sound.

Then came the grand gestures of a vaudeville comedian plying his trade. Poe was aghast. Here was Roderick Usher, one of his greatest characters as well as one of his most somber, performing a slapstick comedy routine.

With a final pratfall, Usher offered a closing bow and took his place behind his stone. The mime, obviously serving as master of ceremonies, extended his hand to the next in line, and Lady Ligeia came forth for her moment in the spotlight.

As Poe watched, each one in turn, stepped forward to deliver their stand-up routine, wordlessly telling jokes, mugging, and dancing with canes and top hats, all done in pantomime. With each punch line, the other characters laughed and applauded, but as with the mime, there was no sound.

C. Auguste Dupin was the last in line and performed an amusing routine concerning an incompetent detective trying to find his magnifying glass. It brought forth roars of silent laughs from the gallery. He took a bow, resumed his position behind his grave, and turned to Poe.

They all turned, from Roderick Usher to tiny Hop-Frog, looking at Poe in expectation.

Waiting.

Quiet.

Very quiet.

The seeds of some uncomfortable idea had already sprung to Poe's mind. He tried his best to ignore it as even a possibility, but with all of his creations staring him down, it appeared to be inevitable. He looked at the mime who rose and gestured to a spot center stage.

"You're putting me on," said Poe.

Again the mime pointed to a spot on the stage.

"And what do you expect me to do, tell jokes?" Poe snapped.

At this, they all nodded, enthusiastically clapping their hands in unison. The mime ran to Poe, took his hand, and led him to the foot of the stage, facing out to the theatre. Poe could now see that something had drastically altered in his surroundings. The auditorium was no longer empty but filled to the brim with patrons.

The audience looked identical, all dressed in skin-tight outfits, similar to what the mime wore, but their faces caught Poe's attention. At first, he thought them all to be the same but soon realized that each and every one wore cardboard masks tied around their heads with a length of string, and with eyeholes cut out to see. Overall, it was an unnerving sight…

Especially since all the masks were of his own face.

Poe looked at the mime as if to say, "What the blazes is this?" but the mime gestured for him to begin his oratory, and in a final gesture, handed Poe a rubber chicken and a Groucho Marx disguise.

For the first time in ages, Poe felt a peculiar sensation, one he had not experienced since his youth. Stage fright. Perhaps the greatest fear of most people, public speaking, came naturally to Poe, who took the podium on many an occasion delivering vocal renditions of his works without the slightest hesitation.

But here, as he looked out upon the sea of faces—his face, a cold sweat took over his body, and he knew he was out of his element. They expected something that was not of his nature. He knew it. They knew it. His legs trembled beneath him, and he found that he could hardly stand.

"Mime-faced figure," Poe exclaimed, "I fear you and your intention more than anyone else I have seen this evening. I'm not even sure that your purpose is to do me good. Before I resort to cheap humor, answer me one thing. Are these the shadows of things that might have been, or are you just pulling my leg? You know, having a 'good one' at the old man's expense?"

The mime now stood impassive, offering no further comment. It simply folded its arms and tapped its foot.

Seconds passed with the substance of molasses as Poe considered the now uncommunicative mime, the cast of his invented characters, and the audience, as well as the rubber chicken in his hand.

"Oh, what the hell," he said to himself, tossed the Marx glasses aside, and cleared his throat.

"Why..." he began, pausing from the immense stupidity he felt. "Why did the chicken cross the road?" He allowed for a proper beat and then continued. "To get to the other side."

United, the audience, as well as the Poe-mimes behind him, burst into silent applause. A few stuck their fingers into their mouths to whistle (also quite silent). Just as quickly, they stopped.

"Why did the elephant paint his balls red?" asked Poe. "To hide in the cherry patch." With the punch line, the audience applauded briefly, then waited for another howler. "And how did Tarzan die? Picking cherries." More applause.

There's the rub. At one time, Poe had commanded the stage with his oratory, reading his works with solemn intent. Any of that dignity drained like so much sewer water as he delivered his next joke, one about the traveling salesman, the farmer's daughter, and a cow in the rafters.

The lewd contents only intensified the peals of silent laughter. He grew very pale but talked more fluently and with a heightened voice and violent gesticulations. He paced the floor to and fro with heavy strides as if excited by their observations. Oh, God! What could he do? Poe foamed—he raved—he swore—he told the one about the leprechauns and the nuns. "And so the leprechaun shouted, 'I knew it! I knew I was fucking a penguin!'" Poe exclaimed. The crowd went wild.

He must laugh or die. "I admit the deed!" he shrieked, then performed the entire "Who's on First" routine while playing both parts.

Oh, but horror of horrors, he discovered to his great shock and dismay that he enjoyed—yes, enjoyed the repertoire. This humor, so base, so trite, and beneath his abilities, brought unexpected pleasure.

In dismay, he stood puzzling. How might this be? It came without ribbons. It came without tags. It came without cumulative sentence structure, juxtaposition, or bags. Then came the thought he hadn't before. Perhaps gaiety, he realized, didn't come from a drunken literary bore. Perhaps it means a little bit more.

To the Devil with eloquence. Damned be respectability. He riffed on a verse by erstwhile poet William McGonagall and of the Tay Whale walking into a bar. "'Give me a harpoon straight up,' the whale puffed and blowed, so the bartender fired at him and he dived below."

Poe lifted a Milton Berle joke, one that itself had been stolen—not that the origin mattered. Berle would not be born for nearly sixty years after Poe's demise, but bad humor was immortal.

For his finale, he used a jest by the immortal bard, Henny Youngman. "Take my wife… Please!" he exclaimed, knowing well that his humor had grown three sizes that day. The audience quickly rose to its feet, applauding wildly. Poe accepted the adulation, bowed, and turned.

The mime walked forward, also applauding, clapping Poe on the back, and gesturing to show his admiration. Then he threw his hands outward in an expression of "Well?"

"It was very nice," Poe answered. "Very… amusing."

The mime responded by reaching into a hidden pocket. He pulled out a small musical triangle along with a striker, held it aloft, and struck it.

A loud bell sounded with a cacophony far more intense than anything the meager triangle might produce. As the sound diminished, the mime struck it once more, and yet again to a total of twelve.

"I guess this is it," Poe said as the stage around him began to spin, growing blurred from the motion. "It's been a real laugh."

"Yes, it has," answered the mime. Soon, the blur consumed everything, sending Poe on to his date with destiny.

CASK FIVE

As the mist parted, Poe realized that the visitation had come to an end. He stood in the familiar void where it all began, still holding the rubber chicken in his hand. Everything was as before, leaving him fluttered and glowing, as light as a feather, as happy as an angel, as merry as a schoolboy, and as giddy as a drunken man (of which he had ample experience). Yes, the eternity before him was his own to do with as he would—yet he was at a loss of what to do.

He was not alone. Facing him were Hamlet and his father, Ophelia, Lenore, Jane, and Rochester.

"Back so soon?" said Hamlet.

"Nice chicken," said his father.

The rest said nothing, as did the chicken.

"What's today?" Poe asked.

"Eh?" returned the group as one with all their might of wonder.

"What is today? Is it Christmas Day?"

"Hallo," answered Hamlet. "You know quite well there is no such thing as time here."

"Or every day is Christmas Day," countered Ophelia. "Take your pick."

"Well, then," answered Poe. "I haven't missed it. The mortals have done it all in one night. They can do anything they like. Of course, they can. Here, my fine friend, have a chicken." Poe handed Hamlet the rubber prop. "I would have gifted you the prize turkey hanging at the Poulterer's in the next street, but I think it was already reserved."

Jane looked at Rochester, who twirled his finger aside his ear, suggesting Poe's state of mind.

"Are you all right," asked Lenore cautiously.

Poe smiled. "I think so."

He took in the sights and sounds around him, so rich and full in their deliciousness that he was astounded to have never noticed before. This sublime mood was ruptured as Rochester let forth a loud belch, and Poe could not contain the laughter. Of all the blithe sounds he had ever heard, this was the blithest in his ears.

Indeed, he was better than his word. He would have no further intercourse with the mortal world, and while he had his moments of funk, he embraced a better nature, and ever afterward, it was always said of him that he knew how to keep a bawdy joke well, if any man alive or dead possessed the knowledge. On occasion, he would even join in on a verse of "Tie a Yellow Ribbon." May that be truly said of all of us.

"Yes," Poe confirmed to Hamlet, Lenore, and the others, "I am quite all right."

It was then that he felt a hand on his shoulder, and turning, he saw the familiar auburn hair and blue eyes—and he knew there was no reason to be somber again.

"Amelia," he said with a smile.

ABOUT THE AUTHOR

David Welling is a writer, artist, and graphic designer. His first book, *Cinema Houston*, was published in 2007 by the University of Texas Press. The non-fiction book chronicles the history of movie theatres in Texas' largest city. It is the recipient of the 2008 Julia Ideson Award and the Society of Architectural Historians' 2009 Antoinette Forrester Downing Award. He has since shifted to fiction. David has written numerous short stories, both seasonal and non, and is developing a set of novels for a series centered on fictional auteur film director F.O. Steiner. He lives in Houston along with his wife, furry pooch, and kitties.

* 9 7 9 8 9 9 9 0 9 3 0 8 0 3 *